# FREE
# FALL

## Books by Nancy Mehl

ROAD TO KINGDOM

*Inescapable*
*Unbreakable*
*Unforeseeable*

FINDING SANCTUARY

*Gathering Shadows*
*Deadly Echoes*
*Rising Darkness*

DEFENDERS OF JUSTICE

*Fatal Frost*
*Dark Deception*
*Blind Betrayal*

KAELY QUINN PROFILER

*Mind Games*
*Fire Storm*
*Dead End*

THE QUANTICO FILES

*Night Fall*
*Dead Fall*
*Free Fall*

THE QUANTICO FILES
BOOK 3

# FREE FALL

# NANCY MEHL

BETHANY HOUSE
a division of Baker Publishing Group
Minneapolis, Minnesota

Published by Bethany House Publishers
11400 Hampshire Avenue South
Minneapolis, Minnesota 55438
www.bethanyhouse.com

Bethany House Publishers is a division of
Baker Publishing Group, Grand Rapids, Michigan

Printed in the United States of America

Library of Congress Cataloging-in-Publication Data
Names: Mehl, Nancy, author.
Title: Free fall / Nancy Mehl.
Description: Minneapolis, Minnesota : Bethany House, a division of Baker Publishing
    Group, [2022] | Series: The Quantico files ; #3
Identifiers: LCCN 2022002389 | ISBN 9780764237652 (trade paper) | ISBN
    9780764240119 (casebound) | ISBN 9781493437283 (ebook)
Subjects: LCGFT: Novels.
Classification: LCC PS3613.E4254 F74 2022 | DDC 813/.6—dc23/eng/20220120
LC record available at https://lccn.loc.gov/2022002389

First Peter 5:6-7 in chapter 16 is from the Amplified® Bible (AMP), copyright © 2015 by The Lockman Foundation. Used by permission. www.Lockman.org

First Peter 5:6–8 in chapter 16 is from the New King James Version®. Copyright © 1982 by Thomas Nelson. Used by permission. All rights reserved.

Psalm 91 and Jeremiah 29:11 in chapter 30 are from THE HOLY BIBLE, NEW IN-TERNATIONAL VERSION®, NIV® Copyright © 1973, 1978, 1984, 2011 by Biblica, Inc.® Used by permission. All rights reserved worldwide.

Cover design by Studio Gearbox

Author is represented by The Steve Laube Agency.

Baker Publishing Group publications use paper produced from sustainable forestry practices and post-consumer waste whenever possible.

22  23  24  25  26  27  28      7  6  5  4  3  2  1

When you have a child, you discover a part of your heart you never knew existed. Then you have grandchildren and realize there's more room there than you ever imagined.

I dedicate this book to my incredible grandsons,
Aidan and Bennett.
I love you to the moon and back.
You're both so special, and I'm so proud of you.
I can't wait to see the incredible plans God has for your lives.
Thank you for letting me be your nana.

Daisy, Daisy, give me your answer do. I'm half crazy . . .

# Prologue

The screams of people buckled into rides designed to either terrify or thrill them rang out in the darkness. Walking through the park had always energized him. And tonight, as the rides spun, colorful lights flashed, and tinny music swirled, he once again breathed in the aromas of buttered popcorn, steaming hot dogs, and sweet cotton candy.

He'd grown up in this environment. His father had been a carnie, and they'd traveled together all over the country working carnivals, state and county fairs, and small amusement parks like this one. He loved it. When his father died of a heart attack a little over three years ago, the carnie bosses said he could stay on. At fourteen, it was the only life he'd known.

Besides, the carnies were a family. His family. He had grandparents somewhere here in Virginia, apparently not too far from this park. His father said they'd visited them once when his mother was still with them. But he couldn't remember that. They never really spoke about her. That was okay. If she didn't want him, he didn't want her either. His memories of her were few and easily forgotten.

His father had mentioned once that his grandparents had

money, but even now, at seventeen, he didn't care. He had everything he needed. Of course, as he got older, he began to really want a girlfriend. He was attracted to one dark-haired girl in particular.

He first saw her at this park three years ago, not long after his father died. She had shiny, long dark hair and a smile that made his heart beat wildly. When she walked, she sashayed back and forth, making him feel warm and funny inside. Sometimes she'd throw her head back and swing her hair as though she had no idea she was being observed. But she had to know how attractive she was and that every boy in the park watched her as she strolled past them.

He wasn't brave enough to talk to her, though. And besides, she was always with other girls. That made it even harder for him to approach her. The group all laughed and joked with one another as if they'd been friends forever. He couldn't help but be envious.

Eight other teenage boys traveled with their group of carnies, but he couldn't relate to most of them. They were coarse and stupid, and the way they talked about women turned his stomach. His father never referred to women like that even though his wife had run off with another man.

Eventually, though, he formed a friendship with Andy, who was just two years older. Andy understood him, liked books the way he did, and he never said bad things about girls. Handsome with blond hair and blue eyes, he always had a girlfriend. Girls stared at him all the time.

But when *he* smiled at girls, most of them acted like he didn't even exist. He tried to quell the anger and frustration growing inside him, but it wasn't easy.

Then tonight he'd decided to take a big step. He was running the Ghost Shack when he spotted the dark-haired girl and three of her friends waiting in line. She looked his way, and he got up the nerve to smile at her. His heart soared when she smiled back.

"Keep the tickets," he said when she arrived at the front of the line. "That way you can ride again if you want."

She wore a pretty white dress with yellow daisies printed all over it, and she smelled like . . . summer. It was intoxicating.

She smiled again. "That's so nice."

"You're welcome." Encouraged, he took a deep breath, then spoke to her in almost a whisper. "I have a break in an hour. Would you like to get something to eat? My treat."

Her eyes widened. They were an incredible bluish gray.

"That sounds great," she said. "Why don't I meet you at the beer garden? Lots of tables there."

His words seemed to stick in his throat, but he was able to spit out, "Yeah. Okay."

She and her friends settled into the ride's car, and he could hear them giggling as the large wooden doors swung shut behind them. Then their laughter turned into screams, a cacophony of terror that echoed throughout the old structure. The Ghost Shack always seemed to frighten anyone brave enough to venture inside.

When the car came out through the double exit doors, he unlatched the metal bar that had kept the girls safely inside. She stepped out, then looked back at him and called, "Don't forget!" She blew a kiss in his direction before walking away, her hips swinging.

He turned his attention to the people next in line, feeling happier than he had in his entire life.

Minutes felt like hours until it was time for his break.

When Buzz finally arrived five minutes late, he was ready to throttle him. But he just handed over the ride and nearly ran to one of the carnie games.

He'd remembered that one of the prizes was a little stuffed dog holding a daisy. When you pressed its paw, it sang *Daisy, Daisy, give me your answer do. I'm half crazy all for the love of you.* He asked the carnie, a guy named Mike who'd been a friend of his father's, if he could have one and pay for it later.

"Is it for that girl you been likin' all this time? I seen her go by here earlier."

"Yeah. She's gonna meet me over at the beer garden."

Mike handed him the stuffed toy and told him to forget about paying for it. He smiled and thanked him. This really was the best day of his life.

Before entering the beer garden, he stopped to smooth his hair and brush off his clothes. He was wearing one of his best shirts because he'd hoped she'd show up while they were here. Then he squared his shoulders and walked to the garden, quickly spotting her sitting at a picnic table. His face grew warm with anticipation.

He sat down beside her, smiled, and handed her the dog. "I got this for you. When you press his paw, he sings. It made me think of you . . . of your dress, I mean."

She pressed the dog's paw, and as they listened to the song, she laughed.

"I forgot to ask your name," he said when the song ended.

But instead of answering him, she looked into his eyes. "Would you like to kiss me?"

He nodded, unable to speak around the lump in his throat. Hadn't she noticed his scar? Would she change her mind if she did?

Then something in her expression startled him, but by the time he realized what it was, it was too late. Someone behind him poured soda over his head, and then both she and the girl who'd doused him started giggling. Several of her friends came out from behind the food stand, and they all began laughing hysterically.

"What a freak," the girl said. "How could you think someone like me would be interested in you?" Then she stood and rejoined her friends, tossing the dog in a nearby trash can. As their laughter grew and others around him joined in, a seed of hatred was planted deeply in his heart.

# 1

Fifteen years later

The abandoned amusement park reminded Logan of an aging bride waiting for a bridegroom who never came. From this vantage point, he and Jeff could see Alex get out of her car and walk toward the entrance of a building that looked like it was ready to collapse at any moment. Why had the FBI given its permission for this to happen? It was too dangerous. With the sun slowly slipping out of sight, the park was beginning to disappear into the dusk.

He glanced at Jeff. If his jaw were set any tighter, his teeth would crack. Jefferson Cole, unit chief of BAU4 at Quantico, wasn't afraid of much. But he and Logan were more than afraid. They were terrified. What if this went wrong? What if Alex didn't make it out?

They watched as she hesitated at the entrance to the dilapidated Ghost Shack, then reached into her jacket pocket and removed a small flashlight. She appeared to look up to where they'd parked. She couldn't have known he and Jeff were there, though. This wasn't protocol. But Logan's feelings for Alex had forced him to be here, at this place, with her. If he'd had his way, it would be him walking into the forsaken building that had once caused its riders to shriek in fear. He could almost hear the frightened cries from years ago reverberate around them.

When he first met Alex, he could see her imperfections. A wide mouth. A long nose. High forehead. She wasn't beauty-queen perfect. But as he got to know her, interest in other women faded away. He could see only her. In his mind, she was the most gorgeous woman he'd ever met. Was that love? He wasn't sure. He only knew he'd never felt like this before, and a voice inside his heart whispered that he never would again.

"This is a really bad idea," Jeff said. He sighed. "But Alex insisted she had to try to save the women if they're still alive. So far this UNSUB's been one step ahead of us. I just wish Alex hadn't refused when the SWAT captain tried to get her to wear a wire. I know she was afraid the guy would find it, but . . ."

Jeff was talking about an unknown subject who had kidnapped several young women. They suspected there were more spread out across the state, although they hadn't been able to tie him directly to their disappearances. Typically, a serial killer had a narrower comfort zone. A place where he felt safe to hunt. Of course, they couldn't actually prove he was a killer. There weren't any bodies . . . yet anyway.

"We should have checked this place out first. Placed agents inside."

"I told you. There wasn't time." Jeff shook his head. "As

much as I hate to say it, this is our first and maybe our only chance to catch him. Alex is smart and well trained. We have to believe she can handle him."

"There she goes," Logan said as Alex stepped through the entrance and disappeared from sight. His whole body tensed, and he silently begged God to bring her back to him. Not that he and Alex were a couple. Not yet.

He'd never known anyone like Alex. She was strong, yet she could also be vulnerable. Sometimes her strength was her greatest weakness. She took too many chances. Could be incredibly stubborn when she thought she was right. That trait had landed her in trouble more than once. He knew where it came from, though. Her commitment to the people she swore to protect burned like an unquenchable fire in her soul.

That devotion was why she was walking into a situation that could easily end her life. The FBI had received a call summoning Alex to this spot, claiming that the location of the missing women would be revealed if his demands were met. The hope that it might be true had brought them all here. There were families who couldn't give up, who were praying that their loved one would return to them. Logan understood why Alex felt she had no choice, but he still wanted to physically pull her out of there. He tried to ignore the fear that she wouldn't come back from this attempt, but it clawed at his mind.

Logan reached into his pants pocket and took out the bottle of pills that went everywhere with him now. He opened the lid, shook two into his hand, and managed to swallow them dry. He was taking too many, but the headaches were blinding, the pain unbearable.

"Logan," Jeff said gently, "you've got to take care of—"

"No!" Logan instantly felt guilty. He hadn't meant to bark at Jeff, but he was determined to be available if Alex needed him. Although she would never admit it, in his heart he knew she depended on him. Yet sometimes all he could do was just be there for her, and he had no intention of letting her down now—even if she didn't know he was close by.

"I'm sorry, Jeff. But if you hadn't told me the truth, it would have been really hard for me to forgive you. This is my choice. I had to be here."

"I know you wanted to stop this," Jeff said. "But it was out of my hands. We both had to follow orders."

Once he knew the truth, Logan had thought about calling Alex, begging her not to do it, but he knew she wouldn't have listened. It would have only distracted her, making it harder for her to concentrate on her mission. And that could get her killed. So even though he hated what she was doing now, he could only watch . . . and pray.

The minutes ticked by like hours. Logan could barely breathe. What was taking so long? HRT and SWAT agents were parked as close to the building as they could get without being seen, waiting for Alex to emerge. They were hidden behind a large sign that promised Magic Land Park would provide "the most fun you've ever had." So far it was failing miserably at living up to its hype.

If Alex received the promised information, she was to exit the structure and wave, letting the SWAT team know it was safe to breach the building. If she didn't wave, they were to stay where they were until she could get back to them. Maybe the UNSUB hadn't shown up. This could be a test to see if Alex would follow his instructions.

"It's been too long. I have a bad feeling about this," Jeff said.

"I do too."

Then they saw the SWAT team get out of their vehicle. They were through waiting. Something was wrong. Alex should have been out by now.

"If she was wearing a wire or had her phone, we'd know if she was okay," Jeff mumbled.

"But besides telling her she had to come alone, he said no gun, no wire, and no phone. Defying him could have gotten her killed. I hope he didn't find the weapon she does have."

Alex had a hard nylon knife tucked inside her sock and boot. It wouldn't show up if the UNSUB had a metal detector. Neither would the specially built tracker they'd hidden in the lining of her jacket. Logan felt better knowing she had a way to defend herself if she needed to.

Jeff cursed. "This is insane. We should have set the parameters, not let this guy do it."

"Hard to say no when the UNSUB threatens to start killing hostages if you don't follow orders. He was smart giving Alex only thirty minutes to arrive. I'm just glad SWAT and HRT were also ready to roll."

Logan got out of the car and walked a few feet away so he could see what was happening more clearly. Jeff joined him, and they stared down at the scene below. The agents were moving toward the structure, weapons drawn. Time seemed to have slowed to a crawl.

"I wish they'd hurry," Logan said.

"You know they have to be careful. Not only for themselves but for Alex. If they move too fast—"

Suddenly, a loud explosion rocked the ground, and in only seconds fire engulfed the building. With Alex still inside.

---

### Nine days earlier

Tracy craved more sleep, but her mind fought the almost overpowering urge. Where was she? How long had she been here? She had no memory of coming here. For a moment she wondered if she were dead, but that couldn't be right. This wasn't heaven. God didn't drug people.

She pushed herself up from the bed and swung her legs over the side. Immediately, the room swirled around her, and she grabbed the edge of the mattress to keep herself from falling off. It took a while for the dizziness to subside. She felt sick. Nauseated. And damp. She looked down and realized she'd wet herself. She was so embarrassed. She hadn't wet the bed since she was a child. Then anger quickly overtook humiliation. This wasn't her fault. She wasn't supposed to be here.

She reached inside her pocket for her phone, but of course, it was gone. Not a surprise.

Then she looked around the room. It was small, and there were no windows. But at least it seemed clean and neat. Besides the bed, there was a dresser, a wooden chair against one wall, a bookshelf with a few books, and a small table with something on it. She stood, wobbling some, and made her way to a note on top of a pile of folded clothing.

*You can change into these or any of the other clothes in the dresser. Clean sheets are in there too. There's a toilet*

*behind the curtain. A plastic receptacle for the bag is next*
*to it and will be emptied every night. Other plastic bags*
*are available for any trash or laundry. Just put it all next*
*to the door at the end of the day. Also put your food trays*
*at the bottom of the door after each meal.*

Plastic bags? A receptacle? Food trays? What in the world? She turned around and carefully made her way to a dark pink curtain that closed off one corner of the room. Pushing it aside, she found the kind of portable toilet her family had used when they'd gone camping years ago. She remembered how it worked. Once the bag attached under the seat was partially full, you disposed of it and put a fresh one in its place. As the note promised, a plastic pail sat next to the toilet.

She took in a small sink and some towels and washcloths hanging on a metal bar. A cabinet under the sink was filled with shampoo, soap, lotion, feminine products, a brush, and a bag with makeup. It seemed he'd thought of everything, but she certainly wouldn't be applying any makeup for this freak.

She stumbled back to the dresser, where she found sheets and pillowcases in one drawer and packages of new underwear and socks in the next one. Jeans and some folded T-shirts had been placed in the last one. She slammed it shut. She had no intention of staying here long enough to use all of this.

But even though she didn't want to agree to anything asked of her, she couldn't stand the way she felt—or smelled. It was obvious she'd been here at least a day, maybe two. She took the clothes from the table, lifted a package of underwear from the dresser, and started to strip off her sweat suit. But then, suspicious, she looked around again. Sure enough, a camera was positioned up in one corner with only the curtained area blocked from its view. She had no intention of giving this pervert a show, so she stepped behind the curtain again.

She washed herself, then pulled on the jeans and T-shirt, which fit surprisingly well. They also looked clean and smelled fresh. She felt better.

She shoved her discarded clothing into a plastic bag, then dropped it on the floor next to the dresser, where she grabbed some socks. The floor was concrete. Cold. She carried the socks to the wooden chair next to the wall, then sat down and tugged the socks onto her bare feet. They were thick and warm, which felt good.

She carried the plastic bag to the door, but when she turned the knob, it was locked. The door was made of metal with a small knob about three-fourths of the way up attached to a small panel. There was a larger panel positioned near the floor.

The walls were made out of some kind of stone. She touched them, and they felt cool to the touch. Where was she?

She was about to try opening the top panel when another wave of dizziness hit her. She made it back to the bed, but it was still wet, so she returned to the chair and waited for the room to stop spinning. When it did, she quickly removed the wet sheets and shoved them into another plastic bag. The mattress had a plastic protector, and she used one half of a towel to wipe it down with soap and water. Then she dried it with the other half.

After that she wrangled clean sheets onto the mattress and slipped a new pillowcase onto the pillow. She checked a tiny closet in another corner and discovered a soft comforter.

There was also a hook with a flannel nightgown hanging from it.

She was so tired. Even though she wanted nothing more than to learn where she was and get out of there, she crawled into the bed and pulled the top sheet and comforter up to her shoulders. Then she allowed herself to start drifting off again, determined to fight back as soon as she could.

**Two days later**

ogan hung up the phone, got up from his desk, and headed to the office of his unit chief, Jefferson Cole. Supervisory Special Agent Alex Donovan looked up from her desk and smiled as he walked by.

Logan returned her smile. When he looked at her, his heart ached. He wanted to tell her how he felt about her, but he was smart enough to realize she wasn't ready. For now, they were friends. Close friends. He wanted that to be enough . . . but it wasn't. A couple of times he'd been tempted to ask someone out on a date, but he'd put it off until he was certain Alex would never love him.

He sighed. That was a lie. He honestly believed he would never love anyone but her. Wanting Alex was painful, but it was a wonderful kind of anguish. He couldn't explain it. He didn't even understand it himself. He pushed thoughts of Alex out of his mind as he opened the door to Jeff's office.

"Go on in," Jeff's faithful administrative assistant said with a smile. Logan had always liked Alice Burrows, even though she protected her boss like a mother lion protecting her cub.

"Thanks, Alice."

Jeff looked up as Logan entered, then closed the door behind him. "Logan, you remember Chief Dixon, right? And Special Agent Lucas?" The local police chief sat in a chair in front of Jeff's desk. Next to him was one of their agents from the Quantico field office.

"Of course." He shook hands with both men and then took the third chair. "What's up?"

Jeff nodded at Lucas.

"We have a problem," the agent said after clearing his throat. "Chief Dixon contacted us about a missing woman. I've taken his statement, and we're looking into it, but he asked to talk to the BAU as well. The chief knows I think it's too early in the investigation to bring our unit in, but . . ."

Logan frowned and looked at Jeff. A missing woman? Why was the FBI involved at all? Usually the Bureau was brought in only for offenders with multiple crimes. People went missing for many reasons—and most of them weren't anything the FBI's elite Behavioral Analysis Unit could address.

"I realize people disappear for many reasons," Chief Dixon said, echoing Logan's thoughts, "but Tracy Mendenhall isn't the kind of person to just take off on her own. She's a single mom who recently graduated from nursing school. She's devoted to her two children, and she's worked hard to provide for them. She just got a great job with a local clinic. Was so excited about it. There's absolutely no way she would just leave."

Jeff leaned forward. "Maybe the pressure of—"

"No. She's a strong young woman. Not someone easily overcome by circumstances. If she weren't, she would have buckled when her husband died. She and the children moved in with her parents while Tracy was in school. They're *very* close."

"When did she go missing?" Jeff asked.

"Early Sunday morning. She was out jogging, something she did at the same time every day. She runs from her house and into a nearby park. She was seen entering, but that was the last time anyone spotted her. Officers found her water bottle off the path, near some trees."

"I know this isn't what you want to hear," Logan said, "but profiling an UNSUB with just one victim is almost impossible."

"Do you have a photo of her?" Jeff asked.

"Yes." Lucas pulled a file folder from his briefcase, then laid a large photo on Jeff's desk. "This was taken at her graduation."

Logan leaned forward to see a lovely young woman posing next to an older couple. She had a nice smile and looked very happy. He prayed she'd be found quickly and would smile like that again. But if she hadn't left on her own, the chances of that were slim.

"We have a list of family and friends," Lucas said. "We've just started questioning them. I can send you our findings as soon as we have them. So far no one seems to know anything, but they've all said Tracy would never just take off." He placed the file on the desk next to the photo.

"Have you used ViCAP yet, Lucas?"

"Not yet."

"We'll do it. Run her description and the details of her

abduction through to see if any other cases match hers," Jeff said.

"That's great," Chief Dixon said. "Anything you can do will be appreciated. I know this isn't the type of case the BAU would normally work, but I really care about Tracy. I'm asking for your help as a favor." The chief's eyes grew shiny. "Her parents are beside themselves. I . . . I promised to do everything I can to find her." He gulped and struggled to continue. "I've known her ever since her family moved here from Kansas a few years ago to be near David's ill mother, who's since passed away. They go to my church. If you could help us look in the right places—at the right people—maybe we can find her. So far we just don't have any leads." He sighed deeply. "Sorry to get emotional, but this hits so close to home."

"We'll see what we can do and get back to you ASAP," Jeff said.

"Good to see you, Chief—although not under these circumstances," Logan said. "I truly hope we can help you."

"I do too."

Lucas nodded and followed the chief out of Jeff's office.

"She probably ran off with some guy and will show up soon enough," Jeff said once the door closed behind their visitors. He stared down at the picture on his desk. "Although she's older, she reminds me a little of Stephanie."

"How's Steph doing?" Logan asked.

"Great. She'll start classes at the University of Virginia in the fall."

"That's wonderful. And how are the two of you getting along?"

Jeff smiled. "I guess the idea that she could have lost me a few months ago made an impact. We're both still working at it, but I've decided she doesn't actually hate me." He shrugged. "She'll be gone in a few months, but at least for now, we're closer than we've been in a long time. She even dumped her anti-law-enforcement boyfriend."

Logan laughed. "Good."

"Amen." Jeff handed over the photo of Tracy and her parents as well as the file folder Lucas had brought. "Go through this and see if anything jumps out at you. And don't forget ViCAP, although I'm sure searching for missing single women will give you way more possibilities than you can use."

Logan thumbed through the papers in the folder. "I don't see anything in here about a missing persons report."

Jeff frowned. "Check on it. Surely the parents filed one." He shook his head. "Lucas doesn't seem convinced this is a kidnapping case any more than I am."

Logan stood. "I'll keep you updated. Okay if I ask Alex to help me?"

He was surprised to see Jeff hesitate. Why? Alex was the best they had.

"Yeah, go ahead," he said after a long pause. "But remember that getting emotionally involved with another agent can cause you to make mistakes."

"I . . . I don't understand."

Jeff met Logan's gaze. "Yes you do. Be careful."

"We're just friends."

"I'm not blind, Logan. And I'm not stupid. Just watch it."

Logan wanted to argue. Tell his boss he didn't have feelings for Alex. But he couldn't do it. He would have to lie, and he couldn't do that to Jeff.

"I hear you," he said softly. Then he walked out of the room and headed for Alex's desk, the file in his hand.

**3**

**A**lex looked puzzled. "I don't understand. We're supposed to come up with a profile based on the disappearance of one woman? This isn't much information to work with."

Logan sat down on the edge of her desk. "I know, but Chief Dixon feels strongly that something's not right about this. It's not like Tracy packed a bag and drove away. She jogs through this park almost every day. She was seen entering, but she never came out. She left her car and her purse at home, and they found her water bottle on the path, near some trees. If you were running away, is this the way you'd do it? Besides, she has two kids that the chief said she adores."

Alex shrugged. "Could this be a way to get some money from her parents? A fake kidnapping? Are her parents rich?"

Logan flipped open the file Jeff gave him, then turned over a few papers before saying, "I don't think so. Her father owns a small insurance company in downtown Quantico. Her mother doesn't work outside the home. They don't sound like people who could cough up a lot of money."

"No, they don't," Alex said. "But it's still possible they had something to do with their daughter's disappearance. Lucas and the chief need to look into that. What else can you tell me?"

Logan glanced at his watch. "Let's grab some lunch and talk about it. I'll drive."

"Sounds good. I'll meet you outside."

Logan nodded and went back to his desk to get his reading glasses. He didn't usually need them, but lately he'd been straining some when he read. He'd also been experiencing a lot of headaches. Although he'd had them occasionally before, this was becoming an uncomfortable trend, even making it hard to sleep at night. He'd set up an appointment with an ophthalmologist. Maybe it was time for stronger lenses. He read forms and reports all day, online as well as hard copies. Then at night he liked to read. Maybe TV for a while. Or audio books. He liked listening to them when he was traveling. Might be a nice change. Probably better than television. He couldn't find much on anymore that he thought was worth his time anyway.

A few minutes later he met Alex at the car.

"Where are we going?" she asked.

"How about Tony O's?"

"Exactly what I was thinking," she said with a smile.

Tony O's was owned by Tony O'Grady, a local man who retired from the Marines a few years ago, after an injury overseas. Not someone to just sit around, he'd turned his love of cooking into the small, intimate restaurant a lot of soldiers and staff from the nearby Marine base frequented, as well as agents from Quantico. Tony had a way with sandwiches that kept people coming back.

It took them about ten minutes to reach the small café. It was packed, which wasn't surprising. Tony was standing behind the counter and waved at them when they came in. Logan waved back and then scouted for a table. He was thinking they should just order lunch and eat it back at the office when a couple got up from a nearby table. Logan hurried over and sat down, then motioned to Alex to join him.

A man who'd entered the restaurant behind them had headed toward the same table. Logan smiled at the man, who then flashed him a dirty look and returned to the front of the restaurant.

A few minutes later a harried-looking busser came over. He quickly cleared the dishes and wiped down the table.

"Thank you so much," Alex said to the man, whose name tag read Larry.

His cheeks flushed pink, and the corners of his mouth ticked up. "You're welcome," he said softly.

Her kindness was something else Logan liked about Alex. Most people ignored bussers, but not her. Words of appreciation and a smile had brightened the man's day. Why was someone his age bussing tables? He looked to be in his early thirties. Surely he could secure a better job.

Logan laughed inwardly. He was profiling. He did it all the time. It was like a disease.

A waitress named Maggie walked up to their table, handed them menus, and then took their drink orders. Logan didn't actually need a menu. He knew exactly what he wanted. He loved the Turkey Supreme with pan-seared turkey breast topped with caramelized onions, bacon, cream cheese, and mild jalapeños.

Alex usually skimmed the menu even though she always settled on the Spicy Tuna Melt with Southwest-spiced tuna, jalapeño cream cheese, and white cheddar on grilled white sourdough. They quickly told Maggie what they wanted. As busy as it was, it was better to order now. They both asked for the homemade potato chips. She scribbled their order on her pad and left with Alex's "Thank you" following her as she went.

Logan's mouth watered just thinking about his sandwich. He noticed that now the line waiting for a table was all the way out the door. He couldn't help but wonder when Tony would finally expand. It was long overdue.

"So if we're going to write a profile for this case, is there any chance we'll have access to the woman's parents?" Alex asked. "I noticed she lives with them."

"I assume the chief will want a list of questions from us so he can interview them himself. Or have Lucas do it. You know we don't do that."

Alex shook her head. "I realize that, but with so little to go on, I'd like to see their reactions to our questions. Listen to them myself. You know how much we can learn from that kind of observation. We need to be certain they aren't involved somehow."

"Yeah, I agree. We can ask."

She nodded. "When we get back to the office, we'll pull up all missing persons cases in the area similar to this one. And run the information through ViCAP."

"Do you really think we'll find something?"

Alex sighed. "Maybe. It's happened before. Too many times."

"You're right about that. I don't know Chief Dixon well. Met him a few times, but he doesn't seem like someone who would be concerned without good reason."

Chief Dixon's heightened concern bothered Logan. The chief wasn't naïve, nor was he an amateur. Although a large number of missing people were found with a girlfriend or boyfriend, others disappeared for sinister reasons. In those cases, most of the time they never made it home.

Maggie brought their drinks, and then Logan noticed Tony coming their way, a big smile on his face. "I'm so glad to see you, my friends. Have you ordered?"

"Hi, Tony," Alex said. "Yes, we did."

They weren't really friends with Tony, but they'd been among his first customers. When they went back to the office and spread the word about how good the food was, lots of coworkers came—and they brought even more people. Tony credited Logan and Alex with making his business a success. Logan had told him more than once that his awesome food had made his restaurant prosper, not their recommendations. But Tony still felt he and Alex had been instrumental in building his clientele.

"Your lunch is on me," he said with a wide smile.

When Logan started to object, Tony waved his comment away. "No, my friend. Once in a while I want to thank you by buying your meal. What is it the Bible says? Give and it will be given to you?" His loud, hearty laugh filled the room. "You must let me do this so the Lord will bless me. Right?"

Logan could see that any argument would end in defeat, so he finally nodded. "Okay, Tony. I wouldn't want you to lose a blessing. We accept."

"That's wonderful, my friend. You've made me very happy."

Then, just as quickly as he'd arrived, he was gone. A few minutes later their waitress showed up with their sandwiches and chips. "Tony says no charge," she said with a smile.

They thanked her, and she left to take care of other customers.

"At least we can leave her a nice tip," Alex said.

"Absolutely." He picked up his sandwich. "Tony's a nice man. I really like him." Then he took a bite, and the flavors exploded in his mouth.

"I like him too. And I think I'm addicted to these sandwiches. Do they have rehab for sandwich addictions?"

Logan laughed. "I have no idea, but if they do, I'll be in the room next to yours."

A few minutes later they'd settled into a comfortable silence. Logan knew Alex was thinking about the case just like he was, trying to pull the few threads they had into some kind of pattern. Although this was perfectly normal for them, he'd noticed that Alex had grown significantly quieter lately. And sometimes she seemed so far away. She always came around, yet it happened enough now that he'd begun to worry about her.

A few months ago she'd been tormented by a truly evil psychopath. A man whose goal had been to kill her . . . and make her suffer horribly before she could welcome death. Although she'd come out of it thanking God for rescuing her, over the past month or so he'd noticed a haunted look in her eyes. He'd tried to draw her out, find out what was going on, but Alex had put up emotional walls to protect herself. This was a pattern he thought she'd broken.

Would it always be this way? He knew she trusted him—to a degree. He was pretty certain she felt more secure with him than she did with any other human being on the planet. But she was still keeping her pain and fear inside as if protecting an old friend. Someone she was comfortable with. Not that anyone but him would notice, but it was there. And by now he knew her well enough to feel sure if whatever this was lingered untreated, it could eat her up inside.

She'd come so far trying to overcome her past. Just after she'd turned her life over to God, he saw such a change in her. A spark of optimism. A willingness to allow others inside. Although she still came to church with him and their friend Monty every Sunday, it was as if what was said from the pulpit just bounced off her.

"Dessert?" he asked after they'd finished eating.

She shook her head and smiled. "Completely full. No place to put it."

"Not even some bread pudding? When we get back, you'll regret it."

"Well, if you get an order to go, I might be influenced to share it with you later."

He smiled and signaled Maggie, who came over. "One order of your incredible bread pudding to go," he said. "And we want to pay for it, please."

"Okay." She grinned. "Just couldn't leave without it, could you?"

He laughed. "I guess not. It's awesome."

Maggie patted her flat stomach. "Yeah, but it's murder on diets."

"Doesn't look like you need to worry about it," he said, realizing she was hoping he'd say it.

She tossed him a shy smile and took off. A few minutes later they'd paid their bill, left a generous tip, and had their bread pudding in hand. Logan noticed Maggie had given them a substantial serving.

"I think you have an admirer," Alex said as they got back into his car.

He chuckled but didn't respond. That might be true, but he wasn't interested. The only woman on earth he wanted to look at him with more than casual interest was this woman who so often seemed to look right through him.

# 4

**A**lex couldn't help thinking about the missing woman at lunch. Where was she? Logan was right. If she'd wanted to run off, there were better ways to do it. Maybe the parents weren't involved, but statistically, family *was* implicated when someone went missing. Authorities usually looked closely at a spouse, but Tracy Mendenhall was a widow.

When they got back to the office Alex requested a check on the parents' financial records. An hour later she got a call telling her there was no sign of an inheritance or any influx of money that might cause Tracy to stage a kidnapping. Nor was there a significant outflow of money. It was awful to think about, but family members sometimes paid hired guns to dispose of troublesome relatives.

She was going through the notes in Lucas's file when Logan came up to her desk. "I think we have a problem," he said. She knew that expression. Something was wrong.

"Four other women are missing in our general area. The descriptions match Tracy's. Young, attractive, long dark hair, same approximate build. I requested information from all the different police stations in Prince William County, but not everyone's gotten back to me yet."

That niggling feeling Alex had turned into a cold stab of fear. She swallowed the bile in her throat, pushing away the images that too often tried to force their way into her mind. The ones that kept her awake at night, making her afraid to sleep because they waited for her to let them in.

"Any bodies?" she choked out.

She noticed Logan's raised eyebrows and took a deep breath to calm herself. Her heart was pounding.

"No. And no leads." He sighed. "This makes five in the same county."

Alex frowned. "If we do have a serial, where are the bodies? Even if they're well hidden, eventually they're found. Of course, Gacy buried twenty-nine on his property and threw four others into the Des Plaines River. And Dahmer had the remains of eleven in his apartment. But they were the exceptions, not the rule."

Logan nodded. "You're right. Maybe this is just a coincidence?"

"I doubt that, and so do you."

"Then maybe we'll see something to help us with our profile when we get the records about the other disappearances."

"We've got to get busy generating a victimology for all the police departments," Alex said.

"Let's start now. We can update it as information comes in. We need to get this done before a body actually does show up."

Alex nodded, the words she wanted to say stuck in her throat. Could Logan tell something was wrong?

"I'll start on the checklist while you let the police at each station know we'll send it to them as soon as it's ready," she finally managed to say. "If they can effectively canvass the neighbors, family, and friends of all the missing women, that will help us determine if we have a pattern here."

Logan stared at her for a moment, but then he nodded and set off for his desk.

Alex knew she needed help, but fear and pride prevented her from asking for it. If she told Jeff and Logan the truth, they'd make her take another break, and she just couldn't go back to the psychologist the Bureau assigned to her. Her job was her identity. Without it, she was nothing. If they made her stop working again, she was certain she'd shatter into a thousand pieces. She prayed every morning, asking God to take away this unreasonable fear that had worsened in recent weeks. But where was He? Why wouldn't He answer? After He saved her from a madman who'd tried to destroy her, she'd had so much peace. The reality that God loved her had been a burning fire in her heart.

So why was she feeling like this now? She felt sick . . . and guilty. God must be so ashamed of her. She should be stronger by now. What did the Scripture say? Be strong in the Lord and the power of His might? She didn't feel strong, though. She was so weak. What was wrong with her?

Yes, she knew she was loved and treasured by God. How many times had she been told that? But she still needed something to define her as a person, didn't she? Surely God wasn't interested in people who were useless.

The psychologist's response when Alex informed her she

was ready to get on with her life suddenly came back to her. "I'm glad to hear that," Dr. Keegan had said. "But just remember this, Alex. Many times relapse is part of the healing process. Sometimes people who've been through severe trauma go through a period of euphoria and believe they've recovered. But the damage done to their inner selves is just hiding in the dark. Waiting to come out. And eventually it will."

Alex remembered the feeling of superiority that caused her to dismiss the doctor's concerns. She didn't understand. Alex was a Christian. She wouldn't relapse. God had healed her, and she would stay that way.

Yet she hadn't been able to banish the images that tortured her. Sometimes she still woke during the night gasping for air, her hands clawing at her neck for a noose that wasn't there. And for a few seconds she was convinced she was still in that warehouse, struggling to breathe, her life ebbing away. Strangely, death wasn't what scared her. The process of dying was what turned her body cold and made her feel out of control. She'd battled images from her childhood for years. But this was worse. Much worse. How much more could one person bear?

She moved to the break room, where her hands shook as she poured coffee from the carafe into a mug. This had to stop. Whatever it took. She would not let a psychotic serial killer rob her of the rest of her life. She just couldn't.

Tracy lay in bed, staring up at the ceiling, waiting for the lights to go off. She'd thought about that day over and over. If only she'd been smarter. Not so gullible. But it wasn't really her fault.

When she was first brought to this place, she could hardly keep her eyes open. Her eyelids felt as if they were weighted down. Little by little, flashes of memories came back to her until she was able to recall everything that happened.

She'd gone for her usual morning jog. When she'd come around a corner, she'd noticed another jogger sitting by the edge of the path, holding his right foot and lightly groaning.

"Are you okay?" she'd asked him.

When he looked up, she saw a good-looking man with blue eyes and dark hair with a casual cut that fit his face.

"I twisted my ankle," he said with a smile. "Should have warmed up. I haven't done this in a long time. Guess I was overconfident."

"What can I do to help?"

"I hate to ask, but could you assist me to my car?" He pointed to the copse of trees behind him. "If we cut through here, it's parked right on the other side."

Tracy hadn't wanted to go through the secluded area, but it would save the man having to hobble through the rest of the path.

"I just moved here from Dallas," he'd said. "My mother died a few months ago, and I didn't want my dad to be alone. He's kind of helpless." He laughed. "Sorry, that's a lot of personal information, but I thought it might help you decide I'm not some kind of weirdo who pretends to sprain his ankle to meet pretty women."

Tracy laughed too. She liked this guy. "I feel perfectly safe. Let's get you to your car."

She reached down and helped him to his feet. He tried to put some weight on his injury and immediately yelped.

"Sorry. That wasn't a very manly sound to make."

She laughed again. He really was funny. "I promise not to make fun of your girly noises. Put your arm around my shoulders and lean on me."

He frowned. "I'm a lot bigger than you. Are you sure you can do this?"

"I'm sure. I'm stronger than I look."

"Okay. Thanks a lot. I really appreciate this."

He'd wrapped his arm around her shoulders, and she'd put her arm behind his back.

She shivered now at the thought.

He'd halted just as they were almost to the other side of the trees.

"You okay?" she asked. Maybe she was making him move too fast.

"I'm fine."

He reached into his pocket, and she caught a glimpse of the syringe only a second before he plunged it into her neck.

Then she'd come to in this place, wherever it was. She still had no idea.

Another memory had slowly surfaced not long after she arrived here. As she'd slumped to the ground, fighting the darkness threatening to overtake her, her abductor had softly sung an old song she hadn't heard since she was a little girl.

"Daisy, Daisy, give me your answer do. I'm half crazy, all for the love of you. . . ."

Fresh tears dripped down the sides of her face onto her pillow. Would anyone ever find her?

# 5

Alex and Logan were called to the conference room at two. Jeff and Special Agent Lucas sat around the large table along with Chief Dixon and Tracy's parents, the Abbotts. Alex's heart fell when she saw the couple. Their suffering was obvious—and real.

Alex had developed a talent for reading people, and although they couldn't be sure the Abbotts weren't involved in their daughter's disappearance until they talked to them and had read all the investigators' notes, their expressions and body language told her these people had no idea where their beloved daughter was.

"Mr. and Mrs. Abbott," Jeff said, "this is Supervisory Special Agent Alex Donovan and Supervisory Special Agent Logan Hart. They're working on your daughter's case. Do you mind if they ask you a few questions?"

"Of course not," Mr. Abbott said. "We'll do anything to bring Tracy home."

"I . . . I still can't believe this is happening," Mrs. Abbott said. "One day everything is fine, and then . . ." She put her hand up to her mouth to stifle a sob. "Matty and Cassie don't understand where their mother is," she said, tears running down her cheeks. "It's so hard to keep the truth from them, but we don't want to frighten them any more than they already are."

"I'm so sorry," Alex said. "I can't imagine how hard this is for you."

"Thank you," Tracy's father said as he put his arm around his wife's shoulders. Their chairs were pushed together as close as possible. "What can we do to help?"

Although Alex thought she already had the answer to her most important question, she asked, "Has there been any tension between you and Tracy lately? How have you been getting along?"

"If you're asking if our daughter ran away," Mrs. Abbott choked out, "the answer is an unequivocal no. We're a very close family. She's been so excited about starting her new career, and she plans on buying a house. Of course, she says she'll miss living with us, but we want her to have her own life. To become everything she was created to be. Besides, she won't be that far away. We'll still be able to see her and the children whenever . . . whenever we can." She leaned her head on her husband's shoulder.

"We're Christians," Mr. Abbott said. "I don't know if that means anything to you, but to us it's just another reason we can confidently say Tracy would never intentionally do anything like this to us or to her children. I have no doubt of that whatsoever."

Mr. Abbott had leaned forward as he talked, the hand not

around his wife lying on the table, open and relaxed. He'd met Alex's eyes and never looked away. No excessive blinking. Breathing steady, regular. He was telling the truth.

"We understand," Logan said. "Does Tracy have a boyfriend?"

Mrs. Abbott shook her head. "She did, but they broke up recently. And not because of anything wrong between them. Evan is a very nice man, but he accepted a job in California, and they decided it was best to end the relationship because of the distance. Tracy cared for him, but she wasn't in love with him. Evan felt the same way. Their breakup was amicable."

Although Alex wouldn't say it, parents usually knew very little about their children's romantic lives—or at least not as much as they thought they did.

"Can you give us his full name and any contact information you have?" She smiled at Mrs. Abbott. "I'm sure you're right about this, but we need to make sure we don't leave any stone unturned. Maybe Evan knows something helpful and doesn't even realize it."

Mr. Abbott nodded. "I see what you mean." He took his phone out of his pants pocket and started scrolling through it. "I have his number because we asked him to call us when he reached his destination. Wanted to make certain he got there safely. We care about him even if he wasn't the one for Tracy." He stopped scrolling and read out a number, which Alex wrote down. "His last name is Prescott. I don't have his new address, but I can get it for you."

"Thank you. Do you know of anyone who might dislike Tracy?" Logan asked. "Anyone who might want to harm her?"

Tracy's mother sobbed again. "No, no one," she managed to say as she tried to catch her breath.

"My wife is right," Mr. Abbott said. "I know people in this situation might say their loved one has no enemies, but in this case it's true. Tracy has always been friendly to everyone. And if someone didn't like her, she'd try even harder to connect with them. Some of her best friends are girls she went to high school with. Girls who used to dislike her. Who were jealous of Tracy because she's smart and very pretty."

"She's a single mother, correct?" Logan asked. "Widowed?"

Mr. Abbott nodded and sighed. "Her husband, Terry, died four years ago in an automobile accident. He was a wonderful man, and she loved him very much. I think he's the real reason she didn't fall in love with Evan. Terry was her soul mate, if you believe in that kind of thing."

He frowned and stared at Alex for a moment. "Excuse me for saying this, but you remind me of Tracy. She has long black hair like yours. She even ties it back like you do. And you have the same build. Your eyes are the same color too. You could be sisters."

Alex shoved aside the "very pretty" description he'd used for his daughter. She knew she wasn't pretty. Her mouth was too wide, and she kept her bangs long to cover a forehead that was too high for her liking.

"What about any strange people in her life lately?" Logan asked.

"You know, the police asked us all these questions," Tracy's father said, glancing at Chief Dixon. "As did Agent Lucas."

"We know," Alex said. "I'm so sorry to keep putting you through this, but it's possible our questions might trigger something new. Something you've forgotten."

"Be patient, David," his wife said. "Let these people do their work."

Mr. Abbott took a deep breath, then let it out slowly. "I . . . I'm sorry. I'm just so worried about her. Where can she be?"

"We can't answer that right now," Lucas said, "but I guarantee we'll do everything possible to find her. These agents with the BAU are the best we have. If anyone can help us locate the other missing women who resemble your daughter . . ."

As soon as the words left his mouth, Alex froze, and it was evident Lucas immediately knew what he'd done. He clamped his lips together and stared at the Abbotts as the chief's face turned red. So did Jeff's.

"Women?" Mr. Abbott said as he shoved his chair away from the table. "You're telling us other women are missing? Women who look like Tracy?"

Before anyone could respond, his face turned white, and he clutched his chest. If his wife hadn't grabbed him, he would have fallen to the floor.

Logan, Lucas, and Chief Dixon all leaped from their chairs and carried the man toward the sofa in Jeff's office. As Alex and Jeff trailed behind them, Jeff pulled out his cell phone and called 9-1-1.

After Chief Dixon and the ambulance carrying the Abbotts left, Jeff tore into Lucas. "What were you thinking?" he yelled. "We don't even know if those disappearances are connected."

"It just slipped out," Lucas said, his expression reflecting his misery. "I had no intention . . . I mean, I can't believe . . ."

"Jeff," Alex said. "It was a mistake. It could have happened to any of us."

Jeff's face was dark with rage. "No. We're trained agents. It shouldn't have happened at all. It's totally unprofessional. I'm sure Chief Dixon wishes he'd never come to us."

Logan was disturbed by Jeff's reaction. It was clear Lucas felt terrible. Maybe Jeff was right, but this wasn't helping. Was he thinking about his own daughter? Was that why he was overreacting? As if reading Logan's mind, Jeff took a deep breath. His color began to normalize.

"Look, it happened," Jeff said. "Let's get past it. We have

to let the Abbotts know they can't talk about this. We have no proof these disappearances are related. It could cause a panic, and our UNSUB could take off. We'd lose the element of surprise." He looked at Lucas. "Get to the hospital. Talk to Mrs. Abbott and the chief. Make sure this stops here, got it?"

Lucas, who appeared to be barely holding on, nodded. As he turned to go, Jeff called out his name.

"Alex is right," Jeff said with a sigh. "Any of us could have made the same mistake, but we all need to learn from this. Even a momentary loss of concentration can cause a lot of damage. Let's just hope we can put our finger in the dike before the flood starts."

"Sorry," Lucas said. "I'll make sure it stays with the Abbotts."

Once Lucas walked out of the office, Jeff turned to Alex and Logan. "Don't say it. I know what you're thinking, but something like this just can't happen. A careless word can make it incredibly difficult for investigators."

Logan shrugged. "I'm not arguing with you, but it's time to move on. We can't go back in time."

Jeff sighed. "It would be helpful if we could." He pushed some file folders across his desk. "Here are three of the reports you asked for on the other women missing in the county. Still waiting on the fourth. Look these over and see what you think. I sent your victimology checklist to the police departments involved. We should be able to connect the dots soon . . . assuming anything links these women beyond their similar ages and looks." He sighed again. "I've got to contact Lucas's Special Agent in Charge and tell her what happened."

"Who is his SAC?" Logan asked.

"Marilyn Stein. She's tough, but she's fair. She's known for supporting her people."

"Good. Lucas will need that," Logan said.

Alex nodded in agreement, then said, "Sure didn't see this coming when I got in this morning."

"Me neither," Logan said. He took two of the folders and pushed the other one toward Alex. "Let's start going through these. See what we can find."

"Well, we already know one thing about our UNSUB. I'm pretty sure he was dressed like a jogger when he abducted Tracy. Otherwise, he probably wouldn't have managed to get so close to her."

"Good point. She would have taken off if he'd seemed threatening. As often as she jogged, she probably could have left him in the dust. He had to find a way to keep her from doing that. Probably faked an injury."

Alex sat back in her chair. "He could definitely be a stranger. If Tracy ran every day, it would be easy to determine her schedule. He wouldn't have to actually know her for that."

"But how did he find her?" Logan asked. "Is he just randomly looking for young women with long dark hair?"

"Good question." She opened the laptop she'd brought with her. After tapping at the keys a few times, she said, "Maybe this is how." She turned the screen toward him.

"'Tracy Mendenhall putting together boxes of supplies for school children in the Philippines,'" Logan read out loud. "Then below that headline, the article begins with 'A local woman has organized a group at her church to ensure low-income children in the Philippines have the supplies they need to succeed.' Looks like it goes on to talk about all the outreach her church does. Yeah, this could be how she turned up on his radar."

"We need to check whether these other women showed up in the media somewhere as well," Alex said. "Then maybe we can learn what links them together."

"I agree," Jeff said. "Get on that. Then do what you can to write a profile. I know the information is thin, but I've seen you both do some remarkable things." Jeff got up and walked out of the room, pulling the door closed behind him.

Logan stared after him. "Thin? How about almost invisible?"

Alex smiled. "There's more here than you think."

"You've said that before."

"And I've always been right."

Logan laughed. "Yeah, you've always been right."

Alex was the most talented behavioral analyst he'd ever known. She could take the smallest fact and bring more out of it than seemed possible.

"Have you heard from Monty?" Alex asked.

"A few days ago. He expects to be back next week." Their friend and coworker Monty Wong had inherited his grandmother's house. But the roof needed to be repaired. In an effort to save money, he took on the project himself. Turned out to be a mistake. Logan was grateful he'd only broken his leg. The fall could have caused a lot more damage.

"I take it he's hired someone to finish the job," Alex said with a grin.

"Yeah. I want to tease him, but he's so embarrassed I just can't do it. It would be like adding salt to a wound."

Alex laughed. "I'll bet you twenty bucks he won't be back for two days before you make fun of him."

"That's a sucker's bet. I might as well just hand you a twenty-dollar bill right now."

Alex shook her head. "You're something else."

"That's true, but at least I keep you on your toes."

Alex laughed again. Logan loved her laughter, but there'd been so little of it lately. His thoughts returned to his feelings about her. Even though he was trained to read people, she was still a closed book in so many ways. And that made it that much harder to tell how she felt about him. Yet sometimes he thought he noticed something in her expression. In her body language. Did she care for him as more than a friend? God would have to tell him when it was time to find out.

"Let me make you copies of these files, and then I'll see if I can find anything that puts them in the public eye. If so, we could have at least a tenuous connection between them." He rose from his seat.

"More than that, in my opinion," Alex said. "I'll go back to my desk and work this profile as much as I can. Let me know if you find something."

"I will."

He'd just sat down when a sharp pain ripped through his skull. It was so bad it took his breath away. He reached into his drawer and grabbed one of the pain pills Dr. Morton had prescribed. He popped a pill into his mouth and swallowed it with the cold coffee sitting in a cup on his desk. Then he closed his eyes to shut out the bright ceiling lights that pierced his brain like tiny daggers. When he was home and one of these hit, he'd pull the blinds closed and turn off the lights until the pain subsided. Couldn't do that now, though.

"We need to get an MRI of your spine," Dr. Morton had said. "You went through a severe physical trauma a few months ago. That jump you took could have done more damage than just breaking your ankle. It may have affected your back, which could be causing the headaches. At some point we might want to give you some injections to reduce pain and inflammation, but first I want to see what's going on. I'll have someone call you to schedule the MRI."

That had been two weeks ago, but no one had called. Maybe he should contact the doctor and find out why he hadn't heard from anyone. He wanted to get on the other side of this as soon as possible. Before it interfered with his job. He grabbed his phone and called the doctor's office. He spoke to his nurse, and she promised to get right back with him. Expressed regret that someone hadn't called to schedule the MRI. Good. Some progress.

Logan picked up his list of the missing women. As he entered the first name into a search engine, his headache was not only better but forgotten. He was now certain they had a serial kidnapper, and he was convinced it wouldn't be long before another woman was abducted.

# 7

**M**errie checked her watch. Shoot. She was running late. Caring for her mother while trying to make enough money to support them both was wearing her down. It wasn't her mom's fault she was sick. The chemo treatments were so hard on her that she couldn't live alone, so Merrie had moved in with her. Into the house she'd left years ago.

She missed her apartment and her social life . . . such as it was. And it wasn't much. Thirty years old and still not married. She'd wasted so many years waiting for Paul to get serious and propose. Why hadn't she realized he was never going to commit? He wanted someone to fawn over him. Stay home and raise a family. Not that it wouldn't be wonderful, but she liked having some independence. Paul never understood why she enjoyed selling real estate. It was a challenge, but when she found the right house for someone, it was not only financially rewarding but also personally satisfying. Watching the excitement on the buyer's face. Seeing a family begin their lives in a nice house she'd helped them find. Of course, she'd like to be on the other side one day. Would it ever happen?

She pulled up in front of the attractive two-story house with the beautiful lawn and blooming rose bushes. Maybe she'd even have a house like this someday.

Merrie got out of the car and hurried up to the man waiting for her on the front porch. When he turned and smiled, her heart fluttered. Dark hair, blue eyes, good-looking. Maybe ditching Paul wasn't a mistake after all.

She suddenly remembered all the warnings her mother had given her about meeting with male clients alone. She had pepper spray in her purse, but thankfully she'd never had to use it. This man hardly looked like a threat.

She greeted him and then began her spiel about the house as she took the key from the lockbox and slid it in. Once they were inside, she remarked on the main floor's open concept. But when she turned to see if the prospective buyer was properly impressed, he was staring at her oddly. Then she froze as he reached for her. Before she knew what was happening, she felt a sting in her neck and slid to the floor.

As she fought the feeling of heaviness overtaking her, she heard the man softly sing, "Daisy, Daisy, give me your answer do. . . ."

"Find anything?" Jeff asked as Alex and Logan entered his office.

"Yes," Logan said. "I searched for the names of the four

missing women on the internet, and I found something for every single one of them."

Jeff motioned for them to sit down. Alex's stomach was tied in knots. Was this really another serial killer? Could she face this again? Part of her said no. That enough was enough. But the desire to stop evil was stronger. She wanted to win. Wanted to send the enemy back into the darkness.

"Sarah Breedlove, thirty-two and a local author, had a book signing at a small bookstore," Alex said. "Her picture was in the local newspaper. She's the one who's been missing the longest, four weeks."

"Amy Tharp was interviewed on TV about summer school classes at the school where she teaches," Logan added. "Marla Bess works for a dog rescue organization. She was interviewed on the same station a couple of weeks earlier."

"And last but not least," Alex said, "Rhonda Brooks, who works for a restaurant in Dale City. A diner left her a tip for a thousand dollars. The local paper picked up the story, and it was also featured on the TV news. These three women have been gone three weeks or less."

"Was Rhonda interviewed on the same station as the others?" Jeff asked.

Logan shook his head. "No. Different channel."

"Well, that's interesting," Jeff said.

Alex nodded. "The police need to know that we have a serial. We have no idea if he's killing these women or simply kidnapping them. If he is, he must have someplace to hold them. Of course, kidnapping several women and then keeping them is really unusual. I've heard of it only once. In Kentucky. A man named Claude Monroe kidnapped four women. They all died before they could be found." She shrugged. "If there's any good news, he kept them alive for several weeks. If this guy is following Claude's example, we have a chance to get them back."

Logan sighed. "Or they could all be dead and buried somewhere around here. Lots of forest area in the county. They would be hard to find."

"Put all this together in a report," Jeff said sharply. "I'll send it to Chief Dixon."

"Will do," Logan said.

"I'm going to suggest they set up a task force. I get the feeling they're going to need all the help they can get. By the way, I heard from the hospital. Mr. Abbott is going to be fine. He didn't have a heart attack. It was just stress." He frowned at Logan. "Speaking of people not feeling well, you don't look so good. Are you feeling okay?"

Logan nodded. "Just a stupid headache. Been having them for a while. My doctor has me on medication that helps. It won't interfere with my work."

Jeff blew out a quick breath. "I'm not worried about your job performance. I'm concerned about you." He glanced at his watch. "Send me that report, but it doesn't need to be too detailed. Then why don't you head home? Take your medicine and get some rest." He focused his gaze on Alex. "Go with him. Make sure he has something healthy to eat and takes it easy the rest of the evening."

Alex was surprised by Jeff's request—and Logan looked rather startled as well—but her concern for Logan outweighed any hesitation. "Sure. I know a place that makes a great chicken noodle soup."

"If it's the grocery store and the soup is in a can, forget it," Logan said with a grin.

Alex noticed that even smiling made him wince, and that worried her. "No, not in a can. I promise you'll love it."

"Okay." He nodded at Jeff. "Thanks, Boss. Sorry about this. I'll be fine by tomorrow."

"You said your doctor has this covered?" Jeff asked.

"Yeah. He thinks I might have injured my back in that warehouse a few months back and it's causing this pain. Not sure why it's kicking up now, but they can do all kinds of things. After an MRI he'll probably give me an injection or something that should help to get me back to normal."

Jeff didn't look convinced. Alex wasn't either. But after quickly putting that report together, all she wanted to do was to concentrate on getting Logan comfortable and away from the bright lights that seemed to exacerbate his pain.

---

As Tracy felt herself rising toward the light, sleep tried to pull her back, its heavy fingers grasping at her mind. She fought against the desire to fall back into the dark where it was safe. She didn't want to face what was happening outside the comforting blackness that had kept her wrapped in its arms.

But then she remembered that a man had decided he had the right to take her against her will. Anger overcame fear, and she pushed the last lazy tendrils of slumber from her consciousness. Struggling to pull herself into a sitting position, she acclimated herself to her surroundings. She was in the same room.

At least her sheets and comforter were dry. Thank God. How weird was it to be embarrassed about wetting her bed in a situation like this? Someone had done this to her, and she was determined to find him and make him pay.

She wasn't a wimpy woman. She'd taken classes in self-defense for the past year, ever since some man robbed her as she walked alone toward her car after school. She'd felt so helpless, and she didn't like it. She'd found some classes offered locally on the weekends, and her parents had encouraged her to take them. Her father had experienced a lot of anger toward that criminal. Learning to defend herself had given him some peace of mind. It was worth the extra stress to her schedule to do that for him. She owed her parents so much. She was blessed to have them in her life and in the lives of her children.

Tracy blinked away tears. What were Matty and Cassie thinking now? Were they wondering if she was ever coming back? How were her parents holding up? She was worried about her dad. He'd had problems with his heart. Was he okay? She was more concerned for her family than for herself.

She pushed herself off the bed, then walked over to the door, put her hand on the upper panel's knob, and slid it open. She was surprised when it moved. She'd assumed it was locked from the outside.

Tracy blinked to clear away the remaining sleep from her eyes. She was looking out on a hallway made of stone. She put her face against the door in an attempt to see as far as she could to the right and then to the left. Her vision was limited because the opening was so small, but it was what she saw across from her that made her gasp.

Another door. Just like hers.

On the way to Logan's apartment, Alex stopped by a favorite deli that made the most awesome chicken soup. She picked up broccoli and cheese for herself and some crusty, freshly baked French bread as well.

Logan was quiet in the car. He leaned back on the headrest, his eyes closed. Alex could tell he was in pain.

"I'm seeing an ophthalmologist on Friday," he said suddenly. He'd been so silent that she jumped when he finally spoke. "Maybe I just need a new prescription for my glasses."

"But you said your headaches have something to do with your injuries in the warehouse."

He turned to look at her and smiled. "I think between the two options, one of them will fit the symptoms. My doctor called while you were inside. He has an MRI scheduled for me tomorrow. So by the end of the week I should know what's going on." He turned his head back and sighed. "Maybe I just need a head transplant. Of course, it would be difficult to find anyone as good-looking as I am, so that might not be an option."

Alex laughed. "Before that MRI, why don't you ask them to check your ego too? It's so large it could be pressing against your brain."

She looked over and saw him grin. "Yeah, you might be right." He hesitated a moment before saying, "Thank you for this. I really think I could have made it home on my own, but I truly appreciate your help. Sometimes when the pain is really bad, it's hard to see. I didn't want to drive like that."

"Yeah, I've seen you drive. People out on the streets are already in enough danger."

"Very funny."

A few minutes later Alex pulled up in front of Logan's apartment. He'd recently moved, and this was the first time she'd been here. Although she wasn't fond of apartment living, she was surprised to find that he lived in an older, refurbished building. Its classical design was a throwback to the early twentieth century with what looked like four separate residences. Six lovely American redbud trees lined the walkway leading up to the main entrance.

"I like this," she said as she turned off the engine. "I don't know what I was expecting, but it wasn't anything this lovely."

"So in other words, you think I have no taste? What did you have in mind? A dilapidated lean-to?"

"No. Not dilapidated."

Logan sighed and opened his car door. "I'll get the food."

Alex came around the front of the car as Logan reached into the backseat to pull out the bag. But it slipped out of his hand, crashing to the ground outside the car. Alex quickly picked it up and checked it out. Thankfully, the tops had stayed on the soup containers.

"It's fine," she said. "Not a problem."

She closed the car door and stared at him. "You okay?"

"Of course. I just didn't get a good grip on it."

Logan's tone was sharp. Was he really upset? Why? Everyone dropped things once in a while.

"I know," she said soothingly, trying to calm him. He was probably just touchy because of his headache. She was grumpy when she was in pain. "Let's get you inside, okay?"

He didn't say anything, just nodded. She followed him to the main entrance, where he slid a keycard into an electronic reader. She heard a click, and then a green light came on. Logan pushed the door open and then waited for her to enter in front of him.

He led her down a hall to a door with the number one on it, and then he unlocked it too. Alex entered a nicely decorated living area. Logan had bought new furniture, contemporary but leaning toward traditional. The couch was gray with white and gray throw pillows and a soft white afghan thrown over one arm. The tufted chairs sitting across from the couch were the same gray and had matching ottomans. A large glass coffee table with metal legs sat in front of the couch.

On the other side of the large room was a dining set made of dark wood. The chair seats matched the couch. She didn't see many pictures on the walls, but a beautiful metal-framed mirror had been hung over a large electric fireplace. Two photos in gray-toned frames hung on either side of the mirror. They were probably of family, but Alex wasn't close enough to see them clearly.

She carried the food bag into the small modern kitchen. She was surprised at how spotless it was. It wasn't that Logan's other place had been messy. It wasn't. But he was obviously trying harder to maintain his new apartment. In fact, the entire first floor was clean and shiny.

Alex thought back to her own house. She considered herself very neat. She'd had to learn to keep things picked up and clean when she was a kid. Yet before running out this morning, she'd tossed her pajamas on the floor in the bedroom. And after a quick bowl of cereal, she'd left the dish and spoon on the kitchen counter. It was funny to discover that Logan was clearly a better housekeeper than she was. It also felt a little disconcerting. She pushed the thought from her mind. Right now, all that mattered was taking care of him.

"If you want to disinfect my apartment, there's some spray under the kitchen sink," Logan said.

He was referring to the problem she had with germs, but she was pretty sure germs had no chance of survival here.

"I don't think that will be necessary. Frankly, after seeing what you've done here, I think I need to hire you to clean my place."

He shrugged. "I was never a slob, you know. But I guess I care more about this place than my last one. This is the kind of apartment I've always wanted." He sighed. "You know, I feel I've been judged wrongly. You should be ashamed of yourself."

"Yes, I'm very embarrassed," she said, laughing. "Now, sit down. What do you want to drink?"

"There's tea in the refrigerator. I'll take that."

Alex had assumed he'd argue with her, tell her he'd take care of the food. That's how he usually was. But when he gingerly lowered himself onto the couch without argument, she began to really worry.

She walked back into the living area. "Are you sure we shouldn't go to the emergency room? Or at least an urgent care clinic?"

He shook his head. "No. Like I said, the MRI is tomorrow. I'd rather let them do their thing." He looked up at her. "Could you get my pills, though? The bottle is on the night-stand next to my bed. The bedrooms are upstairs."

"Sure." She hurried up the stairs and found two bedrooms. One looked like a guest room. Very basic and rather bare. She opened the door to the other room and discovered a pleasant room with dusty blue walls and a king-sized bed with a cream-colored comforter. In the corner on the other side of the room sat an overstuffed chair.

A mahogany bookcase was next to the chair, and Alex stepped closer so she could see what books it contained. She smiled when she realized Logan's reading choices were similar to hers. One shelf held nonfiction books about profiling and case studies of serial killers. The other two shelves were devoted to novels. Suspense and mystery. Alex had read almost every single one of them.

She picked up a framed photo sitting on top of the book-case and saw several people smiling for the camera. Had to be Logan's family. He stood behind two older people who resembled him. His parents? A young man stood on one side of the group and a younger girl on the other side. Brother and sister?

As she set the photo down, a wave of shame washed over her. Logan had spent so much time trying to help her through her problems, yet they'd never talked much about his life.

She suddenly realized he was waiting for his pain medication and here she was dawdling, going through his belongings. She hurried over to the nightstand next to the bed, where she found both a bottle of over-the-counter pain reliever and another bottle of prescription medicine. She picked up the latter and read the label. Hydrocodone? A high dose. He must really be hurting. He wasn't the kind to take something like this unless he had to.

Once downstairs, she put the bottle on the coffee table in front of him. Then she poured a glass of iced tea and took that to him too.

"Soup will be ready soon," she said. "You just relax. I'm not leaving until I know you're okay."

Logan nodded and opened the medicine bottle. She was alarmed to see him shake not one but two pills into his hand and then toss them both into his mouth. Hadn't he taken pain pills back at the office? It hadn't been that long ago. He picked up his glass and took a drink before she could say anything.

"Logan, just how much pain are you in?"

"A lot. I hope I didn't break anything in my back or neck. I really don't want to be out of work for an extended period of time."

"Look, forget work. Just concentrate on getting better."

He didn't argue with her, just kicked off his shoes and swung his legs up on the couch. Alex positioned the couch pillows behind him to support his back and head. Then she grabbed the afghan on the arm of the couch and covered him with it.

"My grandmother made this for me," Logan whispered. "She was incredible. I miss her so much."

"Just see this as her hugging you even though she's in heaven now."

Logan smiled. "I will. Thank you."

In the kitchen Alex found bowls for the soup and small plates for the bread. After locating butter in the refrigerator, she carried everything into the living room on a tray. But Logan was already sound asleep, so she took his food back to the kitchen and put it in the refrigerator. She'd heat the soup for him later. But for now, she leaned against the counter, closed her eyes, and began to pray.

**J**eff was looking over the report Alex and Logan wrote, carefully reading the information about the missing women. He was surprised the police hadn't found a body yet. But as they'd mentioned, Virginia had lots of places to secretly bury someone. Sixty-two percent of the state was forestland.

There was a knock on the door. "Come in."

Alice stepped partway into his office. "Chief Dixon is here. He insists on seeing you."

Jeff frowned. He didn't like people just showing up. Why hadn't Dixon called first? He sighed and closed the file. "Okay, send him in."

She nodded and closed the door. A few seconds later it swung open again, and the police chief walked in. The muscles in his face looked tight.

"We've got another one," he said flatly. "Just happened earlier today. And there's more."

"Tell me."

"We've got eight others, Jeff. This has been going on for almost six years."

---

Tracy sat on the edge of her bed for what seemed like hours. There was only silence in the hallway. Where was the man who'd taken her? Finally, she got up and went back to the door. She slid open the small panel and looked out into the hall again. She listened for a moment but couldn't hear anything. She decided to take a chance and call out.

"Is anyone there?" she said softly. Her voice was raspy. She suspected it had something to do with the drugs she'd been injected with. She tried again, this time a little louder. "Can anyone hear me? My name is Tracy Mendenhall. Is anyone else out there?"

After a few minutes, the small panel on the door across the hall from her slid open.

"Shut up," a female voice hissed. "They can see you."

"Who?" Tracy said. "Who are you talking about?"

Again, silence.

"Look," Tracy said finally. "I want out of here. We need to work together if we're going to go home."

"We'll never escape," someone else said. Her voice was so soft Tracy could barely hear it.

Tracy was shocked to hear another metal panel slide open farther down the hall. "They're watching. You need to get away from the door. If they see you we could all be punished."

Tracy put her hand to her chest and fought to catch her breath. "All? How many of you are there?" She waited for an answer but none came. "Can they hear us?"

"No. The cameras in our rooms don't have audio, and those of us who have been on *dates* have checked the hall outside. Nothing. I guess they don't feel the need to listen to us since there's no way out of here."

"How many are here?" she asked again.

"We're not sure," the woman across from her said. "At least four. Sometimes they take them out and never come back."

"Is he. . . is he killing them?"

No answer. Tracy heard several metal doors slide shut, including the one across from her. Then nothing. What was going on? Did someone mention *dates?* What did that mean? Something kept pricking at her mind. What did this remind her of?

Then it came to her. A movie she'd seen a long time ago. It was about a man who kidnapped women and held them in some kind of underground prison, keeping them in separate rooms. Even though the title escaped her, she definitely still recalled the fear she felt when it was over.

Her friend Mary Ann had watched it with her. "That could never happen," she'd said when the movie ended. "What kind of underground place could hold that many people? Someone would know about it."

They'd argued for an hour about the believability of the plot. Tracy was willing to believe that the bad guy had some special place to put the women he'd kidnapped, but Mary Ann wouldn't accept it. Tracy had suggested abandoned mines and underground tunnels built to help slaves escape to freedom. Not wide enough, Mary Ann said. Wouldn't have rooms. Although Tracy was annoyed with her friend's almost obsessive focus on this one part of the movie, she realized later that it actually helped get her mind off the fear the movie ignited. Even with Mary Ann's misdirection, Tracy had experienced nightmares for a couple of weeks afterward.

Now she could see that Mary Ann's argument about abandoned mines was right. Those tunnels were only large enough for the cars they used to move whatever was being excavated from the mine. There certainly wasn't room for cells on both sides of the passages. Besides, those walls weren't made of this kind of stone.

So what was this place? Had it been created just for this? That didn't make sense either.

She sat down on the bed and gazed around the room. Just a few books, and no TV, phone, or computer. Was that on purpose? What was this guy trying to do? What did he want? She was certain she hadn't been molested. Was that coming next? She wished the woman across the hall would talk to her. She still had no idea what day it was. She was abducted early Sunday morning, and after she came to, she'd slept for a long time. But how long? She couldn't be certain. Was it Tuesday? Wednesday?

Tears filled her eyes. She'd missed getting together with her special women's group at church. She loved her church. Besides her charity work there, she went every Sunday with Matty, Cassie, and her parents. The kids had their own service, so Tracy sat in the sanctuary with her mother and father. She loved sharing church with them. Although she'd planned to start looking for a house for her and the kids soon, she knew she'd really miss them. They'd been so good to her and their grandkids.

*My parents. What are they thinking? Do they think I'm dead?*

Tracy wiped away the tears streaming down her cheeks.

She had to stay strong. Be on her guard. If she was going to get out of this, she had to be at her best. She lay down on the bed and tried to think of some way to escape.

Before long she started drifting off again. She fought it as long as she could, then finally gave in.

Alex finished her soup and decided she'd like some hot tea. She was pleased to find Logan had some of her favorites. After making some Earl Grey and adding a little milk, she made her way into the living room and placed her mug on a coaster on the small table between the two chairs. After retrieving her laptop from its bag, she put her feet up on the ottoman and began to work on the profile.

So far, the UNSUB had abducted five women—all Caucasian, all around the same age, with long dark hair and about the same color eyes. They couldn't yet prove that all the cases were related, but for now they had to move forward with this as the prevailing theory.

She grabbed the file she'd brought with her. All the women had different jobs and interests, but nothing that intersected. A single mom who'd just graduated from nursing school. A waitress. A self-published author. Someone who volunteered for a dog rescue group. A teacher. At least two of them appeared to care about children, but their concern manifested in different ways.

Alex thumbed through all five reports more than once, looking for something, anything that would help them with the profile. Three of the abductees went to church, but not the same ones. Two were married. Three weren't. The only thing she could find to link them was a brief mention in the

media. He was probably hunting his prey online since not
many people read hard copies of newspapers anymore. Three
of the women had been on television while the others hadn't.

She closed the file and sighed, then leaned her head back
and shut her eyes. There had to be something about this guy
that would help the police find him and the missing women.
Targeting them only because of their age and looks would
mean he had no access to their personal information, the
kind that might help him be more selective about whom he
took. Of course, that didn't leave many people out. People
in law enforcement, those who worked at banks or at the
IRS—although Alex doubted the IRS was kidnapping people.

She chuckled quietly. She was really getting off course.
She needed to concentrate. So what was this guy looking
for? The women probably reminded him of someone, but
without knowing what he was doing to them, they couldn't
figure out if he was taking them out of some kind of twisted
revenge or because of some other kind of obsession.

Her cell phone buzzed. She'd put it on vibrate so its ringing wouldn't wake Logan.

"Yes," she answered quietly.

Jeff's voice came over the receiver. "How's he doing?"

"Better, I think." She spoke almost in a whisper. "He's
been sleeping awhile. He hasn't eaten anything yet. When
he wakes up I'll try to get some soup down him."

"Okay, good. I thought you'd want to know we have another abduction. Same physical characteristics."

Alex's heart fell. "Oh no. Any details yet?"

"Some. I'll have everything ready for you in the morning,
but I think Logan needs to take a few days off. When is he
getting that MRI?"

"Tomorrow. I'll tell him you think it's best to stay home until after the doctors have had time to figure out what's going on. I'll try to talk him into waiting until at least Monday to come in."

"All right. If he fights you, let me know. I can read him the riot act."

Alex laughed lightly. "Yes, I know how effective that is. I've been on the receiving end a few times."

Jeff chuckled. "I'm sure it was for good reasons."

"It was."

Alex said good-bye and then ended the call. Another one? That made six missing women—that they knew of. How many were still alive? And how many were dead?

They had to get this profile right. The authorities needed to find this man before they started discovering bodies.

# 10

**W**hen Tracy woke up, a tray with a metal lid had been pushed through the bottom panel in the door. She rose and approached it slowly. Lifting the lid, she was surprised to see a plate of lasagna and an Italian salad with a breadstick. There was even a small bowl of what looked like chocolate mousse, a bottle of water, and a cup of hot tea.

Although she didn't want to eat anything the man who'd abducted her gave her, she was really hungry. She hadn't eaten anything since before her jog Sunday morning.

After carrying the tray to the little table, she pulled the chair sitting against the wall over and sat down. She found some utensils rolled up in a napkin, then cut off a small piece of the lasagna and put it into her mouth. It was delicious. She finished all the food in record time, then chugged down the bottle of cold water.

Still thirsty, she picked up the cup of tea. Delicious. When she was done, she put all the dirty dishes on the tray and covered it with the lid. She was reminded of a deluxe hotel. But this wasn't a hotel. She couldn't allow herself to get sucked in by any kind of manipulation her kidnapper might use in an effort to control her. She had no intention of becoming complacent or grateful to the criminal who'd abducted her and the other women here.

She'd just deposited the tray on the floor when she heard something from outside her room. She slid open the upper panel in the door and saw someone walking past her. A man with longish blond hair that hid his face. He was carrying a woman with long dark hair in his arms. He was talking to her, trying to reassure her even though she was obviously unconscious. It was almost as if he cared about her. But if he was working with the dark-haired man who'd abducted her, he had no real compassion. If he did, he wouldn't be helping him imprison people.

The woman's face was turned away, so Tracy couldn't see her features. In just seconds, they were no longer in her line of sight. She heard a door open down the hall to her left, and then a few minutes later, it closed.

Once again, the blond man walked past her. She still couldn't see his face. Who was this guy?

"Let me out of here," she called, trying to control the rage she felt. "You have no right to do this to people. It's wrong."

His footsteps stopped, but he didn't look at her.

"I can't help any of you," he said. "He's really angry. People shouldn't be treated so cruelly. Someone has to pay."

Tracy was confused. Was this someone she knew? She couldn't recall treating anyone badly, including the man who'd drugged her. Who could be this angry with her?

"I have no idea who you are," she said, "but I try hard to treat people well. Could you have confused me with someone else?"

He was silent for a moment. "He'll keep looking until he finds her."

"So you're looking for one woman, but you're willing to kidnap all of us on the off chance you'll find her? That's not right. The woman you're looking for might not even be here. You know that, right? What if all these women are innocent?"

As soon as she finished speaking, she realized her words most likely meant nothing to him. He was working with someone who wasn't connected to reality. They were looking for someone specific, and everyone who looked like her was not only suspect but guilty by their association with the female species.

He sighed. "I don't know, but you're his first choice. I suggest you be very careful."

"If either of you tries to rape me, I'll kill you," Tracy said. She couldn't help the tears that filled her eyes. "I mean it."

"He has no intention of touching you . . . that way."

Tracy wiped her cheeks with both hands. "Who are you talking about? The man who took me? I don't know him, I swear. Please, I'm not the woman you're looking for. Really. I just want to go home to my children."

His steps came closer again. "I'm sorry. I really can't help you. Step back." When she did, he pushed an envelope through the slot. Then she heard him walk away.

"Please, please," Tracy pleaded. "Please don't leave me here."

The man didn't respond. He just kept heading back the way he'd come. A few seconds later she heard a door close.

He was gone. She didn't want to give these men the satisfaction of knowing they made her cry, but she was frightened.

Whoever was behind all this was crazy. Where was he? And who was in charge? The man with the dark hair and blue eyes? Or this blond guy? None of this made sense. These men were carrying out some kind of vendetta against a woman who must have hurt one or both of them, maybe a long time ago. But they obviously didn't know her name or exactly what she looked like. This was insane.

She picked up the envelope and took out a folded sheet of paper.

*Each night you'll be given a cup of tea with dinner. It will have medicine in it to help you sleep. Consume the tea in front of the camera and then turn the cup upside down so we'll know you drank it. If you try to pour it out or hide it, we'll know, and then everyone will be punished. You will also follow all the other instructions given you. If you don't, again, everyone will be punished.*

At least now she knew what time of day it was.

She was walking away from the door when the first wave of drowsiness hit her. She struggled to make it to her bed, then collapsed onto it. The tea. She didn't know whether to pray that she'd wake up from this . . . or that she wouldn't.

# 11

When her alarm sounded the next morning, Alex rolled over and hit the button to turn it off.

Krypto grunted and pushed on her back with his nose. Her white pit bull hadn't been happy with her last night because she'd stayed out so late. She'd just wanted to make sure Logan was okay before leaving him alone. He'd finally eaten his soup, and by the time she left, he seemed to be feeling better.

She told him Jeff didn't want him back in the office until Monday. Logan had grumbled about it, but Alex made it clear that if he came in, Jeff would probably just send him home again. Finally, he gave in. "I guess Jeff will assign someone else to work on the profile with you," he'd said. It was obvious he wasn't happy about that, and neither was Alex.

Monty was still off work, so someone else from their team would be assigned to help her. She could do it by herself, but it was best to have another analyst to bounce ideas off of.

Several times in the past Alex had changed her mind about a profile after feedback from another agent in her unit.

When she got up and headed toward the kitchen, Krypto followed her. She fed him, then turned on the coffee maker. She always prepared it the night before so she wouldn't have to do it when she was still sleepy.

Krypto was waiting by the back door to go outside, and Alex was working on her first cup when her phone rang. She picked it up and saw Logan's name. She prayed he wasn't feeling worse.

But it was just the opposite. After she said hello, his voice boomed over the receiver. "Just wanted you to know I woke up feeling great. Don't know what you did, but I think it fixed me." He laughed. "I plan to go in today. That way you won't have to work with anyone else on the profile."

"You better talk to Jeff. He was adamant that you stay home. I'm really glad you're feeling better, but maybe you should wait until after your MRI."

"Not necessary. I think I must have had a slipped disc or something. That's what was causing my headaches. Maybe I slept on it the right way last night, but for the first time in days, I feel good. I'll call Jeff and talk to him, but if he says it's all right, I'm coming in."

"Okay. But if he wants you to wait, don't get upset. He's just trying to look out for you."

"I know. Hey, thanks for taking care of me last night. I really appreciate it."

When Alex ended the call, she wanted to feel happy that Logan was doing better. But she couldn't get rid of an uneasy feeling. Why did she feel that way? She really wanted Logan back at work.

When Alex got to the office, Logan wasn't at his desk. She was just about to sit down when her phone rang. It was Alice. "He wants to see you."

Alex thanked her and headed toward Jeff's office. When she opened the door, she found Logan sitting in front of Jeff's desk. Was this about Logan showing up to work? Was Jeff blaming her because he'd come back early? But the expression on Jeff's face made it clear this was about something else.

"Have a seat, Alex," he said.

She sat down and waited, unsure what to expect. Jeff rubbed his forehead, and Alex realized how tired he looked. The past few months they'd had one case after another. No time to catch their breath. Was it beginning to wear down her boss? Could that be the problem with Logan as well? She hadn't thought about it until that moment, but stress could certainly cause headaches. Yet she was convinced that what she'd seen in Logan's face last night was caused by more than simple stress.

"I told Logan he should go home," Jeff said. "But he refuses, and I don't feel like pulling rank today. There's too much going on." He took a deep breath and let it out slowly as if trying to calm himself. "Logan, last night I told Alex that we have another missing woman who fits the description of the other women abducted. So that brings us to six."

He sighed. "But I didn't tell her this. Chief Dixon found eight more missing women across the eastern part of the state, all about the same age when they went missing. All Caucasian, all attractive, all with a similar build and approximate height, all with long dark hair. Four in Richmond County, one in Rappahannock, one in Culpeper, and two in Gloucester." He looked at Alex. "I didn't want to tell you about this last night. I knew you were concerned about Logan."

"I . . . I don't understand," Alex said. "I thought something was sent out to law enforcement all over the state."

"It was. But the request was for *recent* abductions. Some of these missing women were taken almost six years ago." He shook his head. "It's shoddy police work, and they know it. It took Chief Dixon getting on their backs and forcing them to look through old cold cases. But now we know. Of course, this doesn't mean these are all connected to our current situation, but we have to look at them as if they might be related."

"Could there be more?" Logan asked. "I mean, maybe they should go back even further."

"Now that they're aware of the connection between these eight, they're combing through their files, looking for others. But nothing's turned up so far."

"So fourteen women are missing?" Alex asked.

Jeff nodded. "Six years is a long time for someone to be kidnapping women, but the police plan to investigate each case. They're setting up a command post with staff from departments in each one of the involved counties as well an agent in charge to coordinate the FBI's work. I've requested their files. I know you need them for your profile, and I'm sorry it's taken so long to get you what you need."

Logan shook his head. "Six women. That's troubling."

Alex turned to look at him. "No, it's fourteen, Logan. Six from here, and eight from other counties."

Logan frowned at her. "Fourteen. I know. That's what I said."

Alex studied him for a moment. It wasn't like Logan to get confused about something this important. But maybe she was being ridiculous. Everyone made mistakes. She was so concerned about him that perhaps she was seeing things that weren't there.

Someone knocked on the door. "Come in," Jeff called, irritation in his tone. He didn't like to be interrupted during a meeting.

Alice opened the door and stepped inside with a phone in her hand. "The media has the story," she said, then touched something on her phone.

Alex heard a woman say, "We've asked for more information, but police chief George Dixon says this is an ongoing investigation and he can't give us any details. This morning, however, we interviewed Carol and David Abbott. Their daughter, Tracy Mendenhall, has been missing since Sunday morning. They're asking anyone who may have seen her to contact the police or the FBI. It's also possible that other women who resemble Tracy have gone missing recently."

Then Alex heard Carol Abbott's voice. "Please, please, help us find Tracy. She disappeared while jogging through the park near our home. Here's a photo of her."

The reporter's voice returned. "If you've seen Tracy Mendenhall, please call one of the numbers you see on the screen below. If you can't get through, call the station, and we'll make certain your information gets to the right person. Right now we don't have any details about the other missing women, but all women in our area should be cautious about going out in public alone. WADA will continue to investigate and bring you updates on this important story."

Alice touched the screen again with one of her red, manicured nails. "This isn't the only station talking about Tracy Mendenhall," she said, her expression grim. "Looks like we have a major problem on our hands."

Jeff sighed. "Yes, we do. Thanks, Alice."

"I'd say you're welcome, but I know this wasn't anything you really wanted to hear."

"You're right about that."

Alice left the room, closing the door quietly behind her.

Jeff swore softly. "So much for Agent Lucas getting the Abbotts to stay quiet about the other abductions. This is the last thing we need. Now every Tom, Dick, and Harry will be phoning the police, saying they know where Tracy is." He sighed. "They'll have to set up something at the CP for the calls coming in."

"Can you blame the Abbotts?" Alex said. "They're frightened. They probably think getting the media involved will help."

"Unfortunately, this will just make it harder for law enforcement. I wish people would listen to the experts instead of taking things into their own hands."

"Well, at least women will be careful," Alex said. "Maybe this will help keep them safe."

"You two work on the profile," Jeff said. "I'll tell you more about the woman who disappeared yesterday as soon as I get the information. For now, all I know is that her name is Merrie McDowell. She's a real estate agent. Her office said she got a call from a potential buyer and went to show a house. Never came back. Her purse was found on the floor of the house, which was left unlocked, and her car was still parked in the driveway. The property is rather secluded, so of course no one saw anything. Her picture is on billboards and ads. I think that's why she became a target. She matches the description of the other women."

"Her colleague reported her missing?" Logan asked.

"Yes. And when he described her, the police dispatcher put it right through even though she'd been gone only a few hours."

"They've been warned not to speak to the press, right?"

Jeff nodded. "Of course."

Alex leaned forward. "Will you want us at the command post, Jeff?"

"Not sure. I'll check with the agent in charge once they assign someone. If they decide they want you on-site, I'll send you over. It might help if they have questions about the profile."

"The sooner we can get the information about the other eight women, the sooner we can give you something that might help," Logan said.

"I agree. Get to work. And let us know what the doctor says after your MRI today."

"Yeah, and next time you jump from a nine-foot-high window onto a concrete floor," Alex said with a grin, "please be more careful."

"Hopefully, there won't be a next time. Once was enough for me."

"For all of us," Jeff said, smiling. "What time is the MRI, by the way? I should have asked you that before."

"Later this afternoon. I have time to work on this."

Jeff put his hand on his phone. "I'll request that additional info for you now. Let me know if you need anything else."

Alex got up and turned toward the door. Logan did the same but somehow stumbled over his chair. He laughed. "Nothing like making a cool exit."

As he walked out of the office, Alex glanced at Jeff. His expression made it clear he'd noticed. What was going on?

# 12

Alex and Logan spent several hours going through the reports on the other missing women in Virginia. They all had long dark hair and resembled the women from Prince William County. Each case had been investigated, friends and family questioned. The police in charge of two of the cases had suspects, but each one was ruled out for good reason. It was as if the women had simply vanished from the face of the earth.

After looking through the last file, Logan closed it and sighed. "Well, I think we have to consider alien abduction, don't you?"

"Very funny, but it would be nice to have an option." She leaned back in her chair and rubbed her face. "He's smooth. Knows what he's doing. No clues. No clear suspects. No eyewitness reports. And no reason to explain the abductions except that our UNSUB is looking for women who fit a certain description. I guess women with long dark hair should get haircuts. Maybe that will keep them safe."

"How do you feel about a trim?" Logan chuckled, but Alex could see he was slightly serious.

"Not just yet," she said with a smile. She shuffled all the files into a stack. "So here's what we know. The UNSUB took these women without any struggle. No blood, no signs they resisted him. Once they vanished, no one heard from them or saw them again. We have no bodies, but I find it hard to believe he's holding fourteen women. You'd need a pretty large place for that. Regardless, he had to transport the women to wherever he's keeping them, which means . . ."

"He probably sedated them," Logan finished. "A stun gun wouldn't do it. He'd definitely have to use a drug he knew would keep them out for a while."

"Dangerous in the hands of someone who doesn't know what he's doing," Alex said with a frown. "He could accidentally kill one of them."

"You think he has medical training?"

"No, I don't think so. I mean, it appears that this guy finds his victims in the media—or at least that's how he found the last six. It seems like a doctor would hunt in hospitals . . . or even choose his targets from his own practice. But nothing in these files links the women to a doctor or medical facility. Since he seems to be comfortable online, he probably read about whatever drug he's using and is administering doses based on that."

"But where did he get the drug? Could he be a pharmacist?"

"Maybe." Alex chewed on her lip as she thought. "Investigators need to look at robberies from pharmacies in Virginia. Especially in the areas where women went missing."

Logan picked up his cell phone to call Jeff, but before he could click on his number, the phone rang. Logan answered and listened for a moment before saying, "Okay. We're on our way." He disconnected the call. "I guess we can tell him in person. He wants to see us again."

Alex and Logan headed back to Jeff's office. Alex prayed there wasn't another missing woman. That would be pretty fast after the last one. The UNSUB would barely have had time to secure his previous victim. Maybe he'd been captured. That would be incredible news.

Alice ushered them into Jeff's office.

"Just need to know when you think you'll finish your profile," Jeff said. "I'm getting pressure from the governor. It seems he knows the Abbotts. Met them through some church group or something. That will make things tougher for us, I'm afraid. But I still want you to do this right. Don't let me rush you. That's how we get it wrong."

"We understand," Alex said.

Logan explained their conjecture that the UNSUB had used some kind of drug to subdue the women he'd kidnapped. "Can you request that investigators check for robberies of pharmacies, clinics, and hospitals in Virginia over the last six years? Especially in the counties where the women went missing. You know the usual suspects. Propofol, Sodium Pentothal, Xenon, Rohypnol—"

"Yeah, I get it." Jeff made a note on a pad of paper. "You don't think we're looking for someone in the medical field as a possible suspect?"

"The way he finds his victims tells me no," Alex said. "We

can't rule it out, but I think someone who works with the public wouldn't be finding his prey online and in the newspapers."

"Okay. I'll get back to you. By the way, Chief Dixon mentioned that they followed up on Evan Prescott, Tracy Mendenhall's ex-boyfriend. He's been ruled out." He frowned at Logan. "Why are you still here?"

"I'm leaving right away." He stood and looked at Alex. "I should be back in a couple of hours."

"If you need more time, take it," Jeff said. "I can get someone else to help Alex."

Logan's face reddened. "Why do you keep trying to get rid of me? Maybe you should just replace me if that's what you really want." He swung around and hurried out the door, sweeping past Alice, who looked at him with her mouth open.

"What just happened?" Jeff asked.

"I don't know," Alex said slowly, "but something is obviously wrong. I'm really getting worried."

# 13

I t was almost four o'clock when Jeff walked up to Alex's desk. "Have you heard anything from Logan?"

Alex shook her head. "Not yet. After the MRI, the technician has to analyze it. Then they have to contact Logan's doctor. It could take a while."

"Yeah, I guess you're right. You know, it's not like I want anything to be wrong, but when they find out what's causing his pain, I'll be relieved. At least we'll know what we're dealing with."

Alex nodded. "I feel the same way. He's certainly not acting like himself. I think he's in more pain than he admits, and it makes him testy. He'd usually never talk to you the way he did."

"I know that. I'm not upset. I just hate to see him like this. Especially if his injury came from his attempt to save you and Kaely."

Kaely Quinn was an analyst who'd worked for the BAU

for a short time. She and Alex had both been targeted by the serial killer who left them to die in that warehouse. Thankfully, Kaely's then fiancé and now husband, Noah Hunter, along with Logan and several of the analysts who worked in their unit, had gone looking for them. They'd found them with only minutes to spare. Logan's jump from a high window to save them had caused his broken ankle, and now it seemed he may have been injured more severely than they'd known.

Alex felt guilty about what happened. No one else seemed to blame her, but she kept thinking that if she'd been more careful maybe she wouldn't have placed herself in a situation that put Logan, Kaely, and Noah at risk. The mistake was hers and hers alone. Between the nightmares and Logan's injuries, sometimes she felt like she was free-falling into a black abyss and couldn't find a way to stop her descent into the darkness.

"Alex?" Jeff said. "Did you hear me?"

Alex shook herself out of her thoughts and looked up to see Jeff staring at her, a strange expression on his face. "Sorry. Just thinking about Logan."

Jeff leaned back in his chair and crossed his arms. "I wish he'd stay home until this is resolved, but I doubt he'll listen to me."

Alex grunted. "He doesn't want to let you down. Besides, I don't think he can accept that something might really be wrong with him. I guess he doesn't believe he has the right to be less than one hundred percent."

"Yeah, I think that's it. I hope he's right and that this is something that can be easily fixed. If not, it will be difficult for him."

"We'll be there to support him."

Jeff nodded. "Let's hope that will be enough."

---

Logan wasn't claustrophobic, but he could understand why some people didn't like having MRIs. At least this machine was open on both ends. His mother had told him they were closed years ago. She'd once had an MRI because of an injury to her foot. "It felt like I was in a coffin," she'd said. "And I couldn't get out. It was awful." Logan had teased her by asking how she knew what it felt like to be in a coffin. She wasn't amused. It was clear she'd been really disturbed by the experience.

Although this was certainly better, he still felt a little stab of alarm as the table he was on slid inside the tube. He'd been told not to move and to keep his hands by his sides. That didn't help. What did help were the headphones they gave him before he went in. He'd been allowed to choose any music he wanted, so he'd asked if they had any Christian songs. Surprisingly, they did. Logan had been prepared for them to say they had only secular music.

Just then "Hold Me Jesus" by Rich Mullins came on. Logan struggled to control his emotions. Although Rich was in heaven now, he was one of Logan's favorite musicians. This song in particular meant a lot to him. He hadn't been able to admit to anyone how frightened he really was. He kept telling himself there wasn't anything to worry about, that he'd always been healthy, that this was something simple. Yet a negative voice kept whispering words of fear into his mind. He was fighting hard to ignore them.

He murmured a prayer as Rich's voice urged him to fall down on his knees. In his heart, he did exactly that.

Alex continued working at her desk, trying to nail down a workable profile of their UNSUB. She was fairly certain about some things.

He was most likely attractive because of how he'd been able to approach the women he abducted. He clearly wasn't threatening or he never would have managed to get so close to them. She also believed he'd abducted Tracy Mendenhall by pretending he was a jogger, which meant he was probably in his late twenties to middle thirties. Although older people jogged, a younger man seemed a more likely suspect. Someone Tracy could identify with.

They also believed he was most likely alone when he abducted Tracy. They couldn't prove it had anything to do with this case, but one of the women who'd disappeared almost six years ago was seen talking to a good-looking young man just before she went missing. He'd had dark hair, a medium build, and was of medium height. Of course, they couldn't be certain he was their UNSUB, yet the idea that he was nice-looking tied into the profile. The same thing had worked for Ted Bundy. As far as Alex could tell, this was the only time the UNSUB may have been seen by someone else, which meant he was clever. Organized.

Also, their UNSUB was either psychologically drawn to women of a particular description or he was angry with them. Maybe a mother who'd hurt or deserted him? The rest was more difficult. Where were the women? No bodies. The bodies would tell them much more. Was there overkill? Were there signs of remorse? There was no way they could be sure about his motivation.

It was hard to believe that the women he'd abducted years ago were still living. Surely he wasn't keeping them for this long. It would be unprecedented. Some serial killers had kept victims alive for a while so they could assault them, though. Alex prayed this wasn't what was happening, but if these women were still alive, it was a likely scenario.

Alex suddenly remembered a movie she'd seen years ago about a man who'd kidnapped women and kept them alive in locked rooms somewhere underground. Interesting plot, but unrealistic. Women were almost always abducted because the man who took them wanted to harm them. Keeping them around to amuse himself just wasn't reasonable. Authorities probably hadn't found bodies yet because of so many dense forest areas in the Virginia area. Cadaver dogs could find what people couldn't, but they needed a search area, and they didn't even have that. The dogs were pretty remarkable though, able to sniff out bodies buried twelve feet under the ground. They could also locate remains in water.

This UNSUB bothered Alex. It was almost as if he was looking for someone in particular but didn't know where she was. And except for a loose description, he didn't know exactly what she looked like. Didn't know her name. Alex shook her head. That was just too bizarre. She was wandering off track again. Why was she having such a hard time with this profile? Of course, she knew the answer to that question. It wasn't just that this case was odd. No matter how hard she tried, she couldn't stop thinking about Logan.

# 14

ogan had been inside the MRI machine for a while when the table began to slide out and he was met by the technician who'd helped him inside. He pulled the headphones off his ears.

"Your doctor has asked for some additional pictures," she said. "So we're going to turn you around the other way. I'll also be administering some contrast fluid."

"I don't understand. What kind of additional pictures?"

"Images of your brain." She smiled. "Nothing to be alarmed about. When someone experiences severe headaches, it's just a precaution."

Logan got up from the table and turned around. The technician gave him a soft sculptured headrest to help hold his head still and brought him a warm blanket, which felt great, before inserting an IV, which didn't. She injected fluid that felt cold and made his mouth taste funny.

Then the table slid his head back into the MRI machine. Although he couldn't wear the headphones this time, Logan thought of another one of Rich's songs that reminded him that people were not always as strong as they thought they were. At that moment, that particular song seemed to fit. Why would Dr. Morton ask for images of his brain? Was the tech telling the truth? Was it really just a precaution?

The fear Logan had been trying to ignore all day intensified. Was his life about to change forever?

Alex decided to go out for a burger since she'd missed lunch and was getting hungry. She could have grabbed something from one of the vending machines, but she felt the need to get out for a while. To breathe some fresh spring air. To take her mind off Logan. A good burger place was just up the road, so she headed there in her car.

When she arrived, she went inside to order, intending to just pick up her food and head back to work. She hated eating alone in restaurants. It made her feel conspicuous. Were people wondering why she had no friends? No one to eat with?

She was waiting at the counter behind an elderly lady when someone else came in and stood behind her. A few seconds later she felt a tap on her shoulder. She turned to find a young blond woman smiling at her.

"I'm so sorry to bother you," she said, "but I've never been here before. I'm picking up an early supper for me and my son. What do you recommend?"

Alex smiled. "I'd go with the double cheeseburger. If you like onions, ask for them grilled. And the onion rings are outstanding. Their chocolate shake is also the best I've ever tasted."

The woman's eyebrows shot up. "Thank you so much. That's really helpful." She stuck out her hand. "I'm Portia."

Alex shook it. "Alex."

"Short for . . . ?"

"Alexandra. But no one calls me that."

Portia smiled. "Even so, it's a beautiful name. It's nice to meet you. Do you live in Quantico?"

Alex nodded. "I work with the FBI, so I live close to work." She turned around to check on the woman in front of her. She was busy counting out her change. This could take a while.

"Wow, the FBI," Portia said. "How interesting."

The door opened, and a man carrying a bag came in. They would have a long line soon if the woman in front of her didn't speed it up. Alex was thinking about paying for the woman's food herself, not only to bless her but to get her out of the way. Before she had a chance to offer her help, though, Portia said something that made her forget that idea.

"So you must know something about the woman who's disappeared. My daughter looks a lot like her. Tracy . . . someone. I can't remember her last name."

"I wouldn't worry," Alex said. "Everyone just needs to keep their eyes open and play it safe."

"But on the news Tracy's parents said young women who look like their daughter should be especially careful. Frankly, women who resemble you. Any truth to that?"

Feeling distinctly uncomfortable, Alex just shrugged. "Like I said, everyone needs to do whatever they can to stay safe."

She suddenly realized the man standing behind Portia was

aiming a camera at her. "What are you doing?" she asked him. He refused to make eye contact.

"Look, Agent Donovan," Portia said, "people just want to know what's going on. You don't have the right to keep important information away from the public when lives may be at stake."

"Who are you?" Alex asked rather loudly.

"Why, honey, that's Portia Meadows from channel 5," the elderly woman said. It seemed she'd finally counted out enough change to pay for her order. "I thought everyone knew her." She leaned toward Portia and smiled. "I never miss you. I just love you."

"Thank you," Portia said, her tone decidedly dismissive. "But, Agent Donovan—"

"It's Supervisory Special Agent Alex Donovan. And I have nothing to say to you."

"So if someone else goes missing, you won't feel bad that you didn't warn the public?"

"If anyone sees something that concerns them, they need to contact Police Chief George Dixon." Alex spoke in clipped tones. "That's all I have to say."

Although she really wanted that cheeseburger, Alex stepped out of the line, opened the door, and quickly headed back to her car. Out of the corner of her eye, she saw the guy with the camera coming after her, Portia scurrying behind him in her high heels. Alex got into her car and sped away, leaving them gesturing for her to stop. She understood that the public was worried now, but this wasn't the way to get information. Ambushing someone without acknowledging your identity was pretty low. When she got back to the office, she'd let Jeff know what happened. He wouldn't be happy.

Alex headed to another restaurant, one with a drive-through. She ordered her food, paid for it, and then drove back to work. She waited a few minutes before getting out of her car just to make sure no one had followed her. Once inside, she sat down at her desk and called Jeff.

Based on the stream of profanity she heard, she was pretty sure the owners of channel 5 were about to get an earful.

She sighed. Jeff probably wouldn't be able to stop Portia Meadows from showing what they'd filmed, but she had to hope he could do something. She was embarrassed to have been taken in by that wolf in high heels. She really hadn't given them any information, though, so maybe they wouldn't air what she'd said after all. Surely they'd rather interview someone who would actually answer their questions. But it was almost impossible to second-guess the media.

Some local news stations were great to work with. They were respectful and accommodating. But others, like channel 5, were only out for ratings, and they'd do almost anything to beat the other stations in the area. Alex didn't watch much TV, but she should have recognized Portia. She'd actually seen her a couple of times. She must have been distracted thinking about Logan.

She finished her meal and then went back to work on the profile. She discovered that each missing woman had been seen in public like the ones recently abducted, although not necessarily in the media. One of the women worked with her father in an auction house. Another was a hostess in a popular restaurant. A third was in a local theater group. However, her face had been on posters all around town.

This information made her wonder if the UNSUB had only recently searched for victims online. That could explain why he'd abducted eight women over several years but six in the last month.

Alex had just looked up the work history for a fourth woman—discovering that she'd worked as a checkout clerk in a grocery store—when she noticed the time. It was after six. She didn't want to interfere with whatever Logan had to do, but she was beginning to worry. She picked up her phone and sent him a text.

*Everything okay? Let me know.*

She went back to the files, but her stomach was tied in knots. She whispered another prayer for Logan, asking God to help him.

# 15

ogan was just getting into his car when his phone rang. He took it out of his pocket. Dr. Morton's office. Strange. The technician said he probably wouldn't hear from anyone until sometime tomorrow. This was quick.

"Hello?" he said as he closed the car door.

"Logan?" He'd expected to hear the receptionist's voice. Or maybe his nurse's. But it was Dr. Morton himself. Was he making sure he'd had the MRI?

"Yes?"

"Is it possible for you to come to the office?"

Logan swallowed. "When?"

"Now. I want to go over your test results."

"You . . . you have them already?"

"Yes. It's important I speak to you right away."

Logan glanced at his watch. Jeff had told him he didn't have to come back to work today. He might as well go to the doctor's office.

"I'll be there in a few minutes," he said. When he ended the call, his mind raced. Had they seen something in his back that required surgery? But why couldn't he have told him that over the phone? He thought of another possibility, but he didn't want to seriously consider that. It made him feel like throwing up.

As he drove out of the hospital parking lot, he turned on his favorite Christian radio station and let the music minister to him, reminding himself that he belonged to God and God loved him. He wasn't alone. Still, he wanted to call Alex and tell her what was going on. He wanted her by his side. But that was ridiculous. They didn't have that kind of relationship. Besides, she needed to concentrate on getting herself strong after everything she'd been through. She couldn't pick up his problems too. It was selfish of him to even consider that.

He finally reached the doctor's office. He turned off the car's engine and sat in the parking lot, gathering his thoughts and praying for God's strength and protection.

When he was ready, he went inside.

Tracy woke up with a headache. She had no idea what time it was, but she felt as if she'd slept for more than just one night. Was that because of the tea? Or did she still have some of whatever had been in that syringe in her system as well? Either way, she was tired of being drugged.

She forced herself to sit up. Immediately, she felt the bed. It was dry. Thank God. She wasn't sure why it mattered so much, but that experience had made her feel helpless. Weak. After stumbling to the bathroom, she relieved herself. The plastic bucket was back, and the bags from yesterday were gone. She washed and dried her face, then walked back into the room and saw that someone had delivered another tray of food. She had no intention of eating it—or drinking anything. She picked up the tray and threw it across the room. A cup and carafe shattered. The food and coffee made a mess on the cement floor, but she didn't care.

She sat down in the chair. How could she get out of here? She tried to recall how the woman escaped in that movie she'd seen, but it was just a dim memory. Maybe she'd attacked her kidnapper and made her way out of the underground maze. Was that it?

Suddenly, she realized she'd made a tactical error. Her abductor was drugging her because he couldn't trust her. He was aware that if he came into the room while she was awake, he was vulnerable.

She needed to get his guard down, even if it meant allowing him to continue giving her drugs. But what if he made a mistake? Unless he was a doctor, how could he know exactly how much to give her without killing her? But the truth was unless she could get out of here, she didn't care that much about staying alive anyway.

There was only one thing she could do. She had to quit fighting. Although fury toward her abductor burned like a fire in her belly, she had no choice. To defeat him she had to make it look as though he'd won. Until she knew what he wanted, it was too risky to make him angry. Not only could it possibly put her in danger, but it could also bring harm to the other women. The note said they could all be punished, and she didn't want to make them more vulnerable because of her. It was clear that she had to play it smart and do whatever it took to get them all out of here alive.

Tracy quickly cleaned up the mess she'd made before placing the tray near the bottom of the door, in front of the panel.

After that, she changed clothes and made her bed, hoping her abductor was watching. Maybe he'd think she was feeling defeated and giving in to her surroundings.

She selected one of the books in the bookcase. Jane Austen's *Persuasion*. Her last novel. Tracy had read it when she was sixteen and loved it.

She sat down in the chair to reread the touching story of Anne Elliot. As she got into the story, she was inspired by Anne's strength, and it gave her courage.

In an effort to stop thinking about Logan, Alex worked until almost seven, trying to figure out how the missing women were connected besides their ages and looks. She sighed as she closed the file. Some people had a wrong concept of what the BAU did. They didn't understand that BAU agents don't run around chasing serial killers and shooting people. Their work was done by going through files and sitting through endless meetings. Actually, it was rather monotonous and not even close to the way TV shows portrayed it.

She finally decided to call Logan since he hadn't responded to her text. She clicked on his number and listened to his phone ring. No answer. She'd had enough of this. She'd drive to his apartment and check on him.

By the time she got there, she'd moved from being worried to feeling afraid. This wasn't like him.

She was just getting out of her car when it started to rain. It had been raining a lot lately. Oh well. Supposedly April showers would bring May flowers.

Alex checked Logan's parking spot and was relieved to see his car. She hurried up to the main door and pressed his buzzer. No response. She pressed it again and spoke into the speaker. "Logan, if you don't open the door, I'll call the police. I mean it!"

A few seconds later, the entrance unlocked. She went inside and knocked on the door to his apartment. It opened slowly. Alex almost gasped. She'd never seen Logan look the way he did at that moment. His face was pale, and something in his eyes frightened her.

"This isn't a good time, Alex. I'm sorry. Bad headache. I just called Jeff to explain why I didn't come back to work."

"Let me come in and help. I won't talk to you. I'll just make sure you have something to eat and—"

"Not this time. I'll be fine. I just need to lie down for a while. Go home. I'll see you tomorrow."

"Do you need any medicine picked up? What about food?"

The sides of Logan's mouth ticked up a little. "No, but thanks. If I need anything, I'll call you, okay?"

"I guess," Alex said. "But I really think I should stay—"

"I'll see you tomorrow," he repeated firmly. Then he closed the door.

Alex stood in the hallway for a while, not sure what to do. Finally, she walked back to the building's entrance. The rain had picked up, and she wished she'd brought her umbrella with her. It was still in the car. Great planning.

She took a deep breath and ran into the downpour. By the time she reached her car, she was soaked. She quickly slipped inside and closed the door behind her. She started the engine and turned on the heater, hoping it would warm her up. Instead, it blew cold air as she sat there wondering what was actually going on with Logan.

Was it really just a headache? It was possible, but her gut

told her it was something more. Something to do with his MRI? But surely he couldn't have the results already.

She shivered as warm air finally enveloped her. At this point she had no choice but to believe what Logan had told her. She sighed, put her car in gear, and drove away.

# 16

Logan stood by the front window, holding the blinds back just enough to see Alex get into her car. She sat there for a while, her car running but not moving. Finally, she pulled out of the parking lot.

He wanted to call her back. Desperately wanted her to stay with him. Talk to him. But he had to deal with this by himself.

He returned to the couch, where he'd been sitting ever since he'd arrived home. The doctor's words reverberated in his mind over and over.

"We found a brain tumor," he'd said. "It's what's been causing your symptoms. Besides the headaches, you may experience dizziness, instability, problems with your eyesight and memory." He'd paused and stared at Logan for a while, as if making sure he understood.

Logan had felt as if his mind was frozen. He couldn't quite process the doctor's words. This couldn't be right. Surely he was mistaken. But by the expression on his face, Logan knew he wasn't.

Then Dr. Morton said, "It has to come out, Logan. At this point I don't want to hazard a guess as to whether it's benign . . . or not. Let's wait until we know for certain. I've already run the scans past a surgeon who says she's fairly confident she can get it all out—if you move right away. We have no idea how fast it's growing, but the suddenness of your symptoms concerns me. You should have had that MRI last week. I'm sorry my staff dropped the ball. We can get you into surgery on Wednesday but only because the surgeon had a . . . cancellation. Please don't put this off. Dr. Schmeidler's one of the best with these kinds of cases."

*Had a cancellation?* Logan could tell by the doctor's body language that the cancellation hadn't come about because someone was mysteriously healed and flew off to the Caribbean for an impromptu vacation.

Logan started to breathe quickly and realized he was having a panic attack. He'd only had one other in his entire life— when he'd heard that an evil man had kidnapped Alex with the intention of killing her. He struggled to get his breathing under control, but he finally did, although it took a while.

He suddenly realized that he hadn't prayed since he'd talked to the doctor. Why was his first reaction to panic? Shouldn't he have cried out to God first?

"I'm sorry, Lord," he choked out. "I always thought I'd be stronger if I heard something like this. To be honest, I never really thought I would. I don't know why." He took a big gulp of air and tried to calm down. "I . . . I've told people facing tough things that they need to release their problems to you. Sometimes it helps, and other times it seems as if they don't want anyone telling them what they should do. Several said they just wanted someone to listen to them. God, forgive me, but I think I've seen that as unbelief. I was wrong. Right now I wish Alex was here and I could talk to her. Just lean on her. Have someone with me who cares. But the truth is she's still dealing with what happened to her. How can I ask her to walk me through this? Wouldn't that be selfish?"

He took another deep breath, trying to push away the temptation to panic again. Maybe he didn't have a person here to talk to, but he did have God.

Logan picked up his Bible and opened it. The pages seemed to turn themselves. When they stopped, he found himself looking at 1 Peter 5:6–7. *Therefore humble yourselves under the mighty hand of God . . . casting all your cares [all your anxieties, all your worries, and all your concerns, once and for all] on Him, for He cares about you [with deepest affection, and watches over you very carefully].*

Logan liked the way the Amplified Bible shared this Scripture. He read it several more times, then prayed again. "So I humble myself by giving all my problems to you, God. All my anxieties, all my worries, and all my concerns because I'm . . . I'm not you. My shoulders aren't big enough, but yours are. Help me do this right. I know I can't get through it without your strength."

Logan put the Bible back on his coffee table and did something he rarely did.

He cried.

<br>

When Alex got home, she let Krypto out right away. The rain was down to a light sprinkle, which he completely ignored. He ran into the backyard with enthusiastic fervor. He loved being outside. During the week, her neighbor Shirley let him out around noon, and when her kids came home from school, they took him for a walk. They loved the big white dog, and he adored them too.

After sniffing almost every inch of the backyard as if there had been a circus performing there that day, he finally did his business and came running back to Alex. They sat together on the steps of the covered porch for a while, Krypto's wet head in her lap, the rain continuing to fall. Alex loved spring—the scent of the burgeoning flowers, the leaves sprouting on the trees, the fragrance of new growth carried on light breezes. And now the scent of rain in the air.

She stroked Krypto's large head and told him how much she loved him. Alex knew they'd have to say good-bye someday, but she couldn't deal with that now. Still, it was like a little bug wiggling around in her brain, trying to get her attention. Trying to get her to face something beyond her ability to comprehend.

"Let's get you something to eat," she finally said.

Krypto jumped to his feet and wagged his tail so fast it was almost invisible. As much as he loved the outside, he was even more excited about food. If Alex let him, he would eat 24/7. She was pretty sure that was because his previous owners hadn't fed him much. He'd been extremely abused and was so broken by the time he was dumped at a local shelter that the staff there planned to put him down. But Alex recognized the look in his eyes. She'd seen it in the mirror when she was younger, and she decided she would save him the way she'd been saved.

She went to the shelter every day, talking to him, sitting

near him, until one day he rose from the corner where he cowered almost all day. He walked over and put his head on her leg. The staff was amazed. A day later, Krypto was home. It took a while, but he became a changed dog. No trace of the pain he'd endured. Clear proof of what love could do.

Alex smiled to herself as she watched him devour his food. Krypto and Alex had changed together. Her love had changed him, and God's love had changed her. The Lord had done so much for her. Why was she having such a struggle with what happened in that warehouse? It was as if she were saying God's power wasn't enough to completely heal her, and she knew that wasn't true.

She suddenly remembered a chance encounter not long after she'd finished with the psychologist the Bureau had arranged for her. It was with the assistant pastor at the church she, Logan, and Monty attended — Pastor Bryant. She hadn't planned it. She'd gone by the church to pick up the Bible she'd left behind on a Sunday morning and ran into him. She wasn't sure why he invited her to have a cup of coffee with him in his office, but she found herself sitting across from him, suddenly wanting to talk. He'd waited quietly as if he knew she needed to talk. After telling him what she was going through, he nodded.

"God has heard your prayers, Alex, and He's healing you," he'd said. "But you must remember that just like a physical injury needs time to get better, our internal hurts may need time as well. Wounds need air to heal. Hiding your feelings won't help you. Air them out. Come and talk to me anytime you want. That's why I'm here."

He'd leaned forward then and earnestly gazed at her. "Alex, the devil wants to make you feel guilty, as if you're weak in faith, letting God down somehow. But God doesn't see it that way. Yes, He wants you to have faith, but it won't come through guilt. It comes through learning to trust Him and allowing Him to do His work in you in His way and in His timing. Just like you must get to know someone before you can trust them, time with God will build the kind of relationship you need right now. Read the Bible every day and let God speak to you. You and God have to navigate this together. Learning to do that will make you stronger. And the next time something happens, you'll have more confidence in His ability to meet you where you are and get you where you need to be."

He'd smiled at her. "Believe me, God knows exactly how you feel, and He's capable of handling it. You're not a disappointment. He loves you unconditionally. He wants to help you, not make you feel ashamed."

As she ran Pastor Bryant's words through her mind, she was comforted. How could she have forgotten about that meeting? Although his comments had been more God-centered, they echoed some of the same things the therapist had said. She sighed. Time for her to listen now.

She made a sandwich, poured some tea, and sat down on the couch. As she ate, she read her New King James Bible, stopping when she reached 1 Peter, chapter 5, verses 6 and 7: *Therefore humble yourselves under the mighty hand of God, that He may exalt you in due time, casting all your care upon Him, for He cares for you.* It was as if the words were burning like fire in her heart, and she had to blink away tears. She read on to verse 8: *Be sober, be vigilant; because your adversary the devil walks about like a roaring lion, seeking whom he may devour.*

It was exactly as Pastor Bryant said. She'd been feeling ashamed of her weak faith, but that was what the devil wanted. She'd been playing right into his hands.

Alex finished her sandwich, then after cleaning up the kitchen, she went back into the living room and curled up on the couch with her Bible, Krypto lying next to her. She read until she began nodding off.

Suddenly, she was inside a large house. Some of the rooms were clean and beautiful, but the doors to other rooms were shut. Somehow she knew something dark was behind those doors. Something she didn't want to see. She looked for a way to exit the house, but she couldn't find one. Instead, she found herself trying to squeeze through small tunnels that led nowhere. How would she ever find her way out? She was so afraid she was going to get stuck in one of them that she cried out to God. She finally made her way into a larger hallway and found a Man clothed in white standing there, watching her. He extended His hand, and she took it.

"I'll help you find your way," He said.

He led her toward a glowing light Alex knew would lead to freedom. But then He stopped and looked at her. It was strange, because she couldn't see His face, only His eyes. His gaze made her feel warm. Loved.

"Logan needs you, Alex. Help him in his journey the way I'm helping you now."

A moment later she found herself standing outside in a beautiful field full of purple flowers, Krypto sitting beside her. She looked down at him, and he stared at her, his tail wagging and his mouth open in a doggy smile. He looked so happy. She knelt and put her arms around his neck. Somehow she knew that when the day came she had to say good-bye to him, their separation wouldn't be forever. Someday they'd sit together in a field just like this one where there would no more good-byes.

She was aware that Jesus had been the Man comforting her, and she was overcome by His love for her.

When Alex woke, tears were streaming down her face. And yet she was smiling.

# 17

Before heading into the office the next morning, Logan called the surgeon's office and confirmed that his surgery was scheduled for the following Wednesday. He also canceled his appointment with the ophthalmologist. He had no choice but to tell Jeff what was going on, but he'd decided to wait until next week to let Alex know. He was aware that it would upset her, and he wanted to put it off until he had no choice but to tell her the truth.

Even then he planned to make light of it. Tell her it wasn't any big deal, just a growth that needed to come out. Although he couldn't be certain it wasn't cancerous, he hoped and prayed it wasn't and tried his best to cast the care of it onto God. If humbling himself meant he had to let go of the worry and the stress, then so be it. But if he'd really done that, why was his stomach so tight?

Logan arrived at the office early. Jeff was in, but Alex wasn't. He called Jeff and asked if he had a few minutes. A short time later, he was sitting in his boss's office. Although it was rather hard to get out what he needed to say, he finally did.

Jeff's look of compassion moved Logan, but he steeled himself to stay focused and unemotional. He didn't want to appear weak to his boss. He was concerned that Jeff might send him home. He just couldn't sit alone any longer, thinking about the upcoming surgery. He needed distraction to help him not obsess about what he was facing.

"Are you absolutely sure you should be here?" Jeff asked.

"Yes. I'm fine. I have medication for the headaches. I . . . I need to work, Jeff. Please."

He hadn't planned to beg, but he couldn't help it. He prayed Jeff would understand.

"Okay, we'll play it your way, but if you need to go home at any point, just go."

"I will."

Logan stood. He needed to leave Jeff's office. He was having a hard time holding it together.

"Thanks, Jeff," he said before walking out. He could feel Alice's eyes on him as he hurried past her, but he didn't trust himself to speak. He headed to the men's room and quickly stepped inside. Thankfully, no one was there. He stood in front of one of the mirrors and stared at his reflection. He was shocked by what he saw. Who was that man looking back at him? His skin was pale, and there was something unsettling in his eyes. Was it fear?

"I'm sorry, God," he whispered. "I'm trying to trust you, I really am. I don't believe this situation is your will for me. I know it's an attack from the enemy, but to tell you the truth, I'm scared. I don't want to die. I realize heaven is wonderful, but there are things I want to do here. I want to tell Alex I love her. I want to get married, and I want to have children. Please hold me, Jesus. Don't let me go."

He grabbed a paper towel and wiped the tears off his face. This was getting to be an uncomfortable habit. He heard someone's hand on the doorknob and hurriedly stepped into one of the stalls before closing the door. He leaned against it and continued to wipe his face until he was able to breathe again. Then he walked out of the stall, threw the towel into the trash, and left, heading for his desk.

When Alex got to work, she noticed people staring at her oddly. What was that about? She'd just reached her desk when her phone rang.

"My office now," Jeff said. Then he hung up. What was going on?

When she reached Alice's desk, the woman simply cocked her head toward Jeff's office. Strange.

Alex walked through the door and found Logan waiting there too. What now?

"What's going on?" she asked as she took the seat next to Logan.

"Quite a bit," Jeff said. "Let's start with this." He punched a button on his laptop and nodded toward the large TV screen on the wall. Immediately, a news report began to play. It was Portia Meadows from channel 5.

"Look, Agent Donovan," Portia was saying, "people just want to know what's going on. You don't have the right to keep important information away from the public when lives may be at stake."

"It's Supervisory Special Agent Alex Donovan," Alex said. "And I have nothing to say to you."

"So if someone else goes missing, you won't feel bad that you didn't warn the public?" Portia asked.

"Everyone just needs to keep their eyes open and play it safe."

Then it showed Alex getting out of line and walking out of the restaurant. The video cut back to Portia, who shook her head and looked distressed. "Seems the FBI isn't concerned about our community, telling us we're on our own—that we should watch out for ourselves." She paused to look deeply concerned, then said, "This is Portia Meadows reporting from Quantico, Virginia, where several women have gone missing. Please, be careful out there, especially if you look like Tracy Mendenhall. We're praying for your safe return, Tracy."

Then the camera lingered on a photograph of Tracy while her mother's voice played at the same time. "Please, please, help us find our daughter. . . ."

Jeff shut off the feed and stared at Alex.

"That's not how it happened," she said. "They've edited it to make it seem as if I couldn't care less about Tracy . . . or anyone else. I swear that's not the way it went down. I told her twice that people needed to be cautious and watch out for anything suspicious. I also told her people should contact Chief Dixon if they saw anything that concerned them."

"We've dealt with the media before," Jeff said. "I believe what you're saying, but we've got to stay out of the public eye. This won't help the investigation."

"I know. I was ambushed. I had no idea who she was when she approached me. I thought she was just someone in the community who was concerned. She said her daughter re-sembled Tracy, and she sounded worried."

"I know something about Miss Meadows," Jeff said, disgust in his tone. "She doesn't have any children."

Alex just shook her head. She felt stupid for walking into a trap, but now she was angry as well. It was clear that Portia Meadows wasn't concerned about anything but her ratings.

"Can I ask why you didn't know who she was?" Jeff asked. "Don't you ever watch the news?"

"No, not really. But if I do, I watch channel 9. They seem a little less biased and work harder to simply report the news. Channel 5 likes to actually create it."

"Well, that certainly proved true this time," Logan said. "I've seen Portia Meadows, but I wasn't impressed."

"The problem is we came off as insensitive and uncaring," Jeff said. "Someone higher up will be issuing a statement later today, but don't worry. They have your back. I'm going to let them know what really happened. They'll report it just as you told it to me. Hopefully, Portia won't come off well."

Alex wanted to believe Jeff, but if people got it in their heads that the FBI didn't care about the missing women, it might be hard to change their minds.

"That woman will never get near me again," she said.

"Good."

"I'm a little concerned about something else," Logan said.

"What's that?" Alex asked.

"You. You were just on TV, and you look like the abducted women."

Jeff swore softly before saying, "He's right. You need to be careful, Alex. Stay armed, and don't let anyone you don't know approach you."

Although she knew she should be a little concerned, she wasn't. "The kidnapped women weren't trained FBI agents. I'm sure the UNSUB won't risk being captured." She shrugged. "Although, I have to say, I wish he would come after me. I could take him down, put a stop to this, and maybe find out what happened to those women."

"I appreciate the sentiment," Jeff said, "but you're a behavioral analyst, not a field agent. I don't want you forced into a position like that. You've been put in enough danger."

Alex didn't argue with him, but she'd kept up with her training. She was one of the most accurate shots the FBI had, and she was proficient in hand-to-hand combat. She'd love to get the chance to confront this guy, but Jeff was right. It wasn't her job.

"Is your profile ready?" Jeff asked.

"I think so." She looked at Logan. "I've been working on it, but I'd like to go over it with you before we turn it in."

"Okay. We can do that this morning."

"Then we'll have it to you by noon," Alex said to Jeff. "I wish we had more information about the other missing women. But because most of them were viewed as having taken off for their own reasons, there isn't much in their files. Not yet anyway."

"Just do the best you can. As it turns out, Bethany and Nathan are working a case, and I have another one for Robin and Todd. Monty won't be back to work until next week. So for now it's up to you."

Alex nodded. It would be hard to walk away from this case once their part was done. It was happening right in their own backyard, just like the case they'd handled a few months ago. Alex pushed images out of her mind that tried to force their way in. Not now. Not in Jeff's office.

Alex stood, and Logan did the same. As they headed back to their work area, Logan said, "Do you want us to work at your desk? Or should we go to one of the conference rooms?"

"Conference room. I can't handle all the files on my desk." She stopped and grinned. "I notice you never say we should work at your desk."

Logan shrugged. "I'm one of those people who can only create in the midst of chaos."

"Yep, that certainly describes your desk," she shot back.

"Funny. Let's grab those files and get a room before someone else thinks of it."

A few minutes later they were settled in a small conference room. As they finalized their profile, Alex couldn't help but glance at Logan from time to time. He hadn't even mentioned last night or his MRI. Something wasn't right, and it bothered her. God wanted her to help him, but how could she do that if he shut her out?

───

When Tracy opened her eyes, she reminded herself that she had to be good. That's why she'd drunk the tea last night, the only thing they'd brought her.

She still wanted to talk to the other women, but she had to be careful. She needed to find the right time.

When she sat up, she saw a food tray on the floor. Hoping her punishment was at an end, she first got up and used the toilet, then washed up and changed clothes, once again thankful for the curtain. The guy in the hallway didn't like to talk about sex and probably felt the same way about watching his captives clean or relieve themselves. He'd said *we*, so she assumed both men felt that way. Could she use that somehow?

She carried the tray, which felt lighter than usual, to the table, then lifted the lid. Nothing but a note.

*You have one more chance. If you don't do as you're told everyone will be punished. No food, nothing to drink except tea, and no lights for three days.*

She stared at the note, thinking. This was how they kept the women from fighting back. So she would be a good girl. Do what they asked until she could formulate a plan to get everyone out of here safely. Whatever it took, she would put an end to this and make them pay.

# 18

"So what now, Rider?" Brent asked the man sitting across the kitchen table from him. "You barely punished Tracy. Do you have anything else planned?"

"I warned her. If she does it again, they'll all be sorry. Including the next one to join us. The woman I just saw on TV."

"But why bring another one here so soon? We've had so many."

"Don't question me." Rider glared at him. "Why shouldn't I bring another woman here? Because you work so hard? All you do is cook and take care of the laundry. Andy does almost everything else."

"I'm the one who got them here. I even sang the song you told me to—even though it seemed silly."

Rider's glare intensified, making Brent's stomach turn. "You were living on the streets before I took you in. You can always go back to that."

Brent shook his head. "No, I can't live like that again. Please don't make me leave. I'm sorry."

Rider studied him as though he wondered if he meant what he'd just said, and that frightened him.

"I told you she fits the description," Rider said. "I want her brought here."

"But how? She's an FBI agent."

"I have a plan."

"Of course you do." He shook his head. "Don't be mad at me. We need each other."

"I know that. But I haven't always been completely sure you do."

Brent did his best to satisfy Rider, but this had been going on for years. His life was lived at Rider's beck and call. The man didn't allow him to watch TV or listen to the radio. When he went to town he was careful to stay away from newspapers or anything that might tell him what was going on in the world. He'd wondered more than once if he could get away with a quick peek in a newspaper. But his fear of Rider outweighed his curiosity. Brent wasn't sure how much longer he could take this. Was it possible one of the new women might be the one? He hoped so. They had to find her soon. Once they did, maybe life would be more enjoyable. At least these other women wouldn't have to suffer any longer.

Brent got to his feet. "I guess we'll have to clear out room four. We can put her in there." He sighed. "I wish you'd listened to me about installing something so we can hear them talking. This FBI agent will try to get them out. You know that. We need to know her plan."

Rider laughed. "Why should we care about what they're saying? Nothing they can cook up will succeed."

"I hope you're right."

"I am. Trust me. I'll take care of things just like I always do. You don't need to worry about it."

He stared at Rider for a moment. "You always let them go, right? Make them understand they can't tell anyone about us?"

Rider frowned at him. "Of course. I promised you I would. They've never betrayed us, have they?"

"No, I guess not." No one had ever come looking for them, so he assumed Rider had kept his word.

Rider stood and patted him on the shoulder. "Don't worry. Just let me handle this. I'll have Andy clean the room and get it ready for her. This new one will come to us. I've got a really good plan. I just need you to help me pull it off."

"Okay. Tell me what you want me to do." He looked at Rider for a moment before adding, "I feel sorry for them sometimes. I wouldn't want to wake up and find myself locked inside a strange room."

"We take good care of them," Rider said, his tone soothing. "You have nothing to feel bad about."

"I guess so. Well, I've got to go into town now to get those supplies."

Brent turned and left the room. He was thankful for Andy and everything he'd done for him. He trusted him. But Rider frightened him even more than he wanted to admit.

---

Alex and Logan worked for a few hours refining the profile. They still didn't have as much to work with as they would have liked, but at least they felt more comfortable that they were going to give investigators something they could use.

So far, the search for missing drugs had yielded too much information. Alex had been surprised at how many robberies and reports the police had found during their search. No wonder America had a drug problem. Although they were still trying to narrow down the information, the police and the DEA weren't hopeful they'd be able to give them what they needed. A lot of stolen drugs were illegally resold to buyers they couldn't trace. This was probably the way the UNSUB had obtained his supply.

He clearly had issues with women of a certain description, but they'd ruled out a mother figure. In those cases, women were usually killed immediately, their deaths driven by rage. Also, the killer would most likely pose them in a way that, in his mind, would humiliate them. Then he'd leave them where they could be found right away. He would be proud of what he'd done and want the world to acknowledge his power.

He was also looking for someone in a specific age range. They knew this because the first woman he'd abducted had been about six years younger than the average age of those recently kidnapped. In other words, he understood that who-ever he was looking for had aged just as he had. That meant he could have been in his early twenties or even in his teens when the trigger occurred that led him to begin abduct-ing women. This confirmed their earlier belief that he was younger because he was able to pose as a jogger when he'd approached Tracy Mendenhall.

They were just about finished when Alex said, "What time is your appointment with the ophthalmologist?"

"Canceled it. I knew we needed to finish this, and I wanted to be here."

"Okay. When do you get the results of the MRI?"

"You know how slowly the world of medicine works."

"Will you tell me when you hear something?"

Logan smiled at her. "I'll tell you what I know as soon as I can, okay?"

Alex was about to press him when Logan's phone rang. He picked it up and identified himself, then waited a moment before saying, "We're on our way."

"Jeff wants to see us," he told her.

"For crying out loud," she mumbled. "We might as well work in his office."

"Probably wants our finished profile. There's a lot of pressure on this case. The governor getting involved doesn't help."

"I know everyone's worried, but they really need to just let us do our jobs."

"I know. I'm sorry I was missing in action last night. If I'd been available, we could have completed this earlier."

"Don't blame yourself. No one else is. Jeff and I wanted you to stay home and rest."

He smiled. "I know. Thanks."

They got up and headed to Jeff's office.

As they sat down in front of their boss's desk, Alex noted his expression was grim.

"We may have heard from the UNSUB," Jeff said.

"Seriously?" Logan said. "He's silent for all these years and suddenly decides to contact someone?"

"He hasn't been mentioned in the news before," Alex said. "Maybe it fueled his ego, so he decided to step into the spotlight."

"Makes sense, I guess," Jeff said. "But I'm not sure you can call this communication." He pushed a piece of paper toward them.

Alex stared at it. Gibberish to some people, but not to her.

"We've sent the original to the lab. They'll check it for

fingerprints and DNA. Hopefully CRRU can figure it out. Obviously, this is some kind of code. He's trying to show us he's smarter than we are."

The Cryptanalysis and Racketeering Records Unit supported law enforcement and the intelligence community by analyzing cryptic communications. Foreign and domestic terrorists, organized crime, gangs, prison inmates, violent criminals, and human traffickers many times used their own codes to shield their operations and financial records. Alex knew CRRU had been instrumental in uncovering hidden operations and bringing many criminals to justice.

"Why don't you work on this?" Logan said, looking at her.

Jeff frowned. "You have training in cryptology, Alex?"

She laughed. "No, but I'm pretty good at word games. I actually decoded a message sent to the police from a serial rapist when I was in Kansas City."

Jeff's eyebrows shot up. "I remember that case, but I had no idea you were the one who deciphered those letters."

Alex shrugged. "It's usually not that complicated. You figure out the symbols used the most often and assume they're either $e$, $a$, $i$, or $o$, then you look for the nouns that start with $r$, $t$, $n$, $s$, or $l$. It can take a while, but when you decipher one or two words, the rest is usually easy."

"Maybe for you," Jeff mumbled. He handed her the paper. "Here. See what you can do. The sooner we know what it says, the better."

"Okay. Just remember it took fifty years to crack the Zodiac Killer's code, so don't expect too much."

Jeff grunted. "Thanks for the warning, but none of us will be in the FBI in fifty years. Hopefully, we can figure it out before we all retire."

# 19

When they sat down again with their profile, Logan said, "You can't wait to work on that, can you?" He knew her well enough to know she'd love to try her hand at breaking the code.

"It's calling my name, but Jeff's right. The profile should come first. CRRU can take care of this." She paused a moment. "The problem is this message may change our conclusions. I mean, now we know he wants attention. Wants to prove he's more intelligent than we are. That makes a difference."

"I think so too. Look, you work on that while I clean up what we already have. Then if we need to adjust our profile, we will. After that, we'll take everything to Jeff. Sound good?"

"Sounds great."

They worked quietly for a while. After a few minutes, Alex said, "I've got it."

Logan looked up at her in surprise. "Already?"

She nodded. "It wasn't complicated. Actually, it was simple. Really simple." She frowned. "I'm a little confused. Something about this doesn't feel right."

"He's been clever enough to get away with kidnapping women and going undiscovered for a long time."

"That's what makes this a little baffling."

The door to the conference room opened, and Jeff stood there. "It occurred to me that this message could affect our profile. Sorry. I should have realized it sooner. The pressure is getting to me."

"We understand," Logan said. "We were just saying the same thing. Alex worked on it while I fine-tuned what we've done so far. It really didn't take any time away from our work."

Alex pushed a piece of paper toward him. "Here's the code." She'd written it down so Jeff could clearly see the translation.

$$A B C D E F G H I J K L M N O P Q R S T U V W X Y Z$$
$$Q 6 ? L 9 \# Z 4 * X 2 @ C 8 ! F 1 \mathcal{G} G 3 \$ N 5 \% T 7$$

After the alphabet, she'd added the message *I am coming for you. No one can stop me.*

"Nothing unique or interesting here," she said. "Just the same threatening verbiage we've seen before from criminals fueled by their ego."

"I can't believe you did this so quickly," Jeff said after scanning the page.

"It's not complicated, which tells us something about our UNSUB."

"You think it shows our guy isn't as clever as we thought?"

Jeff shook his head, a frown on his face. "That doesn't match with the way he's pulled off these abductions. Very well thought out. Clever."

"That's exactly what we were thinking. It's almost as if . . ." Alex started.

"It's not really from the UNSUB," Logan finished for her.

Alex looked at him and smiled. They frequently finished each other's thoughts. Still, it always surprised Logan when it happened.

"What are you saying?" Jeff asked. "You think we have a pair of UNSUBs?"

"It's not unprecedented," Alex said. "Think of Henry Lee Lucas and Ottis Toole. Kenneth Bianchi and Angelo Buono. Leonard Lake and Charles Ng."

"Some of the sickest serial killers who ever lived," Jeff said. "Let's pray this UNSUB and his partner, if he has one, don't take after any of those animals."

Jeff's phone rang. When he answered it, he listened for a while, then told whoever was on the other end to email him their findings.

"You win, Alex," he said, putting the phone down. "That was Special Agent Lucas. They just got a message from CRRU with the same results you came up with."

"Like I said, it's a really simple code. I'm sure they figured it out before I did. It just took them a while to contact the team."

"You're being modest, but the important thing is we know what it says."

"But why send this now?" Alex asked. "It's such a break in his MO. I mean, I guess being on the news may have triggered his desire to get attention, but he's been so secretive up to now." She looked at Logan. "I don't think we should change our profile based on this."

"I agree."

"Jeff, let us know what the lab finds on the letter," Alex said. "Either our UNSUB has changed his MO, or there are two of them. Or—"

"Or this isn't from him at all," Jeff said. He looked back and forth between them, then swore and left the room.

"You think this might be the result of our friend Portia's reporting?" Logan asked her.

"I do. She's stirred up a hornets' nest, I'm sure. Maybe someone's decided to insert themselves into the investigation."

"I hope the lab finds something so we can figure out who did this."

"Let's finish this profile and get it to Jeff," Alex said. "If we decide the message really is from the UNSUB, we'll adjust the profile. It's certainly not the first time we've had to change one, and it won't be the last."

Within an hour they had the profile ready and had delivered it to Jeff so he could distribute it to Chief Dixon and those gathered at the command post.

When they left Jeff's office, Alex said, "Hey, it's almost lunchtime. How about grabbing a bite somewhere?"

"I'm sorry," Logan said, "but I think I'll ask Jeff if I can knock off early. If we get a case, I'll come back. I'm just tired. It's been a tough week."

Alex frowned at him. "Do you have another headache?"

"No. Like I said, just exhausted. I think the newest meds the doctor prescribed have that effect."

"Let me go with you. I can pick something up for both of us."

Logan smiled. "Thanks, Alex. Really. I appreciate it, but I want to be alone so I can sleep. It's not really a two-person thing."

Alex hesitated a moment but then shrugged and walked away. Logan knew she cared about him. That she really wanted to help him. A few months ago, when Alex was in the hospital, she'd been given morphine for her pain. As she'd drifted off, she'd told Logan she loved him. He'd wondered about it ever since. Was it some kind of brotherly love? Or was it possible she actually cared about him in a non-brotherly way? He wished it was the latter, but he couldn't ask her. If he was wrong, he could lose her friendship, and he couldn't imagine his life without Alex.

He called Jeff and told him he wanted to go home.

"Of course, and if you need anything, please let me know."

"I will. And by the way, Alex is getting suspicious. Please don't let her wheedle anything out of you. I don't want her to know until I feel it's the right time. There's nothing she can do."

"All right, but I think you're making a mistake. If she finds out you didn't tell her right away, it might hurt her. You two are close friends. I'd hate to see this drive a wedge between you. She might think you don't trust her."

"It isn't that. It's just . . ."

"Logan, if you think she'll pledge her undying love for you out of pity—"

"That's not it," he said sharply. "That never entered my mind."

As soon as he'd denied Jeff's premise, he realized his boss was right. He didn't want Alex's pity. He wanted her love, and this wasn't the time for her to express it. If she actually did have romantic feelings for him, he wanted to find out when the playing field was level. He had no intention of forcing her into a corner so she'd say something she might not mean. It had to be real.

*Give me patience, Lord.*

"Look, I understand," Jeff said. "But don't wait too long. Sometimes being too careful in love is a mistake. You have to jump into the water without knowing if you'll sink or swim. There's never a guarantee on this kind of thing."

"I keep telling you we're just friends."

"And I keep telling you I'm a trained analyst too. You're not fooling me."

Logan sighed. "I'll see you on Monday."

"I wish you'd just stay home and get ready for your surgery on Wednesday. I can tell Alex if you want me to."

"Thanks, Jeff. I appreciate it, I really do. But it has to come from me. I owe her that. I'll tell her on Monday. I don't want her worrying all weekend. I won't wait any longer than that. You're right. I don't want her to feel as if I don't trust her."

"Your family coming out?"

Logan sighed. "I don't think so. That's going to be a tough conversation, though."

"I'm sure they'll want to be with you."

"That would be great except my dad recently had a stroke. My mother says he's doing okay, but this still isn't a good time for them. I was planning to fly home to see him soon. Now that visit will have to wait."

"All right."

There was a pause, and Logan wondered why Jeff had fallen silent.

"Look," Jeff said finally, "after everything we've been

through together, I think of you as a friend. A good friend. Why don't I come by and pick you up tomorrow? Let's go somewhere and just hang out. You don't have to talk about the operation if you don't want to. I could pick you up about eleven? We'll go to Moxie's and play some pool?" Jeff hesitated a moment before adding, "If you're up to it, that is. If not, I understand."

Logan felt a sudden burst of emotion and struggled to control himself. "That sounds wonderful. I'd really rather not be alone this weekend. It might be best to call before you come over, though. I'm never sure about these headaches."

"Look, if you're not feeling up to going out, we'll just hang out at your place. Whatever you want to do. No pressure."

"Thanks, Jeff. I really appreciate that."

"Nothing to thank me for. I just want to prove I can beat you at pool."

Logan laughed, said good-bye, and ended the call. He felt better, but knowing he would soon have some tough conversations with his family and with Alex sat like a rock in the pit of his stomach.

ogan was getting ready to leave when Alex heard his phone ring. He listened for a moment, then disconnected the call and said, "Jeff."

"You almost made it," Alex said with a grin. "Just a few more minutes . . ."

Logan sighed. "I'm sure it's important or he wouldn't have called us."

Once again they headed to Jeff's office. This was certainly getting to be a habit. "Go on in," Alice said. "Whatever it is, he's not happy."

Alex's curiosity was triggered. What now?

They found Jeff standing behind his desk. Never a good sign.

"Sit down," he barked. Then he took a deep breath as if trying to calm himself. "Sorry, but I'm angry."

"What's going on, Boss?" Logan asked as he and Alex both took a seat.

"Heard back from the lab. They found DNA on the envelope used to mail that coded message to the police."

That should be good news. What was going on?

"It's David Abbott's."

Not much truly surprised Alex about people anymore, but this certainly did. "I don't understand. He's not our UNSUB." Investigators had already concluded that Tracy's father had not only not kidnapped his daughter but couldn't possibly have abducted the other women.

Then it struck her. "He sent the letter because he thought it would make the authorities try harder to find Tracy. Get more attention to the case." She shook her head. "I thought the code was just too simple. Now I know why. I'm praying he hasn't sent a copy to the media."

Jeff sat down. "Thankfully, we stopped that in time, but it would have been his next step if we hadn't responded the way he wanted."

"If he'd done that before we found out he'd written the note . . ."

"It would have been a disaster. And very embarrassing for a couple desperate to find their daughter."

"Why is his DNA in the database?" Logan asked.

"One of those family heritage sites. He and his wife sent their samples in months ago."

"Surely no one thinks he's a suspect because of this," Logan said.

Jeff shook his head. "No, but now they have to follow up again. A waste of time and resources."

"So Lucas is handling this?" Logan asked.

Jeff nodded. "He's talking to the Abbotts now. Hopefully, he can get David to realize what a mistake this was. If investigators had accepted the note as real, they could have been misdirected, which could have resulted in it taking longer to find Tracy."

Alex sighed. "I feel sorry for the Abbotts. They obviously don't feel we're doing everything we can."

"I realize that," Logan said, "but let's hope they don't send a copy of that code to the media."

Alex looked over at him. "We just said they were stopped before they could do that. Are you okay?"

Logan frowned at her. "I'm fine. Sorry. My mind must have wandered for a moment. It's been a long week."

Alex glanced at Jeff. She couldn't quite interpret the expression on his face, but he looked concerned. "You're right, Logan," he said, refusing to meet Alex's eyes. "Why don't you both go home? We'll meet again on Monday."

"Okay," Logan said. He hesitated a moment before saying, "You know, at some point the police may actually need to go to the media to warn people. Especially women who fit the description of the victims."

"You could be right," Jeff said. "But we'll have to let whoever's in charge decide that. I've been told the command post will be up and running by Monday afternoon."

Logan stood. "Sounds good. See you Monday."

"Hey, wait up for me, will you?" Alex said. "I'll walk you out, but I want to speak to Jeff first."

Logan stared at her for a few seconds before saying, "Sure. I'll be at my desk."

After Logan left the office, Alex fixed her gaze on Jeff. "What's going on?"

He stared at her blankly. "I don't know what you mean."

"Yes, you do. Something's wrong with Logan, and I want to know what it is."

Jeff looked away for several seconds, then said, "I can't tell you. It has to come from him." He met her eyes. "I mean this, Alex. I won't change my mind no matter what you say. Talk to him, but don't badger him. He needs to handle this his way. Please allow him to do that."

Alex got to her feet. She had no intention of pushing Jeff any further. It was obvious he wouldn't bend. But her concern had now turned into a cold fear that made her chest feel tight.

She walked out of Jeff's office without saying another word, passing Alice without acknowledging her. Her mind felt locked up by one thought. Logan was in trouble. Real trouble. She believed God had told her to help him, but how could she do that if no one would tell her what was going on?

She found Logan waiting near his desk. "Ready to go?" he asked.

She nodded wordlessly, then grabbed her things and started following him to the front entrance. But she suddenly stopped and watched him as he walked a few feet away before turning back to frown at her.

"Forget something?" he asked.

"No, I don't think so. But I believe you did."

His frown deepened. "I'm sorry. I don't understand."

"You forgot we're friends. You forgot everything we've been through together. And it seems you also forgot how many times I opened up to you and talked about things I've never discussed with anyone else. You forgot all of that."

She could feel the tears on her cheeks, but she couldn't stop them. It was as if they had a mind of their own.

Logan stared at her for a moment before walking back to

where she stood. Todd Hunter and Robin Wallace passed them on their way out the door. Todd hesitated for a moment before Robin grabbed his arm and gently guided him outside. Alex was grateful she'd realized they didn't need any interruptions.

Logan stared at her silently before saying, "I'm sorry. I guess I also forgot that it's almost impossible to hide anything from you. Can we do this somewhere else?"

She nodded. "Your place."

"Okay. Wait for me there. I'll grab some food from somewhere first. What do you want?"

"I couldn't care less."

Logan smiled. "Well, that narrows it down."

Alex knew he was trying to lighten things up, but there wasn't any space inside her to accept that. Instead, she headed for her car. When she got inside, she put her head on the steering wheel and tried to rein in the emotions that surged through her. She couldn't help Logan if she failed to get control of herself. But she knew things were about to change . . . and not for the better.

# 21

Alex had been waiting outside Logan's apartment building almost fifteen minutes, sitting on the steps leading up to the main entrance, breathing in the scent of the flowers growing in the flowerbeds that lined the front of the building. Someone was tending them, and they were doing a beautiful job.

She didn't know much about flowers, but she recognized a few of them, like the red mandevillas. Her aunt Willow had bought them every year for her front porch. Of course, she hadn't watered them or tended to them at all. That had fallen to Alex. Still, she'd grown to like the delicate flowers that attracted hummingbirds.

She looked up as Logan's car pulled into a parking space reserved for those who lived in the building. When he got out, he pulled a couple of bags from the passenger seat. Must be their dinner, but Alex couldn't imagine eating right now. She wanted to find out what was going on with him. Until then, she couldn't think about food. She could barely think at all.

He smiled as he walked toward her, and she was suddenly hit with a truth she'd been hiding from, pushing it out of her mind and refusing to deal with it. She'd grown to love Logan. And not just as a friend. But she couldn't tell him now. Couldn't ask him to think about that now when he was clearly facing something serious. Honestly, she wasn't completely sure what love was anyway. She'd never been loved. Really loved. She just knew she had to have this man in her life. That without him, the world would be smaller. Grayer.

What if Logan didn't feel that way about her? If she made a mistake and told him how she felt, she could lose him. She couldn't allow that to happen. She didn't want to be alone again. The idea terrified her.

"Went by that new Mexican place and got enough food to feed us for a month." He shrugged. "I'll put whatever we don't eat in the fridge. When I need something, I'll just nuke it."

She stood up and waited silently for him to unlock the entrance to the building.

He put the bags down and opened the door, then snatched up the bags with one hand and held the door open with his other.

As Alex walked down the hall to his apartment, a voice in her head told her to leave. Now. Before Logan said something she didn't want to hear. But she stayed where she was. She had to see this through. Had to know the truth. Had to find out how she could help him.

Once inside his apartment, Logan put the bags on his kitchen table.

"What do you want to drink?" Alex asked him.

"I made more iced tea. It's in a pitcher in the fridge."

She took some glasses out of a cabinet and put ice in them. Then she filled them with tea and carried them to the table.

Logan had grabbed plates, forks, and napkins. Once they'd both sat down, he removed tacos, enchiladas, chips, and queso from the bags. Even fried cinnamon sticks. Alex was certain everything was delicious, but at that moment the smell made her stomach turn over.

Logan said a short prayer while Alex watched him. Somewhere inside she knew what he was going to say. She'd suspected it almost right away, but she hadn't allowed herself to believe it. He kept saying the problem was in his back. But back problems don't cause confusion and forgetfulness.

Logan put some food on his plate, then pushed an enchilada and the box with tacos toward her. "Eat something, Alex."

"I can't. Not until you tell me what's going on."

Logan took a bite of his enchilada, then chewed and swallowed it without looking at her. After a sip of his tea, he finally met her eyes.

"I have a brain tumor. Wednesday I'll have surgery to have it removed. The surgeon will request a biopsy to determine if it's malignant."

Although Logan was only confirming what Alex expected, she was still shocked to hear the words. She felt as if someone had punched her in the gut. For a few seconds she couldn't catch her breath.

Logan's eyes widened, and he looked surprised. "Are . . . are you okay?"

She wanted to say yes, needed to say yes, but the words just wouldn't come. She was horrified to realize she was crying. Again.

Logan got up, pulled a chair up next to her, and sat down. "I'll be all right, Alex. The tumor is most likely benign. Even if it isn't, there's treatment for it." He took her hands. "I'll be all right," he said again.

"You don't know that," she said, her voice shaking.

"God is a good God," he said gently. "It's not His will for me to suffer. I'm choosing to trust Him. It's all I can do, isn't it?"

Alex turned her head and gazed at him. "I'm sorry I'm acting like this. I'm not sure why . . ." She couldn't finish the sentence because she really did know why. She'd lost her father, her mother, and her aunt. She couldn't lose Logan too. She just couldn't. She laid her head on his shoulder. "You're my best friend," she said. "If anything ever happened to you . . ."

He laughed lightly. "Trust me, you'd find another friend. Besides, you have another best friend. One who sticks closer than a brother. If you hang on to Him, you'll be okay. You'll always make it through, no matter what happens to me."

She lifted her head and straightened up in her chair. "I'm so embarrassed. This isn't the way a tough FBI agent should act."

"You should have seen me when I couldn't find you. When I learned that a sick serial killer had abducted you." He took a quick breath and held it for a moment. When she looked into his eyes, she saw something. Something she couldn't deal with right then. She pushed herself away from him.

"We need to eat this food before it gets cold," she said in almost a whisper.

For a moment he stayed where he was, but then he returned to his chair. "You're right," he said.

When she glanced at him, she noticed the hurt in his expression. That was the last thing she wanted to see, but what could she do about it? Right now she could only cry out to God and beg Him to save Logan. She wanted to ask if they could pray together over his upcoming surgery, but she couldn't get the words out. She knew she'd break down if she said anything at all.

They ate in silence for several minutes before Logan said, "I'm not rushing you, you know. No pressure. Ever."

In that moment, she knew what he was trying to say, and she wanted to tell him she felt the same way. But she couldn't. Instead, she took a deep breath and choked out, "I've lost everyone important to me. I just can't . . ." She couldn't finish, but she didn't need to. She saw instant recognition in his face.

"I get it. No matter what, I'll always be here for you, Alex. I'm not going anywhere."

Could he really promise that? She didn't know the answer, but his words comforted her. And feeling a little better, she took a bite of an enchilada.

**W**hen Tracy woke up, she lay in bed for a few minutes, thinking. Last night she'd left the upper panel in her door open after drinking the tea because she didn't like being in the dark. It must be daytime now since the ceiling light in her room was on.

She'd been dreaming that she was home. Her parents were sitting at the kitchen table when she came downstairs for breakfast.

"Made your favorite waffles," her mother said.

Tracy had smiled. Pecan waffles. She could hardly wait. "Smells great." Before sitting down, she grabbed a mug from the cabinet and poured some coffee. Then her mother brought her a plate she'd kept warm in the oven.

"Your mother is a great cook," her father said with a smile. "You won't get this kind of food at college."

"I know, Dad," she'd said, smiling back. "I'll come home a lot. You'll get sick of me."

"That will never happen," he said with tears in his eyes. "Just come home, Tracy. Just come home. Please."

His voice grew louder, and she realized he was frightened. But why? That was when she woke up and remembered where she was. She tried not to think about home. Matty, Cassie, and her parents. Would she ever see them again? Being with her family in a dream wasn't even close to reality. She had to find a way out of here.

But right now, she was hungry. She forced herself to sit up even though she really wanted to go back to sleep. As she swung her legs over the side of the bed, she sniffed the air. A familiar aroma. She walked over to the tray near the bottom of her door and carried it to the table. When she lifted the metal cover, she found waffles and started to cry. She must have smelled them and then inserted them into her dream. Or maybe it was God reminding her He was with her. That her heavenly Father would provide for her no matter where she was.

She whispered a prayer, thanking God for His love and protection. "Help me trust you," she said aloud. "To not be afraid. I believe you will deliver me, and that I'll see my parents and children again."

Her prayer gave her inner strength, and the lingering effects of the drugged tea seemed to dissipate, making her feel stronger. At that moment, in her heart, she knew she would find her way home.

---

"This is ridiculous," Brent said as they ate breakfast. "We're never going to find her this way. It's been years."

Andy stabbed his waffles with his fork. "There's nothing we can do about it."

"Maybe she cut her hair. Or dyed it. There's no way to know." He glared at Andy. "So what next? This can't go on forever."

Andy put down his fork. "We're safe as long as we don't do something stupid."

"But I don't like Rider's new plan. I don't want to risk losing everything we have. I can't be poor again." He fought to dial down his frustration. He couldn't get along without Andy, and he knew it. Theirs was a friendship forged out of need.

Andy hesitated a moment before saying, "Why don't you go on a date with the newest girl? Tracy. Maybe she's the one."

"I guess so, but I have my doubts." He paused and stared at Andy for a moment. "Hey, I realize how hard you work, and I truly appreciate everything you do. Just be careful about the drug Rider gives you for the tea. I'm trusting that it's okay when I add it. We had some problems in the past."

Andy frowned. "Rider told us not to talk about that."

"I know, and I'm sorry. I just don't want to see it happen again."

"I agree, but you need to keep your concerns to yourself."

"You're right. I know you've worked hard to fix the problem. Thank you."

Andy stared at him for a moment before going back to his waffles and bacon. "So when would you like to have this date?"

"Day after tomorrow? That will give us time to get everything ready."

Andy nodded. "Okay. I'll need to check with Rider, of course."

Brent hesitated. "Please do everything you can to keep her safe."

"I'll do my best."

"Good. I don't know what I'd do without you."

Saturday evening Alex called Logan to see if he planned to go to church the next morning. She'd go alone if she had to, but she'd rather ride with Logan and Monty. They always ate out after the service, and she really enjoyed their time together. She almost felt as if she had a family. Maybe not the same kind most people had, but for her it was a real blessing.

Logan didn't sound good when he answered his phone. Not like himself.

"Helloooo . . ." he mumbled.

"Were you asleep?" she asked.

There was silence for a moment. Then he said, "Naaa . . . Don know . . ."

"Logan, I'm on my way over." She disconnected the call, quickly changed from her sweats and T-shirt, said good-bye to Krypto—who didn't look happy—and hurried to her car. She'd just started the engine when her phone rang. It was Logan.

"I'm sorry," he said when she answered. "I'm okay. I was reading and dozed off. You don't need to come, but thanks."

"Are you sure? I'd be happy to pick up some food."

He laughed lightly. "Sounds great, but to be honest, I just took a pain pill and I'm going to lie down. Jeff and I spent some time together today, and it wore me out. Besides, I still have plenty of leftover Mexican food. Thanks anyway."

"Okay, if you're sure. I don't mind staying while you sleep."

There was a pause before he said, "That means a lot to me, Alex, but the place is a mess."

That concerned her because his apartment was usually so neat. She wanted to offer to help him clean, but she was reluctant to keep pressing him. "All right, but if you need anything, all you have to do is pick up the phone."

"Thank you. I know you mean that."

"So do you think you'll want to go to church tomorrow? Or would you rather rest?"

"I plan to go. Monty called, and he's back. He'll be hobbling, but he wants to join us."

"That's great. I look forward to it. Why don't I pick you up this time? Then we can swing by and get Monty."

"Sure. I'd appreciate that. The light still hurts my eyes sometimes and makes it hard to see clearly. I'd feel better if someone else drove."

"I'll see you about nine thirty, then."

"Thanks, Alex. See you tomorrow."

"See you."

Alex was encouraged by Logan's assurance that he was feeling all right. She'd done some research about brain tumors online but then decided to stop. Some articles gave her hope, others scared her. Outcomes depended a lot on what kind of tumor it was.

She went back inside the house. Krypto looked surprised but happy. She changed clothes again before sitting down on the couch, where her faithful dog cuddled up next to her and put his head on her lap. Then she turned on some praise music and once again prayed for Logan.

**A**lex had enjoyed today. Seeing Monty was great. He'd
graduated from a cast to a big boot and was getting
along pretty well. And Logan had seemed almost like
his old self, although she could tell he was a little tired. Had
Monty noticed?

It had been a wonderful service. The praise-and-worship
songs had really touched her. The sermon was about not
looking at what's behind us but instead keeping our focus
on what's ahead while we truly believe that God has a plan
for our lives. She'd needed that.

Now at home for the rest of the day, relaxing on her couch
with Krypto, she wondered once more why she'd been having
such a struggle dealing with what happened in the warehouse. Then it occurred to her that the horror of that day
hadn't entered her mind as often since Logan told her about
his brain tumor. Her concern for him had at least lessened
her thoughts about what she'd endured.

Even so, last night she'd awakened suddenly, thinking she couldn't breathe, once again trying to pull the rope off her neck. Thankfully, it took less time than usual to go back to sleep. But she really wanted the nightmares to go away completely, both the ones at night and the ones during the day.

She recalled what Pastor Bryant had told her. "*You must remember that just like a physical injury needs time to get better, our internal hurts need time as well.*" He was right. She was trying not to feel so guilty about having a tough time dealing with her fear.

She sighed. She hadn't wanted to be alone after lunch, but Logan was facing a monumental journey and needed to rest. Monty was still healing from his injury. Going to church had worn him out, and he'd wanted to go home and put his foot up. To distract herself, she began going over their current case in her mind. Was their profile on target? Could she think of anything else that might help investigators?

The Abbotts's faces popped into her mind, competing for space with all her other thoughts. Alex wanted to believe authorities would find their daughter in time to save her, but she was probably already dead. Still, she wouldn't stop praying for Tracy and all the women who'd been abducted, hoping they'd be found alive—or at least their remains discovered.

She made some popcorn, then carried the bowl back to the couch and turned on the TV. Sometimes movies helped her mind to rest. She suddenly thought of the film that had reminded her of this case. Accessing her streaming service, she searched for the title under the name of one of its actors. When she found it, she stared at the screen for several seconds. Was watching this wise? It certainly wouldn't help her get her mind off the case, but for some reason, she felt drawn to it.

She entered her code to pay for the movie, and then as she settled back on the couch, she noticed Krypto eyeing the popcorn. She gave him a piece before starting the film. About halfway through she began to wonder just what kind of place could hold that many women. Nothing she could think of worked.

After the movie was over, Alex concluded that it would be almost impossible to imprison several women underground unless it was in a huge basement where cells could be constructed. Whether the women were upstairs or downstairs, the structure would have to be abnormally large. Should investigators be looking for a big, secluded house somewhere in case the women were alive?

She reminded herself that after studying serial killers for years, she was fairly certain they'd all been murdered. Alex sighed so loudly that Krypto looked up at her. "Sorry," she said softly. "I'm getting tired of seeing all the evil in this world. It's time for a happily ever after, isn't it? How about we find all the women alive and well? Logan's brain tumor disappears? And all my bad dreams and fears go away?"

Although he had no idea what she'd said, Krypto sat up and licked her cheek. It should have made her laugh, but instead, she held him and cried until she had no more tears.

---

Monday morning Alex poured herself some cereal and then sat down in her living room to eat it. She decided to turn on channel 5 just to see what they were up to. Her mouth dropped open when she saw David Abbott. She was certain the police had warned him and his wife to stop talking to the press, but there he was.

"We have no idea how much time she has left," he was saying. He held up a photo of Tracy, one she hadn't yet seen. "We need everyone's help. The police haven't turned up anything."

"Can you confirm that other women are missing as well? Women who look remarkably like your daughter, Tracy?" the reporter asked. Alex was surprised to see that it wasn't Portia. Some man. She didn't know his name.

"Yes," David said. "Women in their late twenties or early thirties with long dark hair and gray or blue eyes need to be very careful. Stay indoors. Or at least don't go out alone."

"Why haven't the police issued this warning?" the reporter asked.

"I don't know, but the case is being bungled. That's why we felt we had to speak out. Ask for help." David looked directly into the camera. "If you look like our daughter, Tracy, you need to be vigilant. And, please, keep a lookout for her. If you see her, or if you see anything that might be related to her disappearance, call 703-555-2836."

Carol Abbott, who'd been standing silently beside her husband, suddenly blurted, "Please help us. We need Tracy back. She's our only child—our life." She barely got the words out before breaking down, her sobs loud enough to make it impossible for the interview to continue. The reporter stepped a few feet away while someone who'd been standing nearby led the couple away.

The reporter ended with, "Again, if you have any information that might help police find Tracy Mendenhall, that number is 703-555-2836."

The feed went back to the studio, where Portia and another man, both looking solemn, continued with other news.

Alex's irritation at the Abbotts's deliberate disregard for investigators' strong admonition to stay away from the media melted. These parents were scared and desperate. They weren't trying to ignore advice from the police and the FBI. They were simply at the end of their ropes. The longer Tracy was gone, the more they feared she'd never come home. Alex felt sorry for them. Had she failed them? If their profile was better, would Tracy have been found by now? Perhaps the others too?

The thought increased the pressure she felt. "It's too much, Lord," she whispered. "It's all just too much."

She started having trouble breathing and worked to slow her large, gasping breaths until they finally leveled out. She couldn't keep giving in to this fear. Besides, other people had real problems. Like Logan. Like the Abbotts and Mrs. McDowell, Merrie's mother, apparently a widow with breast cancer. Alex felt ashamed to be struggling when she wasn't facing anything as awful as others around her were. It was time to grow up and quit being so pathetic. She put the phone down.

"You're going to stop this," she said to herself. She got up and carried her cereal bowl over to the sink. Then she finished getting ready for work, making herself move forward, step by step, as if she were somehow set on automatic.

# 24

When she got to the office, Alex immediately looked over at Logan's desk. He wasn't there. When he still hadn't come in a half hour later, she called him.

"Are you okay?" she asked when he answered.

"Yeah, but after thinking about it, I decided to take today and tomorrow off. I have to get ready for my stay in the hospital. It takes more planning than I'd originally thought. I need to pack a bag, and I have a few things to buy."

"What time does the surgery start on Wednesday?" she asked.

"Bright and early at seven."

"Should I pick you up at five, then? Or is that too early? I don't know how much prep you'll need."

"You're not taking me, Alex."

"I . . . I'm sorry. Is someone from your family—"

"No, that's not it. I decided not to tell them."

"Logan, your family needs to know. How could you not call them?"

He sighed. "They have enough on their plates. My dad had a stroke a few weeks ago. Mom's busy taking care of him, and my brother's helping her. My sister lives in Texas and is about to have her third child. I'll tell them all once I'm home from the hospital."

"Why didn't you tell me about your dad?" She was surprised that he hadn't shared something so important with her.

"Mom keeps saying it was just a light one, that he'll be okay once he's taken it easy for a while and adjusted to his new medication. Besides, we've had a couple of video chats, and he seemed pretty good. I plan to visit him as soon as I can, but you can see why I don't want them to worry about me right now."

"I think you're making a mistake. What if no one had called you when your dad had his stroke, Logan? How would you have felt?"

Another sigh followed by several seconds of silence. "Okay, point taken. I'll think about it."

"Look, I'll be at your place at five a.m. on Wednesday to take you to the hospital. I don't care what you say. And if you don't get into my car, I'll start honking my horn. Your neighbors will hate your guts. Probably ask you to move."

This time Logan laughed. "Okay, okay. Thanks. Monty can't drive until he gets that boot off his foot, otherwise he'd take me. He's relying on a ride into work today from Nathan. Frankly, I'm a little relieved. I was adding up what I'd owe after leaving my car in the hospital garage. I'd probably have to take out a loan to pay for it."

Alex ignored the joke. "So you told Monty?"

"Yeah, he noticed I wasn't completely myself yesterday and called after you dropped us both off. Besides, it's not like I could hide a stint in the hospital from him."

"I forgot to ask how long you'll be there."

"I was told two or three days, five at the most . . . assuming all goes well."

"And when will . . ." She couldn't get the next words out, but he understood.

"The lab results take a couple of days, but my doctor said he's fairly certain the surgeon will be able to tell once she sees the tumor."

"Everything will be okay, Logan. I just know it."

"Thank you. I trust God."

"I am too."

Several seconds of silence passed while Alex struggled with what to say. "Logan . . . I . . ."

"I know," he said softly. "Call me tonight and tell me what happened today, okay? And if you hear anything about the missing women, let me know as soon as you can. I can't stop thinking about them."

"Me too. And I will."

When she ended the call, she stared at her phone for a while. What would she have said if Logan hadn't stopped her? She wasn't sure. "Liar," she whispered to herself. She knew exactly what she would have said. What she wanted to say.

───

When she woke up, Tracy immediately rose to gather fresh clothes, having decided to wait one more day before putting her plan into action. As eager as she was, she needed a little more time to pray and gain strength.

She noticed a piece of clothing folded and lying on top of the dresser. She shook it out to get a better look. It was a sleeveless white dress with yellow daisies on it. Not anything she'd ever wear. It was juvenile and out of style. Like something a teenager might have worn years ago.

On the floor next to the dresser sat white flats. Then she spotted a note on the dresser top as well.

*Fix yourself up and put on the dress and shoes. Tonight is date night. Be ready by dinnertime.*

Date night? Fear stabbed her in the chest like a knife. Was this it? Did he plan to assault her tonight?

Calming herself, she sat on the bed and thought for a while. This was it. She had to put her escape plan into motion now even though she wasn't sure she was ready. Date night changed things a bit. A few minutes more gave her an idea that involved an item she'd noticed in the makeup bag. She stepped behind the curtain, cleaned up, and then dressed in her regular clothes. She prayed this would work. It just had to.

As she sat eating her breakfast, she suddenly acted as if something was wrong and ran back to the sink behind the curtain. Then she put her fingers down her throat and threw up. It wasn't pleasant, but she had no choice. After rinsing her mouth, she took out the tube of red lipstick and rubbed a little onto her cheeks, hoping that would make her look like she had a fever.

After she came out from behind the curtain, she carried her tray with the remainder of her breakfast to the door. Then she made a show of lying down on the bed and stayed there until she heard the bottom panel slip open to retrieve the tray and leave her lunch.

"I don't want it," she called. "I'm not feeling well."

No response, but the lunch tray didn't come through. She listened as the other doors slid open. One, two, three, four . . . She waited for the fifth, but instead simply heard the cart going back down the hall. What did that mean? Had one of the women escaped? Or . . .

She couldn't think about that.

She ran to the area behind the curtain a couple more times. After each deception she lay down again, then wrapped her arms around her middle, making certain the camera could see her do it.

After she heard the cart with the dinner trays start down the hall, a knock sounded at her door. "Date's off for tonight," a male voice said, "but you'd better recover soon or you'll be punished." Then a tray was pushed through the bottom panel.

She didn't say anything because she didn't want to sabotage her plan. She waited a few minutes before bringing the tray to the table. The meal was some kind of broth with saltines, along with a bottle of water and, of course, the drugged tea. How could she make them think she'd downed the tea without actually drinking it? Filling her mouth and then going to the sink to spit it out would be too obvious. Besides, she couldn't hold that much in her mouth all at once.

After thinking about it for a while, she came up with an idea. First she ate her soup and the crackers. Then she went to the sink and removed the toothbrush and toothpaste she kept in a gallon-size zip bag. It was risky, and she wasn't sure it would work, but it was all she could think of.

She hid the bag under her T-shirt, went back into the room,

and took the tea cup off her tray. Then she carried it to the bed, where she got in and pulled up her comforter. She sat with her knees up to her chin and slowly moved the bag until it was between her chest and her legs. After that, she carefully opened the bag and held the cup to her lips while allowing the tea to pour into the bag. Since it had sat for a while, the tea wasn't hot. That made it easier.

She finally got all the tea into the bag, then still holding the cup, she slowly zipped the bag with her other hand so that whoever was watching wouldn't notice that something was going on. Praying the bag wouldn't come open, she slid it under her comforter as she bent to place the cup on the floor.

When it was time for bed, she got up with her back to the camera, the bag clutched to her chest, and slipped behind the curtain. She poured the tea into the sink before washing and drying the bag with a paper towel. She put her toothbrush and toothpaste back inside and returned it to the shelf.

When she carried the dinner tray to the door after gathering the cup by her bed, she prayed no one would pick it up early. If they did, they might notice the butter knife was missing. They'd obviously put it on the tray by mistake since she didn't need it for her soup. Their carelessness gave her hope that they might not miss it. Maybe she really could pull this off.

She got the waste bags and placed them near the door. After that, she lay down on the bed, pretended to go to sleep, and waited.

W hen Alex got home from work, she wasn't hungry, so she sat down to watch the evening news before calling Logan. She didn't want to bother him in case he was eating his dinner.

All the local stations had, of course, picked up the story about Tracy and the missing women, yet tonight she saw nothing more about it. Maybe they'd covered it all at five.

Before she could pick up her phone to call Logan, he called her. She was encouraged when she heard his voice. He sounded good.

"Nothing important happened today," she said. "At least not that I know about. Bethany and I are working on a profile for a guy who shot people in a grocery store in St. Louis this morning and then escaped."

"I heard about it on the national news this afternoon. They don't know who he is?"

"No. He wore a ski mask and gloves. All they have to go on

are his clothes, his height, and the way he moved. Of course, they should know more after the ballistics report."

"Has anyone died?"

"Not that I know of. It's a miracle. Eight people are in the hospital."

Logan paused a moment before saying, "Any idea why he did it?"

"Not yet. The police are checking for connections related to each victim, of course. Also former store employees. But I don't know . . ."

Logan laughed warmly. "You have a hunch?"

Alex smiled to herself. He knew her. Knew what she was thinking. They worked together so well. She blinked back the tears that filled her eyes. Then she cleared her throat to rid herself of the lump that had formed. Finally, she said, "The shootings were so random. I mean, it seems as if he didn't have a specific target."

"So what are you thinking?"

Alex sighed. "I don't know. Maybe I'm nuts, but there's something about this guy. The security tape shows him acting as if he'd rather be anywhere else than in that store. He didn't shoot anyone in the head. Or the chest. He hit legs, shoulders, arms . . ."

"You think someone made him do it?"

"I wonder if it was a gang initiation. Or maybe someone paid him to shoot up the store, like a disgruntled ex-employee. But in the end, he just couldn't kill anyone."

"That's quite a hunch."

"You mean a wild theory. I mentioned it to Jeff. Not sure if he plans to pass it along. He may think I've lost it." She sighed. "It was his body language, you know? He seemed hesitant.

After all, most spree killers are determined. They think they're on a mission to acquire some kind of twisted justice they think they deserve. This guy was just . . . different."

"I wish I was working this with you," Logan said.

"I do too. Why don't I bring over some dinner? We—"

"No."

Alex was surprised by his sudden and emphatic response.

"I appreciate it, Alex," he said. "But I need some time before my surgery. I need to pack, pray, and prepare. Not necessarily in that order."

"But maybe I can help you."

"Thank you. Really. But I need this time to myself. I hope you understand."

"Not completely, but I've never been through anything like this. I'll wait until Wednesday to see you, then. I've asked Jeff for some time off after you get home so I can help you while you recover."

During a long pause Alex wondered if Logan was about to turn down that offer as well.

"I'm really grateful," he said. "Thank you. That would be wonderful."

"Good. Well, I guess I'd better let you get to it. But, Logan, please, if you need me, call. I can be there within ten minutes. I . . . I just want you to know you're not alone."

"Thank you. And I will definitely call my folks sometime after the surgery." He cleared his throat. "I should be feeling rather alone, but having you and Monty . . . and Jeff. . .Well, you're my family too." His voice shook slightly. "It means more than I can say."

"We truly are family, Logan. I feel that, too, and since I've never really had one, it means a lot to me as well."

"I'm glad. Call me tomorrow when you get home from work, okay?"

"Sure. Talk to you then." She ended the call.

She should have felt better, but she didn't. Logan was putting up walls. Was this what it was like to be around her? He'd told her more than once that she'd created barriers of protection around herself. Walls he couldn't get through. For the first time she understood what he meant. Logan wasn't completely shutting her out, but he was allowing her to get only so close. Why?

She sat for a while, stroking Krypto's head, trying to understand what was happening.

*God, how can I help him if he won't let me in?*

Logan leaned his head back against the couch and closed his eyes. He really wanted Alex here, but if things went wrong . . .

He shook his head. No. He couldn't afford to think that way. He needed time to build his faith, and as awful as it sounded, if Alex was with him, he'd be thinking about her rather than concentrating on the battle ahead. It had to be just him and God right now. No one else, no matter how much they meant to him. He didn't even want Alex to drive him to the hospital, but he couldn't see a way out of it. She was so adamant.

"God," he prayed out loud, "I'm putting my faith in you. I've asked you to get me through this operation, and I believe you will. I know you don't want me to be afraid. You want me to live in faith. I intend to do that, but I'm asking one more thing. Please, God, help Alex. She needs freedom in her mind. Don't allow this challenge to hurt her. She means too much to me. Help me be an example of someone who trusts you with . . . well, with their life. You know the thoughts inside my head. Help me turn them toward you. You've always been there for me. I refuse to be afraid, not because of anything good inside me but because I know who you are. A good God. A loving Father. A healer and a deliverer. I love you, Abba."

Then he reached for his Bible on the coffee table.

Tracy lay in the dark, fighting off sleep. She had to stay awake. This might be her only chance to get out of here. She felt silly using an old movie as a model for what she was doing, but what else could she do? She couldn't come up with anything else. Although she clasped the knife in her hand, she couldn't imagine actually stabbing someone. Could she really do it? If it meant going home? She had to be brave and prepared to do whatever it took, not only for herself but also for the other women imprisoned here.

She knew they came into the room at night, because the next morning there were always clean clothes and the waste bags were gone. They clearly waited until they knew the women had fallen into a drugged sleep. But how long did that take? She assumed they didn't hesitate too long since they wouldn't want to take a chance the drug would wear off before they were done.

She wanted to move, but she didn't dare. Finally, after what seemed like hours but couldn't have been, she heard a key in the door. She grasped the knife tightly in her hand and waited for her chance.

# 26

Alex lay in her bed, Krypto next to her, snoring away. Tears ran down the sides of her face.

*God, please help me get past what happened in that warehouse. I need to be there for Logan. I'm afraid he doesn't feel like he can lean on me because he's still worried about me. I understand that it might take a while to heal from the trauma, but I can't wait any longer. Logan needs me now. Please rescue me. I give you the fear, the anxiety, and the nightmares. I want to walk away from that warehouse. Leave it in the past. And, God, please, please heal Logan. Let the tumor be benign. I . . . I love him. I don't want him to leave my life. I've lost so many people. I can't stand to lose someone else who matters to me.*

She lay there a little longer, letting the tears wet her pillow. Krypto had stopped snoring, and Alex turned her head and saw the beautiful white pit bull staring at her. Then he started licking the tears from her face. Alex wrapped her arms around him, praying God would give her the desire of her heart.

———

Tracy lay in bed with her eyes closed. She could hear drawers sliding open. The door was open, and the light from the hallway made it possible for her to see someone leaning over the dresser. She jumped up and ran toward him, grabbed him from the back, and held the knife up in the air. Her sudden move seemed to surprise him, and he turned around quickly, losing his balance. She watched as he fell backward, his head hitting the side of the dresser. He slumped to the floor, completely unconscious. For some reason she stood there for several seconds, trying to figure out what to do next. Then she realized she didn't need to do anything.

She quickly slid on her shoes and ran toward the door. She knew there were two of them. What if the other one was watching her? But she had to take that chance. She slowly stepped into the hallway and quietly closed the door behind her. She paused for a moment, wondering if she should go back, get the man's keys, and lock him in. But she was afraid he'd wake up and grab her. Her best bet was to get out of there as quickly as possible and get help. She couldn't take anyone with her because they'd all been drugged. If only she had her phone, but she had no idea what they'd done with it.

Looking around, she suddenly realized why this place seemed familiar. It was a wine cellar. A large one, with the wine removed and the rooms for different wines turned into cells. She'd visited one once when she was on vacation with her parents. That explained why there weren't any windows.

Expensive wines were kept in temperature-controlled rooms, away from light.

She counted six cells, including hers. One of the doors was open, across the hall to the left of the woman who'd told her not to talk to anyone. She quickly looked inside. The room seemed to have been prepared for someone.

A little way down the hallway, to the right of her own cell, she saw a closed door. That was the direction the blond man with the food cart always came from. What was on the other side? Freedom? Or was her abductor there?

She carefully pulled the door open and discovered a set of stairs. Off to one side was an old dumbwaiter they must be using to send food down for the food cart. She slowly made her way up the stairs, listening for footsteps. But she heard nothing. She pushed the door at the top of the staircase open and stepped into a large kitchen. It was like something out of a home-decorating magazine. Beautiful. Granite countertops, subway tiles on the wall, and a large island with the same granite. Whoever these guys were, they had money. That surprised her. Then she saw French doors that led outside.

Crying, she ran toward them, dropping the knife on the floor. She turned the door handles with both hands, but the doors were locked. No. This couldn't be happening. Then she noticed a small knob above the handles. She turned it, and it made a clicking sound. She tried again, and the doors opened.

Tracy ran out into the night, gulping in fresh air as if she'd been drowning and desperately needed to breathe. She was in a yard with a large privacy fence around it. She couldn't see a gate, so she turned and ran the other way. It was hard to make out much with only one outside light, but she also had moonlight overhead. It was enough to see she was approaching something she couldn't believe. An amusement park! It wasn't large. Several rides, some concession stands, some picnic tables in one area. This was crazy. Where was she?

She was almost at the end of the park, running toward some trees, when lights suddenly blazed and music started to play. What was happening? At that moment she realized she should have grabbed a sharp knife from the kitchen. It was a stupid mistake. The desire for freedom had overcome reason. She refused to look back and kept running toward the trees, but just as she got close, she found herself facing a metal fence. Not seeing a gate here either, she decided to climb over it.

She put her hands on the fence and screamed as an electric shock knocked her to the ground. She felt herself drifting away, but before the blackness overtook her, she saw someone standing over her.

Alex was walking through some kind of maze. She couldn't see anything except high walls all around her. She walked and walked, trying to find her way out. Finally, she saw a light and headed toward it. When she reached it, it was so bright she couldn't look at it very long. But before she turned her gaze away, she could make out large, white, glowing wings. She fell to her knees, realizing she was standing in front of an angel.

"What do you want from me?" she asked.

"You must listen carefully," a voice said. It wasn't male or female. She'd never heard anything like it before. "There is danger ahead. Lives are at stake, including yours. Do you understand?"

"Yes, I understand."

"You must be led by the voice in your heart. Not the voice in your head. Do not be afraid, for I am with you."

Alex started to ask a question, but then the angel was gone just as quickly as it had appeared. The dream began to drift away from her, and she called out to God.

She opened her eyes and lay on her bed wondering what the dream meant. This was the second one that seemed to be warning her something bad was about to happen. She'd started having strange dreams as soon as she'd become a Christian. They seemed so real. She had to believe that God was speaking to her. She remembered a Scripture in the Bible about the last days. That people would be having dreams.

"God," she said aloud, "I don't know what's coming, but I know you're with me. Whatever you need me to do, I'll do it. No matter what."

Then she turned on her side, wrapped her arms around Krypto, and drifted off.

# 27

Alex had just arrived at work the next morning when Jeff called her into his office. As she passed Alice's desk, Jeff's gracious assistant wouldn't look at her. That was new. Had the Abbotts been on television again? She was certain the police were already overwhelmed with calls—most of them unhelpful.

When she entered Jeff's office, he didn't look happy.

"What's going on, Boss?"

He gestured toward the chairs in front of his desk. "Something's . . . happened. I . . .." He shook his head.

Alex couldn't remember ever seeing him like this. She suddenly remembered her dream from the night before and determined in her heart that she wouldn't allow herself to feel afraid.

"Tell me," she said.

"Chief Dixon received a package this morning. It was stuck in the door of his station. There was a security camera, but the package was dropped off in the middle of the night, and the man who brought it was dressed in dark clothes and a hoodie. He didn't look up at the camera. The original note is at the lab so they can check for fingerprints and DNA, but here's a copy of it."

He pushed a piece of paper across the desk, and she picked it up.

*I have the women. They are alive. You will send FBI agent Alex Donovan to the place I indicate tomorrow. If she comes, I will tell her where they are. If you do not follow these instructions exactly, the women will die, starting with Tracy Mendenhall. Merrie McDowell will be next. Just remember that I am not alone. If you betray me, someone else will execute the women, and you'll never get them back.*

*I will call the phone I've included in this package and give you the location. Agent Donovan will have thirty minutes to get there. She is not to be followed. If I see anyone except her, the women are dead. I will check her for a wire as well as a gun. If I find either, you will lose your only chance to rescue these women. There will never be another opportunity.*

*The Ghost Rider*

"We believe this is real. We've been able to keep Merrie McDowell's abduction out of the press."

Alex nodded at Jeff. "I'll be ready."

"I don't want you to do this. You're a BAU agent, not a field agent. I don't want you walking into another dangerous situation. It's too much to ask."

"So we're just supposed to let these women die? He could be telling the truth." She heard the sharpness in her tone, but she couldn't help it. "There's no choice here, and you know it."

"Alex, to be perfectly honest, I'm not sure you're mentally up to it. You haven't been yourself since . . ." He sat back in his chair.

She smiled at him. "At least it's thirty *minutes* this time instead of thirty seconds," she said, referencing the case that had caused her so many nightmares.

"Not funny."

"I realize that, but let's get past thinking we can say no. We can't."

Jeff sighed. "You're not going home until we hear from him. It's not safe."

"I understand. My go bag has everything I need. I just have to call my neighbor and ask her to look after my . . . my dog."

She'd been fine until that moment. Until she thought about Krypto. Would she ever see him again? She pushed the thought away. God had prepared her for this. She'd be okay as long as she listened to Him, and she intended to do that.

She suddenly remembered Logan. "I told Logan I'd take him to the hospital in the morning."

"Too dangerous," Jeff said, his tone making it clear he wasn't going to argue about it. "I'll get Nathan to drive him. We'll make some excuse for you."

"If it's not a good one, he'll know something's up. If he finds out what's going on, he might want to postpone his surgery." She frowned. "Have Nathan take Monty along. I want someone to be with Logan when he wakes up. He and Monty are close."

"Okay."

"I'm supposed to call him tonight," Alex said. "If I don't, he'll be suspicious."

"Then you'll have to talk like everything is okay," Jeff said. He shook his head. "I don't like hiding the truth from Logan. I hope this works."

"If the UNSUB is telling the truth—and we have to assume he is—why would he suddenly decide to release the women?" Alex asked, changing the subject. "He's been doing this a long time."

"Maybe he's just tired of the whole thing and wants a way out," Jeff said.

"Then why not just kill the women and leave their bodies where they'll be found? That would humiliate them and make him feel powerful. That's the usual agenda for serial killers."

"You're assuming at least some of the women are dead?"

"After all these years? Yeah. Besides, if he's looking for someone specific, once he knows one of the women isn't the right one . . ."

"She becomes irrelevant and . . ."

Alex nodded. "He disposes of her."

"Let's not forget you look like the women he's taken. The problem is you've been in Virginia for only a few years. It seems as if he's looking for someone he met years ago."

"I don't think facts matter much to him. His premise is horribly flawed. The person he's looking for could have moved, died . . . or at least cut her hair, for crying out loud. This UNSUB has an obsession that has no reason. No objectivity. I remind him of this woman he's looking for, and that's all that matters. Just like the other women."

"But he says he's not alone," Jeff said. "Surely whoever is working with him is aware of his delusion."

Alex shrugged. "Assuming he's telling the truth, whoever's helping him may not care. Perhaps he's getting something out of this. Security. Money. I don't know."

Jeff hesitated a moment before saying, "He seems organized, yet he has no way to know if any of the women he abducts is his target. At least not until he has them and . . . what? Interrogates them? This really is something new." He shook his head. "I hear what you're saying, but what if he either wants to add you to his collection or trade the women for you? Maybe he's convinced himself you're the woman he wants. And remember, just because he says the other women are alive doesn't mean they are. They could all be dead. You may just be next on his list."

"Well, I guess I'll find out."

"We're going to spend the rest of today getting you ready," Jeff said. "And getting SWAT and HRT prepared."

Although Alex knew SWAT and the Hostage Rescue Team would be employed, she was worried the UNSUB would see them. "You might not be able to use them," she said. "If the UNSUB picks a spot where they can't hide, they'll have to stay behind."

"I'm not taking chances with your life," Jeff said sharply. "My God, haven't you given enough to this job? I won't let you die."

Alex was surprised by his sudden burst of emotion. He was usually calm and collected. She wanted to tell him that God had prepared her for this. That she knew she would be okay. But if she told him the Lord had spoken to her in a dream, he'd assume she was unstable, and then the CP would dress up another agent to look like her and send *her* out there. She knew better than to be overly confident, but she still had more faith in herself to bring the women home than she did in any field agent the Bureau might choose.

"I'll be fine, Jeff," she said, keeping her voice steady. "I have the same training as anyone you could send out there."

"I know that, but he's trying to stack the deck. We've got to make sure you have some kind of a weapon."

"He said no gun."

"You're not doing this without a way to defend yourself." Jeff leaned so far back in his chair that for a moment Alex thought he might tip over. He ran a hand over his face. "Why are we even talking about this? It's nuts. This is probably a complete waste of time."

Alex couldn't argue with his reasoning. Serial killers weren't known for their compassion or for keeping their word. The UNSUB's world was made up of his needs, his thoughts, and his will. Other people existed only to give him what he wanted—whatever fit into his perverted world. Yet for some reason her gut told her that at least some of the women were still alive.

"We can't be sure of that, Jeff," she said. "And we're not going to gamble with these women's lives. Let's stop talking about this and spend our time preparing me."

Jeff crossed his arms over his chest and stared at her. "You'll go to the command post. They'll get you ready. I want you to follow their instructions to the letter, do you understand?"

"When do you want me to leave?"

"Now. But if the lab finds something on the letter or the envelope that could help us, we'll call this off."

"If there's enough time. Unless they can tell us where

he is—and where the women are being held—I have to go through with this."

Jeff didn't reply. There was nothing to say. Alex was right. No matter what the lab discovered, there was almost no chance it would change anything.

"I have to ask this, Jeff. You said you were certain the note came from the UNSUB. But how can you be sure? Maybe someone who knows Merrie McDowell is missing sent it. Like Tracy's father did."

Jeff scooted another piece of paper toward her, and Alex picked it up. It was a copy of a photo. A woman lay on a small bed, her eyes closed. Alex looked closer.

It was Tracy Mendenhall.

ndy put his hand up to the bump on his head. It still hurt. At least it hadn't bled. "What if she'd found a way out of here?" he said. "I should have been more careful."

"It wasn't your fault," Brent said. "We all assumed she was out for the night."

"She put on that act, pretending she was sick, just so she could get out of your date. She's probably not the right one, you know. We need to learn more about them so we only take the best candidates." He shook his head. "I'm the one cleaning their rooms, delivering their food and supplies, emptying out their waste. . . ."

Frowning, Brent said, "I do my share. Besides, you know we can't trade places. It would never work."

Andy was quiet. Brent was right.

"Do you think Rider will punish them all?" Brent asked.

Andy sighed. "I don't know. You know I can't control him.

Maybe he'll just forget about it. He seems pretty excited about this next one."

"But he won't want the others to get ideas."

"You're probably right," Andy said. "I guess we'll find out." He paused. "We'll be full up again at six."

Brent nodded. "Right. Sarah was released so we can bring in Alex." He closed his eyes. "I hope Rider's really sending the women home. Not . . ."

Andy didn't comment. Brent wasn't the only one who questioned whether they could trust Rider to tell them the truth.

Brent stared at him for a while before saying, "Shouldn't I take out the new girl tonight? Before the new one comes? What was her name? Merrie? A nice name."

Andy shrugged. "I'm sure Rider will let you know."

Andy knew Brent was frustrated with how long they'd been at this. He was too. Could this new woman be the one Rider was looking for? The FBI agent?

He hoped so.

---

When Tracy woke up, the light was on, and she realized she was back in her room. Correction. Her cell. This wasn't a room. It was a prison. At least now she had a better idea of what she was facing. What they were all facing. This was some kind of large house—almost a mansion. There was a small amusement park on the grounds, and it was fenced all the way around. Unless you could turn off the electricity to that fence, there was no way out of this place.

She tried to sit up, but when she did, the room swam around her. A reaction to the electric shock? Or had he drugged her again?

Although she didn't get a good look at the man who'd come into her room last night, she'd seen his blond hair. Except for the day when she was taken, she still hadn't seen her abductor. If she didn't remember his drugging her, she'd almost wonder if he was a victim too. But where was he?

She tried to get up again. Still dizzy, but a little better. She looked down at her hands. They were burned. She was lucky to be alive, and she whispered a prayer of thanks to God.

Tracy looked toward the door. No breakfast tray. Not surprising. She expected retaliation, but she hoped the other women wouldn't have to suffer. Still, this couldn't go on. They all had to be brave.

She rose and walked to the door, and after sliding the upper panel open, she called out into the hall as loud as she dared. "Is anyone there?"

She heard several panels screech open, and a few seconds later the eyes across from her were staring, "Shh! I told you—"

"Listen, I got out last night."

"Why did you do that?" came another voice from her left. "Now they'll punish us."

"How?"

"It's only happened once since I've been here." The woman across from her again. "We talked to each other, and they didn't like it. They didn't give us food for three days, and all we had to drink was water from the sink. Didn't pick up the bags from the toilet. And they turned off the lights. We couldn't see anything. Couldn't read."

"But you had this light in the hallway, right?"

"They turned it off too," another voice said, this one to her left as well, a little farther down. "I don't want to go through that again."

"Look, I don't want to see that happen either," Tracy said, "but we've got to get out of here."

"I want to go home. Please, tell us what to do." Yet another voice. That made at least four women.

"I made it to the edge of the property." Tracy was trying to keep her voice down so no one but the women could hear her. "But an electric fence surrounds everything. I touched it, and it knocked me out. He brought me back here."

The woman across from her said, "How far is the fence past the carnival rides?"

That was surprising. "You've seen them?"

"Yes, on our so-called date."

"I was supposed to go on one, but I convinced them I was sick. What's that about?"

"The other guy, not the blond one, takes you to that strange little amusement park. It was weird because he was so nice. I mean, it would have been pleasant if he wasn't insane and I wasn't a prisoner. We rode rides, had dinner outside, and talked."

"What did you talk about?" Tracy asked.

"He asked me questions about my childhood, especially when I was a teenager. I can't remember too much, really. I was trying to figure out how to overpower him. Get out of here."

"But you didn't try?" Tracy said.

"No. I figured the other guy was watching us. And if I did the wrong thing, he'd retaliate. The threats are always aimed at everyone so you feel responsible for hurting the entire group. And sometimes a woman disappears. So unless you're ready to die . . ."

"How do you know they disappear?"

"We don't talk for long, especially after the time we got in trouble, but we still check on each other sometimes. As long as we keep it short—"

"Quit talking!" a male voice said.

The sound of metal panels clanging shut echoed down the hall, but Tracy kept hers open. The blond guy passed by. He was carrying something. Then she heard a knock on a door down the hall and the sound of a panel opening.

"I'm giving you some clothes and shoes," he said. "Put these on and be ready. When you hear everyone else being served dinner, it's time. I'll let you out and take you with me. You're going on a date. Don't try anything. It won't do you any good, and everyone else will be hurt if you cause any trouble. Do you understand?"

Tracy couldn't hear a response, but he must have gotten what he wanted, because the metal panel was pulled shut. As he walked back down the hall, he whistled that song again. She was really beginning to hate it. When she heard the door at the end of the hall shut, she put her mouth close to the small opening in her door. "Can anyone hear me?"

Another panel down the hall slid open. "My name is Merrie, and I just got here. I'm supposed to go on a date tonight. I . . . I don't want to do this. Please, someone tell me what to do." Her voice shook like an old woman's. She was clearly terrified.

"Don't worry, Merrie," the woman across from Tracy said. "Just enjoy an evening out of your cell. It's useless to fight him. Go along with it. You'll be fine. We'll all figure out a way to get out of here together. But during the date . . . that's not the time."

"Okay, but I'm still frightened."

"I promise you'll be okay. And we'll all be here waiting for you. I'm beginning to think we *have* to keep talking to each other. Take the risk. We have to work together."

"Merrie, I think I saw you being carried in," Tracy said. "You have long black hair like mine, right?"

"Yes. Why?"

"I'm wondering if that's just a coincidence. What about the rest of you? And how old are you?"

"I have long dark hair, and I'm thirty-one."

"That's about my age. What about the rest of you?"

After the others responded, they were all silent for a minute. Were they all thinking what she'd been thinking? That this guy was looking for someone in particular?

Then a voice down the hall said, "I'm Marla, and I think they might have taken the woman across from me away."

"Why do you think so?" Tracy asked.

"Because we usually knock on our doors to say good night. We've done it for a while now. But she didn't respond last night. And the blond guy didn't deliver food to her. I would have heard it. Besides, since we started talking today, she hasn't said anything."

"Look, everyone else say your name out loud," Tracy said. "That way we can keep track of each other. And when one of us gets out, we can tell the police who's here. Again, I'm Tracy. And we've heard from Merrie and Marla."

"I'm Amy," the woman across from her said.

"Rhonda." This came from down the hall.

The hall was silent, and then there was the sound of someone knocking on a door. No response.

"Her name is Sarah," Rhonda said. Her voice broke. It was obvious she was worried.

Where was Sarah? And who would disappear next?

Alex tried to make herself comfortable on the couch at the command post. She'd spent the rest of the day there, talking to Assistant Special Agent in Charge Roberta Williams along with the heads of the FBI's SWAT team and Hostage Rescue Team. The ASAC was used to running investigations, but she admitted to Alex that this was something new.

"You understand the psychology of this kind of UNSUB better than we do," she said. "All we can really do is to prepare you for any kind of confrontation. Our main objective is to find the missing women . . . or their bodies. But the other objective is to stop this person from abducting or killing anyone else."

She'd stared hard into Alex's eyes. "You'll have to read the situation yourself, Agent Donovan. If you can obtain these two goals, then we have a win. But if at any time you feel threatened or in danger for your life, get out. We have no desire to bring devastation to another family. Do you understand?"

Alex had nodded, but there was no family to devastate. She just had Logan, and she couldn't even tell him what she was doing.

His surgery was in the morning, and she had no intention of giving him a reason to postpone it. Which is exactly what he would do if he knew about this plan. It was imperative that he have that operation. Alex didn't want anything interfering with that. He needed to do everything possible to protect his life. Jeff told her Nathan and Monty were ready to tell Logan that Alex couldn't take him to the hospital because she and Bethany had to complete their profile on the St. Louis shooter. Jeff seemed convinced this lie would work, but Logan wasn't stupid. If they played it wrong, he'd know something was wrong.

Williams had given her a tough nylon knife to insert into her boot. Nylon guns with nylon bullets existed, but they were too bulky. A pat down would reveal the gun, and Alex had no intention of angering the UNSUB with so many lives at stake. She'd also have a tracking device in the lining of her jacket, and that would be ready before she left for the designated meeting site. Neither the knife nor the tracking device would show up even if the UNSUB had a metal detector.

SWAT and the HRT would be standing by in the morning. Even though they'd have only minutes to find a place to hide, they were determined to be there. The whole operation had to be handled with professionalism and finesse. If the UNSUB spotted the agents, the whole thing could go south. Although Alex wanted to take the UNSUB down and force him to tell her where the women were, if he really wasn't working alone—which was entirely possible—a move like that could be disastrous.

She went over the profile again, wanting to make certain she understood this guy as much as possible before confronting him. Still convinced he was looking for a specific woman, she considered trying to make him believe she was that woman. Maybe he'd free any captives he might still have. But she didn't know enough to pull that off.

The truth was she honestly didn't expect him to tell her where the women were, no matter what he'd promised. Why would he? Jeff was a talented analyst. He probably knew this too. That's why he made sure she had the knife. Most likely, the UNSUB planned to take her, and Jeff wanted her to have a way to defend herself.

Her thoughts switched to Logan, and she began rehearsing options for what to say when she called him in a few minutes. She had to be careful.

She'd been praying for him all day, whenever she had the chance. Logan Hart was a good man, and he'd made such a difference in her life. He had to be okay. She couldn't accept any other outcome.

She decided to pray for him again. Then when she felt something drip onto her slacks, she reached one hand up to her face and found it wet. She was crying again. This had to stop. It was time to get herself together. She had to focus on the UNSUB and prepare for their meeting tomorrow.

She'd called Shirley and told her she had a special operation the next morning. That she might not be home right away. She'd given her Jeff's number a long time ago in case of emergency. She knew to call Jeff if she didn't hear from Alex for a while.

Suddenly the door swung open. It was Jeff. "I picked you up a cheeseburger and fries. I thought you might be hungry."

"Thanks," she said with a smile. "I'd forgotten about eating."

"I thought you might." He pulled a small table over to the couch and put the bag on top of it. Then he handed her a large paper cup with a lid. "Root beer. I know you like it, and there's no caffeine in it. You need to catch some sleep tonight. Tomorrow's a big day."

"Yeah, it is."

"I thought you'd like to know I mentioned your theory about the grocery store shooter to the St. Louis PD. They found the guy. A disgruntled ex-employee kidnapped the daughter of a man he knew, then forced him to shoot up the store by threatening to kill the girl if he didn't. Caught the ex-employee and freed the daughter. We hadn't even delivered the entire profile yet. Good job."

"Wow, that's great. I wondered if I was on the wrong track there."

Jeff smiled. "No, you're just a great analyst. One of the best I've ever known. Not sure even Kaely Quinn could have done what you did."

Alex laughed. "Not certain that's true, but thanks."

"Sure. You doing okay?"

"Yeah. I've been well prepped. I feel confident."

"Have you talked to Logan yet?"

"No. Just getting ready to call. I . . . I can't lie to him. I'm still not sure what to say."

Jeff sat down on the arm of the couch. "You don't have to lie. Act like you're double-checking the time he'll be ready to go in the morning. Just don't tell him you'll pick him up."

Alex raised an eyebrow. "That's still deceptive."

"Once he realizes why you deceived him, he'll understand."

"I'm not so sure. We've always been honest with each other."

"Look, you have to handle this however it feels right to you. No matter what you choose, I'll support you."

"I'm not as worried about you as I am about the ASAC and the team leaders who told me I couldn't tell anyone what was going on."

Jeff grinned. "So you're not afraid of me anymore."

"Oh, I'm afraid. Just not *as* afraid."

He laughed, then stood. "I'm going to leave you alone so you can eat and make that call." He paused a moment before locking his eyes on hers. "Listen, tomorrow you do whatever it takes to stay safe, do you understand? No one's asking you to sacrifice yourself."

"I understand."

He sighed. "I don't think you do, but I can't argue with you now. Just come back to us, okay?"

"Yes, sir," Alex said softly.

Jeff nodded and then left.

Alex pulled out the cheeseburger, took a bite, and did her best to swallow it.

Then she whispered, "Lord, help me do this right. I don't want to lie, but I can't allow Logan to get suspicious. It's for his own good." She took one more bite, chewed and swallowed it, and then picked up her phone.

---

Waiting at the door with the upper panel slightly open, Tracy wondered if she'd get dinner after no breakfast or lunch.

She was hungry. But at least the other women got theirs. She'd watched to make sure.

Then she heard the wheels on the cart squeaking, closer and closer to her cell until the panel at the bottom of her door slid open and a tray was pushed inside.

"You need to be careful." She recognized the voice of the blond guy who delivered their food. "He didn't want you to get anything to eat at all today. Next time I might not be able to help you."

She didn't respond. How could he act as if he cared about her or any of the other women here? What kind of game was he playing?

Tracy listened as he proceeded from door to door, stopping first across the hall and then twice more before she heard his keys. He was probably opening Merrie's cell. "Are you ready?" he said.

She heard Merrie answer him before the door creaked open and then shut. Two sets of footsteps clicked on the cement floor until the sound disappeared. When she heard a door close farther away, she opened the panel near the top of her door. Immediately, she heard the screeching of metal as others responded.

"It's me. Marla. Merrie left with the blond guy."

"No surprise," Amy said from across the hall. "The only time I saw the other one here was on my date."

"Are you sure she'll be okay?" Tracy asked.

"I believe so. I came back okay, and Rhonda and Marla did too. Of course, I don't know anything about anyone who was here before I came."

Tracy ignored the shiver up her spine. "I hope you're right. Please pray for her."

"Prayer hasn't done any good so far." A panel slid shut. The voice had sounded like Rhonda's.

"Forgive her." Amy sighed. "I'm sure she's afraid she'll disappear next. I think she got here after Sarah."

"Amy, are you certain they can't hear us?"

"No, but the cameras in our cells only record video. I have some experience with security cameras, and there aren't any speakers. If they can hear us, they would have to have something in the hallway. When I went out on our date, I looked around, but I didn't see anything. And even if there was something out there, I don't think they could pick up our voices clearly. We should probably try not to speak too loudly, though."

"Okay. I'm going to put off drinking the tea as long as I can so I'm awake when Merrie gets back."

"Good luck," Amy said. "You have to drink the tea in front of the camera. If they don't see you drink it, they'll make us pay. I just can't go through three days like that again."

"I'm getting a little tired of the threats. Have you noticed that the blond guy talks like he doesn't want us to be punished? Maybe it's an act. I don't know."

"I don't know either," Amy said, "but I don't trust him."

"By the way, what's the deal with the dress?" Tracy said. "It looks like something a child would wear."

"I know what you mean," Amy said. "It didn't fit me very well either. I could barely get it zipped."

"Is it possible there's only one?"

"I think so. And the shoes were tight too."

"They were too big on me," Marla said. "I agree that there's only one dress and one pair of shoes. Weird. I doubt we're all exactly the same size."

"Okay," Tracy said. "We'd better stop talking for now. I don't want to push it too far. Good night, Amy. Marla."

As she slid her panel shut, she heard the echoes of the other two women doing the same thing. She decided she'd pray especially for Rhonda tonight. She'd sounded about ready to give up. But right now she couldn't stop thinking about Merrie. What was she going through? It was supposed to be her turn to go on a date, and she felt guilty for getting out of it.

She carried the tray to the table and took off the lid. Thank goodness. Food. Beef stew with veggies, fruit gelatin, and a roll. Butter but no knife or fork. Besides the tea there was a bottle of water and a small bowl of vanilla ice cream.

After eating, she held off on the tea as long as she could. But eventually she sat where the camera could see what she was doing and drank it. Then she held the cup upside down to show it was empty. She'd never get the chance to hide the tea in a bag again. From here on out, she needed to play it straight until she could come up with another plan of escape.

She got ready for bed, opened the upper panel of her door just a crack, and then tried hard to stay awake so she could hear Merrie come back. But before long she felt herself losing the fight as she drifted off to sleep.

30

Logan answered his phone almost immediately. "I wondered when you were going to call," he said.

"Sorry. Had to eat something."

"You skipped lunch, didn't you?"

She chuckled. "Guilty. You know I rarely eat when you're not there."

"So it's my job to keep you healthy?"

"I guess so. How are you doing?"

"Pretty good. Still trying to decide what to take. I don't want to stay in the hospital any longer than I have to."

"You just need the basics, I guess. Pajamas, underwear, slippers, toothbrush, toothpaste, soap, shampoo. Something to read. Music. Your reading glasses. Oh, and a charger for your phone. Kind of like a go bag with extras."

Logan laughed heartily. "I should already know this from the last time we were in the hospital."

"Believe me, I figured it out only after realizing everything I needed and didn't have."

"I hear you. But I'm counting on you to bring me anything I forget. I'll give you a key to my place, okay?"

"Sure."

"And if I have a hankering for a sandwich from Tony O's?"

"Just ask and you shall receive." She was having a hard time responding to him without actually lying. She hated not being completely honest with him. "Did you change your mind about calling your family?"

"No. I still plan to talk to them afterward. In case I'm not up to it right away, I've written down a list of names and numbers for you, if that's okay. Maybe you could call them for me?"

Alex felt like a traitor. He was counting on her, and she wouldn't be there. How could she do this? But she had no choice. Those missing women were counting on her too.

"Alex? Are you still there?"

"Yeah . . . yeah, I'm still here."

"You're not getting emotional on me, are you?"

"No. I'm good."

"I've been worried about you. You don't seem like yourself lately. Can we talk about it?"

*You mean can I tell you about waking up at night, sweating, unable to breathe, feeling like my heart will burst from fear? Can I tell you I feel like I'm falling through space and the only safe place to land is by your side? That I don't know if I could go on without you? That there's a chance you may never see me again after tomorrow?*

Alex took a quick breath. "I'm fine. You're imagining things. Why don't you think about yourself for a change? It's okay to focus on you for a while. I'm tired of conversations about me. It gets boring."

"I don't think it's boring. I'm so glad I've had a part in your life. I hope it's been good."

"What are you saying? *Been?*" Alex choked on her words and couldn't get anything else out.

"I . . . I'm sorry. I didn't mean it that way. Hey, this is a simple operation. It's not life-threatening."

"Logan, the doctor is about to cut your head open. That's not a simple surgery."

"Again, I'm so sorry, Alex. I've frightened you, and I didn't mean to. I'll be fine. I promise."

"That's a promise you'd better keep."

He was quiet for a moment, then said, "I need to tell you something important, but I . . . I need to wait until tomorrow. If I tell you now, I'll worry about it all night."

Alex fought against a surge of emotion that brought tears to her eyes. "Hey, I need to let you pack."

"Okay, but—"

She ended the call before she broke down, then choked back a sob since she couldn't risk anyone in the CP hearing her cry. She tried to finish the burger Jeff brought, but she couldn't get it down. She threw the rest of it away along with the fries.

Logan stared at the phone for a while, then scrolled through his contacts and clicked on Monty's number.

Alex tossed and turned on the uncomfortable couch, unable to relax, afraid her nightmares would attack her as if she was in a war and the enemy was determined to destroy her. Was she losing herself? She suddenly realized there was a lot of truth to that notion. She sat up and began to mentally review a sermon she'd heard about spiritual warfare. She couldn't always rely on Logan to help her when she had personal battles. It was time to learn how to fight back using the tools God had given her.

She reached into her go bag and took out the small NIV Bible she kept in it. Then she looked up the Scriptures Pastor Shook, the senior pastor at her church, mentioned in that sermon.

"You will not fear the terror of night," she said out loud, quoting the 91st psalm. She read further and then said, ""Because he loves me," says the Lord, "I will rescue him; I will protect him, for he acknowledges my name. He will call on me, and I will answer him; I will be with him in trouble, I will deliver him and honor him. With long life I will satisfy him and show him my salvation.""

Then she remembered another verse that had resonated with her and read it. Jeremiah 29:11. *"For I know the plans I have for you," declares the* Lord, *"plans to prosper you and not to harm you, plans to give you hope and a future."*

The first time she'd heard that Scripture, Logan had shown it to her. It was hard for her to take it in then, but when she heard it again in church, she finally understood it. God had a plan for her life. She remembered thinking that if that was true, she had a reason for being alive. She was important to God.

She read the Scriptures over several more times, trying to plant them in her memory. When she put the Bible down, she closed her eyes and prayed.

*God, I want the future you have for me. It's hard for me to believe you love me that much, but I know you don't lie. I'm trusting that no weapon formed against me will prosper. And that Logan will come through his surgery safely, that he will be fine. If You have a future for me, I know you have one for him. And, God, please help him understand why I didn't tell him what I'm doing tomorrow morning. I don't want him to feel like I've betrayed him.*

Even as she said it, she felt assured that Logan would understand because he would have done the same thing in her place. Then she recalled what Pastor Shook asked the congregation to repeat after he read those Scriptures.

"I . . . I believe that your Word is true and that you will perform your Word," she whispered. "Thank you, God."

When she lay down again, she felt an overwhelming sense of peace.

# 31

As Alex walked toward the Ghost Shack in the abandoned amusement park, the voice they'd heard on the burner phone echoed in her head. *Magic Land Park in Ashville. Inside the Ghost Shack. Again, she has thirty minutes to get there and no more. If she brings any law enforcement with her, the women will die. And if she has a weapon or a wire, they will die.*

She was uncomfortable knowing SWAT and HRT were nearby, but after looking at an aerial view of the park, they'd found a spot where they felt they could hide without being spotted. She hoped they were right, but that wasn't her call.

Alex was ready to follow through with what they'd told her at the CP. It wasn't much. Just make sure to keep her jacket and boots on, and if she felt uncomfortable at any point, immediately leave the building. If the UNSUB tried to accost her, she was to take him down and then alert SWAT. They would swarm the building and make an arrest. But Alex didn't want things to go down that way. If they did, they might not be able to find the women in time.

She was also told that under no circumstances was she to leave the area with the UNSUB. But Alex had no intention of following those instructions. If he didn't give her the location of the women he held captive, going with him was probably her only shot at freeing them.

She could feel the knife in her boot. It wasn't very comfortable, but she was glad it was there. It was unusually warm for April, even at dusk, and she was sweating a little inside her jacket. But that didn't matter. She needed the tracker that was in the hem.

The Scriptures she'd read the night before had chased away her fear, and this morning she'd thanked God for answering her prayers. It seemed odd to thank Him for something before He did it, but Pastor Shook explained that faith wasn't believing what you could see but believing what you couldn't see.

What was the Scripture in the book of Hebrews? She'd memorized it from her NKJV Bible. *Faith is the substance of things hoped for, the evidence of things not seen.* For someone who relied on facts the way she did, it was a tough transition, but she was determined to become the person God wanted her to be. And if that meant destroying some of her preconceived ideas, so be it. Her previous beliefs certainly hadn't helped her. She was tired of living in the past and angry that the man who'd tried to kill her in that cold, dirty warehouse was still victimizing her. She didn't want him to be a part of her life anymore. She was determined to eradicate him from her mind.

Something Logan once said gave her strength as well. He'd

referred to a Scripture that talked about how God gives His children beauty for ashes, that says He promises to take the bad experiences in our lives and replace them with something beautiful. "God will give us beauty for ashes, Alex," Logan had said. "But we have to give Him the ashes. If we keep them, He can't exchange them for beauty." She wanted the beauty. In fact, she was determined to receive it.

ASAC Williams had forbidden any outside contact while they waited for the UNSUB to call, so Alex had spent the day wondering how Logan's surgery had gone. The hours had ticked by while the burner phone stayed silent. A little after five, Williams handed her a note from Jeff that said Logan was fine. Although she'd wanted more details, she was thankful for at least that much. Hopefully, Jeff had kept Logan's questions at bay once he was out of surgery. She'd wanted to make it to the hospital before he woke up so she could have explained things to him herself.

Everyone at the CP had been on edge as they waited, as if the entire team had been holding their breath. They'd almost given up when the burner phone finally rang at six.

Right now, however, she had to concentrate on the next few minutes. She thought about Tracy Mendenhall, the woman who now represented all the women this UNSUB had victimized. If she was still alive, Tracy was waiting for rescue, and Alex had no intention of letting her down.

She stopped in front of the dilapidated Ghost Shack and whispered a prayer, then reached into her pocket and took out her small flashlight. Suddenly, she felt a strange urge to look up toward the top of the ridge to her right. She glanced that way before she realized what she was doing. That wasn't where SWAT and HRT waited, but if the UNSUB or someone

he worked with was watching, they might think she was looking for backup.

She quickly refocused on the double entrance doors of
the shack, hanging half off their hinges. She hesitated for a
moment, but then that same peace from last night came over
her. She could swear someone whispered, *I'll be with you.*
Was she just hearing what she wanted to hear? Or was this
connected to the dream she'd had, the one with the angel?
She was determined to listen to the voice of God rather than
to her own mind.

She turned on the flashlight, stepped into the gap between
the doors, then swung the beam of light around in the dark.

No one.

"Hello?" she called. "Is anyone here?"

No response. Then a phone, so loud it made her jump,
rang not far from where she stood. She pointed the flashlight
toward the sound and saw the phone lying on the seat of an
old four-seater car that had once carried people through this
ride. She walked over and picked it up, stepping carefully
since the floor was littered with debris. Injuring herself would
endanger the operation, something she couldn't risk.

She answered and said, "Hello."

"Walk toward the back of the building," the same burner
phone voice said. "You'll see a large piece of plywood covering a hole in the floor. Go down into the hole and you'll find
a tunnel. Keep following it to the end. I'll be waiting there."

"You're supposed to tell me where the women are," she
said. "That was the deal."

"You'll find them if you do what I say. If you don't, no
one will ever see them again. It's your choice. You have ten
seconds to decide."

"Okay, okay."

"Bring the phone with you. And leave your jacket where you're standing."

If she did as he said, the team wouldn't be able to find her with the tracking device. She wondered if she could tear the hem of the jacket and put the tracker in her jeans pocket. But before she had a chance to try, she heard "Ten, nine, eight—"

"All right, all right. I'm taking off my jacket." She shrugged out of it and dropped it onto the floor. She had to find the women. No matter what it took. "I'm putting the phone—" She heard it disconnect.

*Okay.*

She slid the phone into her pocket, then used the flashlight to locate the plywood. She reached down and pushed it out of the way. Sure enough, she stared down into a deep hole. Alex hated the dark, so she was extremely thankful for the flashlight. She noticed a rope ladder on one side.

She turned around and held the flashlight in her mouth while she stepped down the ladder as carefully as she could. She'd probably gone about ten feet when the ladder ended and she jumped to the ground under her. The tunnel was right there. It wasn't very wide, though, and once she started through it, she began to feel claustrophobic. She fought against it by whispering the Scriptures she'd read the night before.

She had to stoop down some to keep moving, and she wondered just how far the tunnel stretched. Then a voice called out, "That's far enough. Turn off your flashlight."

"Listen," she said. "This isn't—"

A loud boom shook the earth around her. Alex fell to the ground, and dirt began to cover her. Then hands reached out and grabbed her, pulling her out of the darkness. Before she could open her eyes, she felt a sting on her neck, and immediately the world began to turn dark.

———

Jeff and Logan drove down to where SWAT and HRT were trying to find out if their agents were still alive. They both got out to help, but the SWAT commander waved them away.

"Get back," he yelled. "We've got this."

Logan ignored him and ran toward the Ghost Shack, which was being consumed by fire.

Jeff grabbed him and pulled him away. "Stop! Killing yourself won't help her. If Alex was still in there, she's gone."

A wave of pain and nausea forced Logan to his knees, where he threw up. Jeff stood by him until the ambulances began to arrive. They'd been standing close by in case they were needed. As the wounded and burned were being loaded for transport to the hospital, Jeff waved EMTs over to where Logan still knelt on the ground.

"Give me the name of your doctor," he said to Logan.

When he didn't respond, Jeff said, "It's in your records. No matter what you do, we'll figure it out. Would you rather we find it while you're still breathing or when it's too late?"

Logan mumbled something that sounded like *Dr. Schneider*.

"He must mean Dr. Schmeidler," one of the EMTs said. "She's a surgeon at Mercy."

"That's the one. He was scheduled to have surgery with her this morning. Do you have a way to get her number?"

As one EMT helped Logan onto a stretcher, the other made a call, then handed his phone to Jeff. "Give the dispatcher a message for the doctor. She'll get it to her."

Thankful for the help, Jeff took the phone and gave the woman his name and number. "Tell Dr. Schmeidler that Logan Hart is on his way in. He put off his surgery this morning, but he needs help ASAP. Tell her I said to meet him in the ER when he gets there."

After he disconnected the call, Jeff realized he'd just given both the dispatcher and the doctor orders, but hopefully they would understand the seriousness of the situation. He handed the phone back to the EMT. "I'll follow you to the hospital. And thank you."

The EMT nodded, then helped the other one load Logan into the ambulance before he jumped inside.

Jeff followed the flashing lights that split the night, sending out a warning that lives were hanging in the balance. He also did something he rarely did. He prayed. For Logan . . . and for Alex. It would take a miracle for them to both live through all this. But he'd been told God still performed miracles.

With everything inside him, he hoped that was true.

ogan tried to convince the EMT sitting beside him that
he was okay, that he didn't need to go to the hospital.
But he was too weak to win any kind of battle, verbal
or physical.

"Just lie back and take it easy, Agent Hart. We'll be at the
ER soon, and then you can tell the docs and nurses you don't
need to be there. But until then you're stuck here with me,
okay?"

Logan nodded weakly. "Do you know anything about who
was injured in the explosion?"

"Some agents have burns and contusions, but I didn't see
anything life-threatening. We don't think anyone was in the
building when it went up."

"But there was an agent inside before . . ." He couldn't
finish his sentence. He felt as if he'd swallowed a golf ball.
He couldn't seem to clear his throat.

"I'm sorry," the EMT said. "I just don't know."

Logan turned his face away so the man wouldn't see the tears rolling down his cheeks. As if he understood, the young EMT put his hand on Logan's arm. His kindness made it even harder for Logan to control his emotions.

"I'll pray for your friend," the EMT said quietly.

Logan appreciated his comment, especially since the man probably wasn't supposed to say things like that while he was working. What was this world coming to when promising to pray for someone could cause you to lose your job?

"Thank you," Logan managed to get out. "Thank you very much."

A few minutes later the ambulance pulled into Mercy Hospital's emergency entrance. The EMT opened the back of the vehicle and then jumped out as the driver came around to help pull out the stretcher.

"We're a little backed up," the EMT who'd ridden with him said. "Let me see if we need to go in through a different entrance. I'll be right back."

No sooner had he walked away than an EMT Logan hadn't seen before stepped up to the stretcher and leaned down. He had bright-blue eyes and red hair.

"Alex wasn't in the building when it exploded," he said. "She needs you to pray for her, but she's alive." He patted Logan's shoulder and left as quickly as he'd come.

When the other EMT came back, Logan asked if he knew the name of the red-headed EMT, adding that he'd told him his friend was alive. The EMT frowned and looked around.

"I'm not sure who you mean. I don't know any EMTs with red hair. And I don't know how he'd know about your friend. The area hasn't been cleared for emergency personnel yet." He looked toward the entrance as the driver came back. "Looks like we're taking you inside this entrance. I'll ask around about the guy you're looking for."

As he was wheeled into the hospital, a wave of dizziness overtook Logan. He closed his eyes, trying to stop the world from spinning. The red-haired EMT had known Alex's name, but Logan hadn't mentioned her name to anyone. Jeff wasn't anywhere nearby, so he couldn't have told him.

Yet somehow he knew what the man said was true. Logan whispered a prayer, thanking God for letting him know Alex was alive. But she was evidently still in danger, and right now praying for her was all he could do.

When the stretcher came to a stop, two nurses came up. "You're Logan Hart?" one of them said, and Logan nodded. "We'll get you into a room as soon as we can."

The other nurse checked his electronic tablet. "You're already checked in. You were supposed to have surgery this morning with Dr. Schmeidler?"

"Yes." He was about to explain why he'd canceled when he realized the nurse was simply making certain he had the right information.

"Okay. Hold on a moment," he said.

A few minutes later an orderly wheeled him out of the ER, into an elevator, and then into a room on the second floor. Logan wished he had the bag he'd packed.

"Can you sit up for me?" yet another nurse asked as she lowered one of the rails on the stretcher.

"Yes, I think so." He held on to the side and swung his legs down. This time the dizziness wasn't so bad.

"Are you able to change into this gown by yourself?" she asked. "Or do you need help?"

"I can do it."

"I'll be right outside the door. If you need help, just call out. Only your underwear and socks under the gown. And let me know when you're finished."

She left the room, closing the door behind her.

Logan was afraid the severe dizziness and nausea would start again, so he was determined to change quickly. The last thing he wanted was for the young, fresh-faced nurse to help him remove his clothes. He stood only long enough to slide off his jeans. The rest of the time he sat on the edge of the stretcher.

Once he had the gown on, he folded his clothes and called the nurse back into the room. She helped him into the hospital bed, then he leaned back against the pillows. The nurse pulled the sheet and blanket over him before carrying his clothes to a small closet.

"No food tonight," she said when she returned. "Your doctor will speak to you in the morning before you go into surgery."

"It's been rescheduled?"

"Yes. Dr. Schmeidler rearranged her schedule so she could get to you first thing. Would you like some water? You can have a little before midnight."

"Yes, please."

He'd taken his phone out of his pants pocket and now put it on the rolling table beside the bed. It was late, but he wondered if Monty could get someone to drive him to Logan's apartment. He really wanted his bag, and Monty was the only other person who had a key.

The nurse put a half glass of water on the table while he dialed Monty's number. As the phone rang, he heard another phone ringing in the hall outside his room. The door swung open, and Monty walked in holding his phone in one hand and Logan's bag in the other.

"I think you can hang that up now," Monty said with a smile. He turned off his phone and put it in his pocket. "And before I say anything else, you need to know Alex wasn't in the building when it went up."

"I know."

"How could you? Jeff called me like a minute ago and asked me to tell you."

"Let's just say I had inside information."

Monty stared at him, then said, "Give me a minute before you tell me more."

He carried the bag over to the closet, where he started unpacking the bag, putting Logan's clean clothes into drawers. When he was done, he carried Logan's toiletries into the bathroom. After that, he grabbed Logan's dirty clothes and put them into one of the plastic bags Logan had packed. Plastic bags were a staple for agents who traveled a lot. They held dirty clothes, shoes, and all kinds of other things.

"You can leave those in the closet too," Logan said.

"Nope. I'll wash them and bring them back." Monty's mind was clearly made up, so Logan decided not to argue with him.

"How did you get here?" Logan asked. "I thought you couldn't drive."

"I can't. As soon as Jeff called, I phoned Nathan. He's downstairs in the car."

Logan frowned. "Why didn't he come up?"

"Because he knew I was going to read you the riot act and it might get a little uncomfortable."

Logan looked away. "I couldn't do this with her in danger, Monty. You know that."

"I shouldn't have told you the truth."

"You didn't. You told me she couldn't take me to the hospital because she had to work on that St. Louis file. But you're a terrible liar. I made Jeff tell me the rest."

"I'm glad you decided not to call her and try to talk her out of it."

Logan sighed. "Even if her phone had been on and I could have reached her, I knew she wasn't going to change her mind. I would have just made things harder for her, and she needed to focus on what she was assigned to do."

"I know that decision was hard for you, Logan, but I think you did the right thing. You shouldn't have put off this surgery, though."

"Look, it's happening in the morning. That's only twenty-four hours later. It's no big deal."

"Alex wouldn't have wanted you to wait even a day more."

"Don't say it like she's dead."

Logan had raised his voice louder than he meant to. It was late and some patients might be trying to sleep. Sure enough, the door swung open, and the same nurse poked her head inside.

"You need to quiet down, gentlemen." She pointed at Monty. "Five more minutes, and then please leave. He has to rest."

Monty nodded. "Okay. Thanks."

She closed the door again.

"She's not dead," Logan said, his voice quieter. "I told you—"

"You need to be prepared, Logan. Even though she wasn't in the building, we still don't know where she is or if she's still alive."

"I understand what you're trying to say, but I refuse to believe Alex is dead."

Monty studied him for a moment before saying, "Okay if I pray for you?"

"I wish you would."

Monty took Logan's hand and prayed, asking God to ensure that the surgery in the morning would be successful, to guide the doctor's hands and give her wisdom. Then he boldly asked for all the news tomorrow to be good. When he began to pray for Alex specifically, asking God to protect her and bring her home, Logan had to fight to contain his emotions. Monty seemed to understand, and his grip on Logan's hand tightened. When he finished, he stared at Logan for a moment, then said, "If we get Alex back, you need to tell her you're in love with her."

Logan let go of Monty's hand and wiped the tears from his face. "Being *in love* with someone suggests more than one person is involved. But I don't think that's true."

"I don't agree. You remember what she told you when she was in the hospital?"

"You mean when she was drugged?"

"It was in her mind, Logan. If it hadn't been, she wouldn't have said it."

"I can't count on that. Maybe she was thinking about . . . you."

Monty snorted. "I don't think so. I've seen the way she looks at you when she thinks no one is watching." He sighed and bent closer to Logan. "Look, man. If they'd found her body today, would you be happy with your decision to keep your feelings to yourself? You need to think about that."

"We're analysts," Logan said softly as Monty straightened

up. "We're not supposed to be in the field. These kinds of things shouldn't be happening."

"You're an FBI agent. You don't have to be out in the field. Sometimes just walking to your car can put you in the line of fire. You and Alex have had way too many close calls." He turned around and walked toward the door. "If you get another chance, brother, take it. Before all your chances run out. I'll see you in the morning."

Monty left and closed the door behind him.

Logan stared out the window of his room. Monty's question echoed through his mind. *"Would you be happy with your decision to keep your feelings to yourself?"*

He knew the answer. And it was no. He swore he'd tell Alex how he felt the next chance he got.

Yet even as he made the decision, doubt tried to enter his mind. Would he really get another chance? What if Monty was right and he might never see her again?

He shook his head. He couldn't accept that. He had to believe that God would keep her safe. He honestly couldn't imagine his life without Alex in it.

# 33

lex was seized with a fit of coughing and sat up. It took every ounce of strength she had to stop her body from convulsing. As the bile rose in her throat, she searched for a place to be sick. She was in some kind of room, but she didn't see a bathroom.

Then she spotted a long, dark-blue curtain in one corner. She got up quickly and pushed the curtain back. Thankfully, there was a small sink. She had dirt in her throat and had to keep coughing it up until she could control her gag reflex.

Slowly, her memory came back. The Ghost Shack, the tunnel, the voice . . . an explosion. When she looked in the mirror hanging over the sink, she was shocked. Her face was streaked with grime, and her hair was filthy. When she looked down she realized just how dirty she was. She washed her hands with a bar of soap she found, then after locating washcloths and towels on a rod, she turned on the water and rinsed out her mouth before washing her face.

She looked in the cabinet under the sink, grabbed a hairbrush, and worked on her hair. It made a mess, but she felt a little better. After noticing a camping toilet, she stepped outside the curtain and surveyed the room. Where was she?

Some folded clothes sat on a small table with a piece of paper lying on top of them. A handwritten note. Was this the same handwriting as in the note that came with the burner phone? Maybe.

*You can change into these. Clean sheets and a blanket are in the dresser. There is a toilet behind the curtain. Next to the toilet is a plastic receptacle for the bag, which will be picked up daily. Just move it next to the door at the end of the day.*

She looked at the clothes. They appeared to be her size. Jeans and a T-shirt. She walked over to the dresser and found underwear and socks. The socks reminded her of the knife in her boot. She looked down and realized she was still wearing them, but they were incredibly dirty. So was the bed where she'd been lying. It seemed someone wanted her to change clothes and get comfortable.

She had no intention of complying.

A wave of dizziness hit her, and she grabbed the edge of the dresser. She gingerly made her way back to the bed so she could sit down and decide what to do. No matter what, she couldn't let the UNSUB think she was being compliant. She had to keep the upper hand.

She gazed around the windowless room and spotted a

camera up in one corner. She looked for a speaker but didn't see one. It seemed her captors were watching but weren't interested in listening to her.

She pushed the only chair in the room under the camera before reaching up, twisting it off the bracket attached to the stone wall, and dropping it onto the concrete floor. Then she jumped down and smashed it with her boot. "You're not going to watch me," she said aloud, not caring that no one could hear her.

She walked over to the only door in the room. Metal. She turned the knob, but it was locked. A small panel at the top of the door also had a knob. She slid it open as quietly as she could, revealing only a slit, and found herself looking into what appeared to be a hallway. All she could see was a closed door across from hers.

"Is anyone there?" she called out. "My name is Alex Donovan. I'm an FBI agent. I'm here to get you home."

No response at first, but then she heard the sound of metal scraping against metal and saw the upper panel across from her open. A pair of eyes looked at her. Someone was alive. Alex almost sighed with relief.

"That might make me feel better if you weren't in the same situation we are," the woman said.

"Who are you?"

"I'm Marla. Marla Bess. Just how do you intend to help us?"

Marla. The missing woman who worked for a dog rescue.

"Don't worry about that now," Alex told her. "Just know the plan is to free you. Is Tracy Mendenhall here? What about Merrie McDowell?" She needed to know how many of the missing women were still alive.

"Merrie went on a date last night."

"A date?" The idea filled Alex with alarm. What had happened to Merrie?

"I'm Tracy," said a voice to Alex's left. "Don't worry about Merrie. He takes everyone out on a kind of date, but they all say he's very nice to them."

Alex was especially relieved to know Tracy was alive. Seeing her parents' fear firsthand had made her abduction feel personal. Now she had to find a way to get Tracy—and the rest of the women—out of here and back to their families. "You haven't been on this date, Tracy?"

"Not yet. I was supposed to go, but they moved Merrie ahead of me."

"Because you fought back," a voice said. "I'm Amy. Amy Tharp."

"Hi, Amy. Tracy, what does she mean you *fought back*?"

"One of them—a blond guy—comes during the night to give us fresh supplies and to pick up our bags. You know, the ones from the toilet as well as our dirty clothes. A couple of nights ago I didn't drink the drugged tea they give us. When he came into my room, I managed to confront him, and he fell and hit his head. He was unconscious, so I ran out and found the door at the end of the hall that leads upstairs."

Upstairs? They were probably underground, then.

"I wanted to find a way to get help."

"But you're back," Alex said. "What happened?"

"This place is surrounded by an electric fence. I tried to climb it, but it shocked me and I fell. Then he drugged me again and brought me back here."

An electric fence? What kind of place was this? "You said *they*. How many are there?"

"Two," Tracy said. "The blond guy and the dark-haired

guy who abducted us. He's the one who takes us out on these
. . . dates."

"You two need to be quieter," Amy said. "He might be
listening."

"There wasn't a speaker on the camera in my room," Alex
said. "How can anyone hear us? Is there a listening device
in the hall?"

"I've never found one. But he could be on the stairs behind
that door, trying to listen to what we're saying."

"Well, at least they can't see me anymore. I pulled the
camera off the wall and smashed it."

There were several seconds of silence before Marla said,
"You may have just gotten us all in trouble."

"You all need to fight back," Alex said. "Don't give in to
what they want. They took you against your will. Stand up
for yourselves. Make them uncomfortable."

No response.

"They're afraid," Amy finally said.

"But if we stand together, what can they do?"

"What they've done before. Cut off our food. Put us in the
dark for days," she said, her voice catching. "Maybe kill us. I
want to make it through this. Get home. I miss my daughter.
I don't want to disappear like Sarah did. You must be in her
room."

"She is," Marla said.

So some of the women were gone. Probably dead. No
wonder they were so afraid. Sarah had to be Sarah Breedlove.

"Look, you all do what you need to do. I won't go along
with what they want, but that's my decision. I want to make it
difficult for them. Make them deal with me as an equal, not

a victim. But you're right. It might make them angry enough to retaliate." She paused a moment before saying, "You said they put drugs in tea?"

"Just at night," Tracy answered.

"Why?"

"So we aren't any threat when they come in with fresh supplies."

"Just one of them comes?"

"Yes. As far as we know."

Good. Now Alex knew when she could overpower one of them. "Tracy, so the blond guy carries the keys? But the dark-haired one, the one on the dates, abducted you? Is that the case for all of you?"

All three of the other women answered yes.

"He's the man who must be in control," Marla said. "In his thirties. Nice-looking."

Exactly what Alex profiled. Again, good.

"You woke up pretty quickly," Tracy said. "Whatever they gave me knocked me out for at least a couple of days."

"I had a tunnel collapse on me, and I inhaled dirt," Alex said. "He must have given me a smaller amount. He was probably afraid I'd die if he didn't."

Alex was about to ask for more information when she heard a sound coming from down the hall to her right. Then she heard metal panels sliding shut. She kept hers slightly open. She wanted to get a look at her captors, but a man walked by so quickly she didn't get a good look at him. After he had checked all the doors, he hurried past Alex again. All she could see was a man with long blond hair. He kept his head down. She couldn't see his features at all.

When the door at the end of the hall shut, she once again

heard grinding metal, first one panel opening and then another.

"Are you okay, Merrie?" Tracy asked.

After a moment, a woman Alex assumed was Merrie finally
answered. "Yes, I'm fine. We did all the things you mentioned
at the amusement park. I . . . I know I shouldn't say this, but
I had a good time."

"Did you tell him you want to go home?" Tracy asked.

"No. It didn't seem . . . right."

"Merrie, my name is Alex Donovan. I'm an FBI agent,
and I'm here to get you out. You need to be careful. Have
you ever heard of Stockholm Syndrome?"

"Yes, but that's not it. I mean, he really was nice."

Alex sighed. "Merrie, that man took you away from your
friends and family without your permission. That's kidnapping. Abduction. And that's not nice."

"I . . . I guess so. No, you're right. Sorry. I just liked getting
outside. Seeing grass and trees. Smelling fresh air."

"You say he has an amusement park?" Alex asked. She
hadn't seen that coming. Was this a connection to Magic
Land?

"Yeah," Tracy said. "I should have mentioned it. I didn't
get a very good look at it, though."

"It's . . . it's weird," Marla said. "It has a small Ferris wheel,
a carousel, a Tilt-a-Whirl, some carnival games, and a train.
And there's popcorn, cotton candy, soda . . . hot dogs too."

"What kind of place is this?" Alex said. "An electric fence?
An amusement park?"

"I looked around the best I could when I was outside,"
Tracy said. "It was dark, but there was a light . . . and the
moon was full. I could tell this is a huge house, and there

are woods that surround it. I didn't notice any kind of street . . . or any other houses. And I know where we're being kept. It had to have been a wine cellar at one time. It's the only thing that makes sense."

Although millionaire serial killers weren't the norm, there had certainly been some. The notorious H. H. Holmes created what was referred to as his "murder castle." It had lots of rooms, trap doors, and places where he tortured his victims. He even built a gas chamber. He opened it as a hotel but used it to kill at least twenty-seven people. Some estimates were much higher, though—even up to two hundred unfortunate souls.

Was this UNSUB another Holmes? At least fourteen women had gone missing. A man with this much money could get away with murder, and it seemed that's exactly what was happening unless women like Sarah were alive somewhere else in the house, which she doubted. And if they had two UNSUBs, the danger was double. Had she made a huge mistake by allowing herself to be taken by these men? Would she simply be added to their victim count?

"Amy, who's here besides you, Merrie, Marla, Tracy, and me?"

"Just Rhonda. As far as I've been able to tell, they have only six rooms down here."

"That's all I saw," Tracy added.

"Rhonda?" Alex called. "Could you say something so we know you're okay?"

Silence.

"Rhonda?" Marla said. "Can you hear us?"

Nothing.

"She might have had her tea already. She's probably asleep. We all should have taken our tea by now. We'll have to drink it soon, or they'll get angry."

"I don't think Rhonda's sleeping," Merrie said, her voice shaking. "I think she's gone."

# 34

ometime later, someone knocked on Alex's door, and the bottom panel slid open. A tray came sliding through the hole. Alex had wanted to open the panel at the top of the door and get a look at him, but he was past her cell before she reached it.

"You said you'd reveal the location of the missing women," she called loudly through the slot. "All of them. That was the deal. This wasn't what we agreed to."

"I don't know anything about that," the man said.

"The FBI will find me, you know."

The footsteps stopped. "I'm pretty sure they have no idea where you are. You can't fool him, you know. It wasn't cold, so why would you be wearing a jacket? It made him suspicious."

"You won't get away with this," Alex said. She realized how cliché that sounded, and it made her angry.

"He'll punish you for breaking that camera."

Alex didn't say anything else, just listened as he continued down the hallway, then closed the door at the end. Who was this guy? He obviously wasn't in charge. She closed the panel, picked up the tray, and carried it to the table. She needed to think. To plan. She had no intention of eating the food. She felt so grimy. She needed to clean herself up. Change her clothes.

After taking the fresh clothes and a pair of new socks behind the curtain, she cleaned up the dirt mess she'd made earlier and then washed herself the best she could. After that she managed to shampoo her hair in the sink. When she was finished, she took the knife out of her boot, put on the clean socks, and rinsed off the boots before sliding them back on, carefully placing the knife back where it had been.

Next she changed the sheets on the bed even though she had no intention of sleeping.

But as she sat at the table, planning, she realized trying to overpower this guy could be a mistake. What if she failed? As much as she hated the idea, she needed to go on one of these dates. She needed a chance to profile both men. See if she could understand them and determine their weaknesses. A date would also give her access to the house. Although the prospect made her sick to her stomach, playing along with them made more sense. At least Tracy's experience gave her the upper hand. She wouldn't make Tracy's mistake.

She decided to eat the food they'd sent, so she took the lid off the tray. Underneath it, she found linguine in pesto sauce with shrimp, still surprisingly warm. A smaller plate held garlic bread, and there was a bottle of water and the cup of tea she'd expected.

The food was delicious. She quickly downed the water but was still thirsty despite drinking from the tap earlier. Then she drank most of the tea. She didn't trust them enough to drink all of it the first night, but she couldn't take the chance that they'd think she'd thrown it out if she wasn't sound asleep when they came in during the night.

After that, she put the plastic bucket with the bag from the toilet next to the door. She also tossed her dirty clothes and sheets into a bag and put that by the door as well. Then she covered the tray and carried that over too. She was a little worried that being submissive so quickly might make them wary, but she needed to get out of this room. No matter what it took. She had to go on one of those dates.

She'd been sitting on the bed for a while when the lights went off. Alex had a fear of the dark. She'd also been dealing with a sensitivity to germs for a long time, but she realized she hadn't thought about that even once since waking up here. Why? Because she was focused on someone beside herself? Or was it because this room seemed so clean? Except for the dirt she'd added, it was spotless. Smelled slightly of disinfectant. Whoever cleaned during the night did a good job.

She fought the urge for a while but finally slid the top panel on the door open. Just the little light filtering in from the hall made her heartbeat slow and her breathing more regular. On her way back to the bed, she swayed and felt dizzy, then collapsed on top of the covers. Before she slipped away, she thought of Logan.

---

Logan was really tired, yet he couldn't sleep. Where was Alex? Was she still alive? He wished she hadn't agreed to the UNSUB's instructions, but he understood. If he'd been in her situation, he would have done the same thing.

In a few hours he'd either get his life back or have to deal with one of the biggest challenges he'd ever faced. Up until now, God had always protected him. Would that continue? But even as he asked the question, peace washed over him. The Bible was so clear. Evil comes to kill, steal, and destroy. God gives life. Yet sometimes it was hard to hang on to his faith when darkness came. Would he ever just simply believe . . . without the struggle?

He thought about the redheaded EMT. Why did God send him? To stir up his faith? As a reminder of who God is? Or was God just giving him something to hold on to? Not because he didn't have enough faith, but simply because he was loved.

He smiled to himself, then thanked God for watching over Alex and for a successful surgery in the morning. He still had things to do, and one of them was to tell Alex how much he loved her.

# 35

A nurse woke him, and Logan was confused. What was she doing in his apartment?

"Agent Hart, it's five a.m. and time for me to set up an IV. Then I'll give you some medication to help you relax. Your doctor will be by to see you before we take you into surgery."

Then he remembered. "Okay. Can I have a sip of water? My mouth feels like cotton."

"After I get you set up, I'll give you a few ice chips. But that's it." She smiled. "Sorry, but we need to keep your stomach empty. Once you get back to your room and you're fully awake, we'll give you something to drink."

"A pot of coffee would be great."

She laughed softly. "I hear you."

"Can I use the bathroom before you do this?"

She nodded. "While you're in there, put on this gown."

"So I'm exchanging one gown for another?"

"Yes, and I have some very attractive socks for you to slip on when you come back. And no underwear."

"Can you explain why I can't wear underwear if the doctor is working on my head?"

"Sure. It's funny when your bum sticks out of the back. We need some kind of entertainment."

Logan couldn't help but laugh even though his concern for Alex made it difficult to feel amused. "Good thing my friends at the FBI won't see me like that. I'd never live it down."

When he was finished in the bathroom, he climbed back into bed, and the nurse put bright-yellow socks on his feet. Then after she swabbed his hand, he felt a light stick.

"That wasn't bad."

"That's just the numbing medicine so it won't hurt as much when I put in the IV."

About a minute later, she slid the needle into his hand, and he didn't feel a thing.

"Thanks. Wish all hospitals did it this way."

She shrugged. "We got tired of the screaming."

Logan forced a smile. "Do you get extra pay for making your patients laugh?"

She shook her head. "No, but it makes me feel better. People going through hard things need some relief, don't you think?"

"I do. Thank you."

She smiled again and then walked away for a moment. When she returned, she covered him with a warmed blanket that felt wonderful. "I'll be back in a bit," she said.

After the door closed behind her, Logan prayed. "I'm putting everything in your hands now, Lord," he whispered.

"Please take care of me and Alex. I'm trusting you to bring her back to me."

―――

Jeff was in his office early. He planned to go to the hospital, but he had some things to do first.

He'd been thinking about Logan and Alex most of the night. They were both in danger, just in different ways. His wife had grabbed his hand about two o'clock and prayed for both of them.

He wasn't a religious man, but he knew Logan believed. Alex and Monty too. And he'd grown to care about all of them. Actually, he cared about his whole team. And since he'd almost died last year, he'd started thinking a lot about God and wondering about the concept of heaven . . . and hell.

His wife had been trying to get him to attend church with her for a long time, and last night as she prayed, he'd decided to go. What could it hurt? Maybe there was a God. Ignoring the possibility was stupid. An intelligent person should want to know the truth.

When his landline phone rang, he was so lost in thought that it startled him. Alice wasn't in yet, so he answered it. Maybe someone had news about Alex.

"Agent Cole, it's Chief Dixon. I need to see you right away. It's about . . . well, it might not mean anything, but it's that amusement park. It reminded me of something that might be related to what's happening."

"Okay. When can you get here?"

"I'm already on my way. I'll be there in a couple of minutes."

"All right. See you then."

He hung up. Now what? This case was driving him crazy.

Jeff barely had time to make himself a cup of coffee when he heard a knock on his door. "Come on in," he called out.

Chief Dixon walked in with a large file under his arm.

"Coffee?" Jeff asked.

"Sure. Thanks."

"How do you take it?"

"Black."

Jeff put an extra cup under the spout, added the K-Cup, and pressed it down. When the coffee was ready, he carried it to the chief. He was already sitting in a chair in front of Jeff's desk.

"How are the Abbotts doing, Chief?"

"About the same. Thanks for asking."

Jeff sat down behind his desk. "Okay. What's going on?"

"I was at the command post yesterday when Agent Donovan left for that old amusement park in Ashville. I remembered something." He shook his head. "I can't guarantee it's connected to this case, but it just seems—"

"Just tell me about it." Jeff didn't want to be rude, but he really needed to get to the hospital soon. Monty phoned last night to tell him he and Nathan planned to be there before Logan was taken to surgery, and Jeff wanted to join them.

"Do you know Magic Land's history?" the chief asked.

"I do now. It was built decades ago by the mine owner who founded the town of Ashville, which was near the park. When his mine gave out, he left, and the whole community pretty much shut down. Now Ashville's basically a ghost town. Two different times the park was purchased by people who thought they could make it profitable, but that never happened. It finally closed down for good about twelve years ago. Between neglect and vandalism, it's in bad shape."

"Right. Except there's more. One of the reasons the last owners walked away was because of the murders. When they heard about it, that, combined with the struggle to keep the park viable, led them to finally abandon the place."

Now the chief had his attention. "Murders? What are you talking about?"

"It happened fifteen years ago, when the park was still open. Memorial Day weekend. The police were called that Saturday evening after they'd closed the park gates. A carnival group had come in to add to the park's festivities, and one of the carnies was missing, as was a teenage girl who'd visited the park that night. It took two days to find their bodies. A lot of woods around that area, but it turned out they weren't all that far away. Just well hidden."

"That's terrible, but I'm not sure why you're telling me this."

"It's . . . it's the girl." The chief opened the file and removed a photo, then placed it in front of Jeff. "Her name was Emily Marsden."

Jeff picked up what was obviously a school photo. Emily was a beautiful girl with long black hair and, he noted, bluish-gray eyes.

"A coincidence?" he asked.

"Maybe." The chief showed him another photo, this one a snapshot. "The carnie was this young man. Thomas Tedder."

Jeff stared at both photos. "Did they catch who did it?"

The chief shook his head. "The police had nothing to go on. No evidence at the scene. No footprints because of thick ground cover, no weapon, and no indication they'd been killed somewhere else and then their bodies dumped there. They suspect the two went off into those woods together and someone followed them. They interviewed everyone who worked at the amusement park the night they went missing, especially the out-of-town carnies. They couldn't find a suspect among them or from any of the neighboring towns." He sighed. "This was a tough one for everyone involved. Emily was a local girl. Both kids were well liked.

"The police finally decided the killer was probably someone from out of town. Someone who'd already taken off. Eventually, they gave up any hope of finding him."

"So the case has been unsolved all these years?" Jeff asked.

"Right. I'm leaving this with you. I gave the same information to the ASAC at the command post, but she isn't sure there's a connection either. I mean, a lot of girls have long black hair, and this was nine years before the first woman went missing. Could those murders be connected to what's going on now? I think it's possible, but you'll have to decide if this could be what you call the trigger for your UNSUB's actions. I hope it helps."

Jeff reached into the file and pulled out some other photos. Two bodies. A young man with so many stab wounds he couldn't count them all. And a girl with so much blood on her white dress that it almost completely hid the bright-yellow daisies.

# 36

The nurse, whose name was Donna, added something to Logan's IV. A few seconds later he began to feel unusually calm. That was fine with him. Hopefully, he'd be asleep soon and this would be over. He couldn't stop thinking about Alex. Right now this surgery was nothing more than an inconvenience. Her welfare was the most important thing on his mind.

He'd just closed his eyes when the door to his room opened and Dr. Schmeidler came in. According to Dr. Morton she was an incredibly competent surgeon. The best in her field. He was surprised to see that she looked about fourteen. Even so, he felt comfortable with her due to her reputation.

"You shouldn't have canceled your surgery yesterday," she said, frowning at him.

"Sorry, Doc. It was really important or I wouldn't have done it."

"This is really important too, Agent Hart. At least you're

finally here. I take it you have no plans to suddenly take off this morning?"

He smiled at her. "Maybe before you gave me this medication. But right now I don't think I could do it even if I wanted to."

She awarded him with a smile of her own. Wow. Now she looked even younger.

"Do you have any questions before we go into surgery?"

"Dr. Morton went over everything really well the other day. But could you do me one favor?"

"What's that?"

"If you find rocks up there, will you remove them?"

"But if I did that, you just wouldn't be . . . you, right?"

"You're funny. Not sure I want a funny doctor, though."

"Well, you're stuck with me." She patted his arm. "I'll see you in a little bit."

As soon as she'd walked out the door, Monty came in.

"Hey," Logan said. "You didn't need to be here so early."

"Had nothing else to do. Nathan and I will be waiting while you're in there."

"You really don't—"

Monty held up both hands, palms out. "Stop. You were there for me when my grandmother died. Just returning the favor."

"Thanks. I really appreciate it. Have you heard anything about Alex? It's been almost twelve hours."

"Not yet. But hopefully she'll be here when you wake up."

Donna returned and approached his IV, holding a syringe. "Sir," she said to Monty, "you can wait for your friend in the waiting room down the hall. The doctor will let you know when he's out of surgery."

"I signed some forms so the hospital and Dr. Schmeidler can release information to you," Logan said to Monty. "I guess you're filling in as my family today. I hope that's okay."

"It's more than okay," Monty said softly. "You're the closest thing I have to a brother. Jeff should be here by the time you wake up, Logan. See you soon."

"See you soon." He'd been feeling a little alone, so he really was grateful to know someone would be here for him when the surgery was over.

"This will start making you sleepy," Donna said as she inserted the syringe into his IV, then pushed the plunger. "We'll be leaving in a few minutes."

"Thanks."

He felt drowsy almost immediately, and within a short time he was moving down the hall, overhead lights flashing in his eyes. As the bed went through some double metal doors, he couldn't fight it any longer and allowed himself to drift away.

"Does the ASAC at the command post know you're sharing this with me, Chief?" Jeff asked as Dixon stood to leave.

"Yes, and she's asking you to send some analysts down there since Agents Hart and Donovan aren't available and this information could be important. Besides, even though it's not protocol, I think she wants to keep you updated since one of your people is in harm's way."

Jeff nodded. "I'll send a couple of analysts down there right away."

"One more thing. An ex-carnie who heard about Tracy on TV says he knows something that might help us. He worked at the amusement park when the murders happened."

"I thought you said everyone who worked there then was interviewed."

"I did. But this guy—Mike something—says he couldn't rat out another carnie back then. He would have lost his job and been blackballed. No more carnivals, amusement parks, or fairs. And it was the only income he had at the time."

"So he let a possible murderer walk?" Jeff said. "Seriously?"

The chief shrugged. "Don't shoot the messenger."

"Have they talked to him yet?"

"No, he's coming in this morning. Do you want to be there?"

"Yes. No, wait. I can't. Logan's having surgery this morning. I need to be at the hospital. He refused to tell his family about it, so we're all he has."

The chief's eyebrows shot up.

"I know," Jeff said. "I think it's a mistake too, but it's not my call."

"I don't know what kind of surgery he's having, but if it's something serious, maybe it is your call."

"You think I should phone them?"

Dixon nodded.

"I've considered it. More than once. But I can't go against Logan's wishes."

"I hear you. I want you to know that I'm praying for your agents."

"Thank you. Me too. And that's not something I've said very often."

The chief smiled. "Maybe you need to say it more."

Jeff stared at him for a moment. "You might be right." He stood and held out his hand. "Thanks, George. I appreciate everything you've done. More than I can say."

"You're welcome. And thanks again for listening when Lucas and I brought Tracy's case to you. Stop by the command post after the hospital. I'm sure Agent Williams will bring you up-to-date on the investigation."

Jeff thanked him again, and the chief left.

So someone might have information on murders connected to the same amusement park the UNSUB chose to meet Alex? That was more than interesting. Could this be the clue investigators needed?

"Didn't think I'd see you here," Alice said.

Her voice brought Jeff out of his thoughts. He hadn't heard her come in.

"I'm headed to the hospital," he said, "but first I need to get a couple of analysts to the command post."

"Who do you want?" Alice asked.

"Monty and Nathan are at the hospital. Let's have Bethany and Todd."

"Where's the CP?"

"Over at that furniture store that closed down by the highway."

"Brennan's?"

"Yeah. Tell them to get ready."

"Okay. And call me when you know something?"

"I will. And I'll make sure someone texts the team when Logan's out of surgery."

"Sounds good," Alice said. "Don't forget to add me."

"Could I forget our mother hen? No way."

Alice grinned. "Not sure I'm old enough to be your mother, but thanks anyway."

Jeff laughed. "Sister hen?"

"Much better. And, Boss?"

Jeff looked up at her.

"I'm praying for Logan and Alex."

"Thank you, Alice."

"In this situation you can call me by my middle name."

"And what's that?"

"Faith."

# 37

The light was back on when Alex woke up. She immediately pulled herself to a sitting position and looked down at her feet. She was still wearing her boots, but she couldn't continue to sleep with them on. They might get suspicious.

She glanced around the room. Another camera had been mounted on the wall. She could take it down, too, but if she was going to make her abductors think she was through fighting them, she'd have to leave it alone. She'd just need to be careful when she removed the knife from her boot to hide it in a better place. It galled her that she had to be more cooperative, but if she had any chance of getting these women home, this was the price she had to pay.

The camera was the same model as the last one. No speaker. Alex had a hard time believing the kidnappers didn't want to listen to the women. Why weren't they monitoring their conversations? As soon as she asked herself the question, she realized why they had no interest in what they might say. Because it wasn't necessary. They knew the women couldn't escape, and they didn't believe it was necessary. Still, if they were looking for a particular person, wouldn't they wonder if one of the women might say something that would prove they'd found her?

Unless that's what the *date* was for. If only she could learn more about the woman he was looking for. If she could convince him she was that person, would he let everyone else go? Or would he kill them? She had no way of knowing.

But right now she needed information about the UNSUB. She trusted the profile she'd given to Jeff, but being here should tell her even more. Knowing he wasn't working alone changed things.

Alex needed to understand the guy in charge. Why did he need help? Was it because he was housing the women for a while rather than killing them immediately? She was still surprised by the clean rooms, the good food—all the effort that went into meeting their basic needs. Where was the anger that usually marked the psyche of a serial killer? She did consider him a killer now since it was obvious most of the women were gone. This guy didn't make sense. Of course, he'd cut off the food and kept the women in the dark to punish them. But in anger? Or just to keep them in line?

She stood but then immediately sat down again when a wave of dizziness hit. The drug in the tea, whatever it was, had side effects. She was thankful she hadn't ingested it all.

After a minute or two, she stood more slowly. This time she was okay. Then she noticed the tray inside the door. She took it to the table and pulled off the cover. Scrambled eggs and sausage with hashbrowns and toast. Wow. Also a small carafe with hot coffee. She quickly poured some into the provided cup and took a small sip. No odd taste, nothing chalky. Just coffee. She wondered if drug addicts felt the same way she did when she drank it down. Wonderful.

She used the bathroom before eating, and when she was done, she washed her face and hands. Then she looked around to see if she could conceal the knife anywhere back there, but she couldn't find any place that made her feel secure. She might be able to hide it at the bottom of the box with the plastic bags, but how long would that last? And what if they brought in a new box? No, she needed something better.

She returned to the table and ate her breakfast. It was hard to believe there were only two men here. Two men taking care of all these women? Washing their clothes. Serving them breakfast, lunch, and dinner. Washing their dishes. Keeping their rooms clean. She'd noticed that someone had even cleaned up the mess she'd made last night.

Once again Alex realized her fear of germs hadn't been triggered. Why? It was a mystery to her. It should be driving her crazy by now, but she wasn't thinking about it at all.

Strange.

She set the tray on the floor by the door, then opened the panel at the top, determined to get a better view of the man who came for the trays.

"Is anyone up?" she called.

A panel screeched open. "I'm here," Tracy said.

"Is everyone else still here?" Alex asked.

One by one Marla, Merrie, and Amy checked in. Then the sound of the door opening at the end of the hall made everyone stop talking. Alex heard the small panels closing, but she kept hers open again.

She could hear something squeaking, like the wheels on a cart. Probably to gather the trays and remove them.

Alex stood on her tiptoes and pressed her face against the slot, trying to see the man as he approached. But just as he reached her, the opening suddenly banged shut. She jumped at the suddenness and tried to reopen it, but it was locked. Her tray was pulled through the bottom panel and then closed. She thought about saying something but decided to stay silent.

After he picked up all the trays and she heard the hall door close, she tried again to open the small panel, but it wouldn't budge. She wanted to talk to the women again. She needed more information, but it was pretty clear they didn't want her speaking to anyone.

She returned to the little table, sat down, and bowed her head to pray. They were probably watching her, laughing as she called on God for help. Little did they realize prayer was what they should fear the most.

Logan tried to open his eyes, but someone had apparently glued his eyelids shut. No matter what he did, he couldn't get them open. Then he realized the doctor had probably placed some kind of covering over his eyes during the operation, so he quit struggling. She'd remove it when she was ready.

He felt a wave of pain in his head that took his breath away. He cried out, hoping someone who could help him was nearby.

"I'm in a lot of pain," he managed to say even though his voice was weak. At first there was no response. Where was he? Where was his doctor?

"I'm here," a voice said. He recognized it. Nurse Donna.

"Donna, I'm in so much pain," he said, gasping because of the horrific throbbing in his head.

"Hold on," she said. "I'm giving you something now."

Logan held on with everything he had, but the pain barely subsided. "Could you double that, please?" he whispered. "I . . . I don't think I can take this much longer." He'd experienced pain in his career, but this was beyond a broken ankle . . . or even a gunshot. It was also much worse than the headaches he'd had before the surgery. But then the pain began to wash away like waves on the ocean. Within a minute or two, it was completely gone. "Thank you," he whispered. His mouth was so dry he could barely get out the words. "Can I have some water?"

Donna patted his shoulder. "Not quite yet. Let's get you out of recovery and back to your room first."

Although he wanted to plead for at least enough water to make his mouth feel like it wasn't practically stuck shut, he didn't want to be a problem patient. "Okay. And will someone remove the bandages when I get there?"

"Bandages?"

"I realize I probably have one on my head," Logan said. "And I don't mind that. But I would like the bandages over my eyes removed."

After a few seconds, Donna said, "We'll have to let the doctor make that decision, Agent Hart."

He heard the catch in her voice. She was worried about him. "Thank you. And thank you for being such a great nurse. I appreciate it."

She patted his shoulder. "You work at waking up enough for us to move you. I'll be back in a few minutes."

He heard her soft footsteps fade and tried to get comfortable. He was tempted to just fall asleep again, but he wanted to talk to Jeff. Find out what was going on with Alex. Was she back yet? Was she okay?

He suddenly felt another hand on his shoulder. "Donna?"

But a male voice answered. "You need to know everything will be all right, Logan. Just have faith. God is with you."

"Thank . . . thank you. Who are you?"

Silence.

"Hello? Are you still there?"

No response.

Must be another nurse, a believer. He wished he could see, but what the man said had comforted him. "Thank you, God, for getting me through the surgery," he whispered. "I believe everything *will* be all right no matter what happens next . . . for me and for Alex."

A deep peace settled on him as he waited for Donna's return.

# 38

lex sat on the bed, turned her back to the camera, and pulled off her boots. Then she palmed the knife and slid it under the blanket. She was confident that if anyone was watching, they hadn't seen what she'd done. She turned around and put the boots next to the bed. Her toes especially welcomed the chance to be free.

She moved to the small bookcase in the corner and picked up a book. *Jane Eyre*. Great novel. She returned to the bed, lay down with the book, pulled up the blanket, and then with her left hand pulled back the bottom sheet and carefully cut a slit in the mattress. She hid the knife there before readjusting the sheet. Now she could get to it whenever she needed to.

She put the book down and studied the room, eager to formulate a foolproof plan. Something that would get everyone out safely. One of the first things she had to do was find a way to reach out to the FBI. She needed backup. She had no intention of taking on the electric fence unless she could get to the controls and turn off the juice first. And right now she had no idea where those controls were.

The real danger wasn't just one man guarding them. She could easily take him out. It was the second man who worried her. She would have no idea where he was or if he was armed. A wrong move could cost her—and everyone here.

Alex lay back on the bed again, and although it looked as if she were reading, she was really planning. But her thoughts kept drifting to Logan, wondering how he was. She struggled to force herself to concentrate on her current situation. The sooner she got out of here, the sooner she could see him again.

Jeff called Monty to see if Logan was out of surgery. He was, but he hadn't been transferred to a room yet. Monty promised to call Jeff as soon as he knew something more. Jeff called Todd and Bethany to see if they were ready to go to the CP. Then he let Alice know they were leaving.

"By the way," she said, "you're sending flowers to Logan."

"But I've never really been a flowers kind of person."

"Well, you are now."

He smiled. "Okay. I guess I am now."

He met Todd and Bethany at the building's entrance, and they all jumped into his SUV. On the way, he brought them up to speed on Chief Dixon's news. A few minutes later they pulled into the CP's back lot. The place looked almost deserted. Some cars were parked in the back. Some down the street. A few in the front, but not enough to make anyone curious. With the attention the missing women had drawn from the media, they had to be careful not to draw unwanted interest. If they weren't cautious, they'd be overrun by reporters looking for their next story.

When Jeff knocked on the back door, an agent opened it. He showed his credentials, and they were let inside.

"ASAC Williams?" he asked.

The man pointed to a woman standing not far from them, staring over the shoulder of an agent working on a laptop. When Jeff walked up to her, she turned to look at him.

"Unit Chief Cole?"

"Yes. Thank you for allowing me to meet with you." He gestured toward his agents. "This is SSA Todd Hunter and SSA Bethany Hostettler. They'll refine the profile written by Agents Hart and Donovan based on recent events."

Williams shook hands with Todd and Bethany. "Happy to have you here. Someone who may be able to provide us with information about our UNSUB is coming in soon. I hope he'll be helpful, but please keep working on your profile in case this doesn't pan out. I'm not very confident he'll be able to point us in the right direction. If he knew who killed Emily Marsden and Thomas Tedder fifteen years ago, why didn't he come forward? He says it was because he was afraid of repercussions from other carnival workers, but I'm not sure I believe that. What does intrigue me, however, is that he worked at the amusement park where our UNSUB directed SSA Donovan to meet him. That's a pretty big coincidence."

"Big enough that I agree it warrants investigation," Jeff said. "When will he be here?"

"Any minute. I sent one of our agents to pick him up—"

The back door swung open, and two men walked in.

"There they are now." She frowned at Jeff. "I'm willing to

let you sit in on our conversation, but you need to be quiet. You're not actually part of this investigation, you know."

"I realize that, and I truly appreciate being included. I'll keep my mouth shut. You have my word."

She called out for a young man who got up from a desk where he'd been working on a laptop too.

"Special Agent Snyder, please take SSAs Hunter and Hostettler to the smaller conference table. They'll work there."

"Yes, Boss."

Snyder motioned for Todd and Bethany to go with him, and they followed him to where they'd be tweaking a profile Jeff hoped wouldn't be needed much longer. Once they'd identified the UNSUB, an analyst's primary job was done — although they could help agents searching for the offender in other ways.

The two men who'd come in the back way reached the spot where Williams waited for them.

"Mr. Tenbrook," the agent said to the man with him, "this is Assistant Special Agent in Charge Roberta Williams."

Williams held her hand out to the large, rather scruffy-looking man. "Thank you for coming, Mr. Tenbrook. We're hopeful you can assist us."

"Ah, ma'am, it's just Mike," he said. "If you call me Mr. Tenbrook, I might start lookin' 'round for my daddy, and you don't want him anywhere near here. Trust me."

Williams smiled. "Okay, Mike. I understand. If it's okay with you, we'll go into my office to talk."

"That'd be jes fine, ma'am."

"Roberta," she said.

"Roberta," he repeated with a smile. "I once knew a belly

dancer named Roberta who worked the midways back when I was just a young 'un."

Jeff had to bite his lip to keep from laughing. He certainly wasn't in a humorous mood, but a picture of ASAC Williams doing a belly dance had jumped into his head and he'd almost lost it.

Williams didn't say anything, but her cheeks turned pink. To her credit she just kept smiling and asked Tenbrook to follow her. Then they all walked behind her like some kind of mini parade until they reached an office that must have once belonged to the manager of the furniture store. Inside was a desk and a black leather chair. Williams sat down behind the desk while the rest of them took their places in the folding metal chairs positioned in front of her. When Mike sat down his chair squeaked under his weight.

Williams opened a file and turned to a small recorder. "Do you mind if I record our conversation, Mike?"

"No, ma'am. I mean, Roberta."

The other agent left, and Jeff scooted his chair back some so he'd be out of the way but could still hear.

"So, Mike," Williams said after she turned on the recorder, "will you please state your full name and your address?"

He did as she asked and then waited.

"You contacted the police in Prince William County and told them you might have information that could help them. Something about the recent abductions in this area. Is that correct?"

Jeff noted she was careful not to let on how many abductions they'd found in the county, nor that others had been discovered in four more.

"Yeah, that's it."

"Can you tell me about that?"

"Yes'm. On TV I heard about that Mendenhall woman and how other women are missin' too, but I didn't think much about it until I saw them talkin' about that explosion over at that Magic Land Park. That's when I started to wonder. You see, I worked that park. More than once. Not when it was open the first time, you know. That was a long time past. But I was there around fifteen years ago. When those two kids was kilt. Do you know about that?"

"Yes, we do. We've wondered if it was connected to what's been going on lately."

"Yes'm. Like I said, that's why I called the police."

"What made you think about those murders, Mike?"

"It was somethin' I saw the same night the kids went missin'."

"And what was that?"

Mike took a deep breath. "There was this kid who worked there with us. Well, he worked with his daddy until he died when the kid was about fourteen. After that, he jes kept travelin' the circuit. Nobody was really checkin' to see if carnies went to school back then, you know. We all jes took care of 'em and made sure they could at least read and write. Bought them some books to read from secondhand stores. We were a family. That's what it's like when you're —"

"And what did you see that concerned you, Mike?" Williams said, obviously trying to bring him back to the main point of their conversation.

"Yeah. Sorry. I get carried away sometimes. Was a carnie for a long while. Don't leave you very easy." He took another deep breath. "This happened durin' a Memorial Day celebration, you see. Sometimes amusement parks hire carnies to come in and add to their rides and things during special events. And that's what happened that time. They'd had us the last two years too. So we went and helped 'em out. Some of our crew ran their rides so regular staff got breaks.

"We also set up games, a beer garden, food carts . . . stuff like that. Well, this same kid I was talkin' about had a crush on a townie who came to the park every time we was there. I know 'cause I'd seen him starin' at her both years before. Well, this night he asked her if he could get somethin' to eat with her at the beer garden, and she said yes. He was so excited. I gave him a stuffed dog from a game I was runnin'. If you pressed its paw, it played a song. I was walkin' into the garden myself when he met up with her. When it happened."

"And what happened, Mike?" Williams asked.

"She was sittin' down with him, and I heard her ask if he wanted to kiss her. But she was just settin' him up, you know? A lot of townies thought they was better'n us. Then a friend of hers snuck up behind him and poured soda on his head. The girl started laughin', and the rest of the girls with her laughed at him too. In fact, everyone sittin' there at the time thought it was pretty funny. He got up and run right past me. I'll never forget his face. Here he was without any family 'cept us, and he was humiliated in front of the townies . . . and some of the other carnies too. It was worse because he had a hard time makin' friends. It weren't that he was uppity or nothin'. He was jes shy. Self-conscious. I think that's why what happened upset him so much."

"And why do you think this event is connected to our investigation?"

"'Cause that night the same girl disappeared along with one of our carnies. Seems she weren't really better'n all of us. Jes some of us. What's botherin' me is that she looked jes like the missin' woman on the news. Tracy Mendenhall."

"And do you know what happened to that girl at the park?"

"Yes'm. She was found two days later. Her and the boy she went off with. Someone kilt 'em."

Jeff was having a hard time remaining silent. If only this guy had reported what happened in that beer garden, he might have saved everyone all the heartache since.

"But you didn't tell the police about the incident in the beer garden?" Williams asked, obviously thinking the same thing Jeff was.

"No, ma'am. I mean, Roberta. I needed to stay with the carnival. I couldn't lose my job. Besides, I truly believed that kid had nothin' to do with it."

"And why is that?"

"If you jes coulda known him. He weren't that kinda kid. And I didn't have no proof, and I didn't want him to get in trouble. I still don't think he did it. Like I said, he was really shy. Had a scar on his lip, you know. Had what they call a harelip? Weren't that noticeable, but it bothered him, I think. Anyways, now that I don't work for the carnivals no more, I figgered it was time for me to tell someone 'bout what I saw."

"And do you know this kid's name?" Williams asked.

Jeff held his breath.

"No. I mean, not all of it. I heard his last name once, but I jes can't recall it. I only remember his first name 'cause his daddy called him by that. Didn't cotton to what the other carnies called him. The name I knew him by."

"So what was his first name?"

"Lum. It was Lum."

"What about his father's name?"

"They called him Junior," Mike said. "Might be 'cause he liked Junior Mints so much. He was always eatin' 'em. Have you ever had Junior Mints, Roberta?"

"What was Lum's handle?" Jeff asked, unable to stay silent.

"It didn't fit him, but he usually ran the same ride wherever we went. In fact, he insisted on it. Since keepin' workers was so hard, the owners of the parks let him do it. So that's how he got his handle."

"Which was . . ." Jeff was getting impatient with the man.

"Ghost Rider, but we all just called him Rider."

Jeff had to leave the investigation to Williams. His analysts were there at the CP, doing whatever they could with the information they had. They'd keep working the profile until they had enough to help investigators identify the UNSUB.

At least they knew part of his name—Lum. Mike had given them a brief description, but except for the scar on his lip, it wasn't very helpful. He'd said Lum had brown hair, wasn't sure about the color of his eyes, and thought he was of medium height.

Williams indicated they'd start contacting carnival owners, both former and current, right away. Unfortunately, many of them weren't great at record keeping. A lot of carnival workers were paid in cash and didn't pay taxes.

But the task force would have to handle that. He was on his way to the hospital, praying again that Logan would be okay and that Alex would find a way to contact them so they could find her and any other women who might still be alive.

When he pulled into the hospital parking lot, he took out his phone and called Monty, who said Logan was still in recovery. Jeff was somewhat relieved. He really wanted to be there as soon as Logan was allowed visitors.

He hurried through the main hospital entrance, and memories of his stay in a hospital much like this one—not far from here—flooded his mind. He felt rather unsettled. Thankfully, both he and Alex had survived a psychopath's attempt at ending their lives. He reminded himself that this was different, but no matter what, he needed to be here for Logan. He really did love his agents. A unit chief wouldn't admit that out loud, but it was true nonetheless.

He located the surgery waiting room and found both Monty and Nathan there.

"Heard anything else?" he asked as he sat down on a couch next to Monty.

"No. And no details yet."

"Will the doctor share them with us even though we're not family?"

"Logan signed a HIPAA form with my name on it," Monty said, "so she'll fill me in at some point. I'll tell you what she says. I know Logan would want you to know."

"It's possible she wants to talk to her patient first," Nathan said. "Maybe she'll advise you after that."

"I guess so. It's just . . . well, why not at least let us know if the surgery went well? Isn't that what doctors usually tell people waiting for information?"

"She hasn't said anything about that?" Jeff asked. His stomach was already tight with worry. Now he felt a little nauseated.

Funny how he could profile the vilest, sickest criminal and not be bothered, but when someone he cared about was in trouble, he turned into a big wimp.

He suddenly remembered when his wife had surgery for breast cancer. The doctor was the same way. Didn't tell him everything was okay when it was over. Waited until later to let them know she had cancer. She ended up enduring more surgery, chemo, and radiation, but thankfully she was fine now.

Could this surgeon be withholding information because Logan's news was bad?

The three of them fell silent as they waited to see their friend and colleague.

Logan woke up again, still a little groggy but more awake than he'd been earlier. He fumbled around for the call button. When he found it, he pressed it. A few seconds later, a voice said, "Can I help you?"

"This is Logan Hart," he said to the woman. "I'm sorry, but I'm not certain what room I'm in."

"It's 342, Agent Hart," she said. "Do you need something?"

"Yes. I'd like to talk to my doctor. And I'm really thirsty."

"What would you like to drink?"

"A large glass of ice water, and an even bigger cup of black coffee would be awesome."

He heard soft laughter, and then she said, "We need you to go slow so you won't upset your stomach, but a small glass of water and a regular-size cup of coffee could be arranged. As soon as we get the okay from your doctor, we'll bring you some food too."

"Thank you," he said.

The nurse clicked off. He could hardly wait for something to drink. He also wanted these stupid bandages off his eyes.

He reached up to touch them, then dropped his hand back down to the bed.

A few minutes later he heard the door to his room open, and someone came in. "I've got both water and coffee for you, Agent Hart." It was the same voice he'd heard when he pressed the call button.

"I need . . . I need to speak to my surgeon immediately," he said, working hard to get the words out.

"Are you in pain?"

"Yes, but that's not what I want to talk to her about." He reached out and found her arm, then held on tight. "I can't see . . . anything. I'm blind."

Must be lunchtime.

Alex heard loud, squeaky wheels. Whoever it was whistled a song that seemed like a tune she should know, but she couldn't recall the words to.

One by one she heard the larger door panels opening, breakfast trays no doubt being picked up and lunch trays substituted. With her panel locked, Alex couldn't even try to see who'd brought hers. It didn't matter, though. According to the other women, the blond man did all the work.

Was the man in the tunnel, the one who brought her here, his partner? Or was it the other way around? She'd profiled the UNSUB as younger and good-looking. She didn't get a good look at the man at the park, but his demeanor seemed to match the confident individual she'd assumed was behind the abductions. Was he the man who'd kidnapped Tracy and Merrie? Was he the Ghost Rider?

After the man in the hallway left, Alex fetched her tray and took it to the table. A ham and cheese sandwich on wheat bread. Potato salad. A brownie. Lemonade and water. It was clear to her that they were treating the women well, trying to foster Stockholm Syndrome. Other than showers, they had just about every convenience except television, computers, and phones.

She knew why, of course. The women could contact the outside world with a computer or phone, and they could watch coverage about their disappearance on TV. Seeing their grieving, worried relatives would destroy the atmosphere the men were trying to create. They wanted them to feel safe. Protected. After a while they'd forget that these same men had taken away their freedom and separated them from their loved ones. It would make them much more malleable. Easier to control.

She was munching on the brownie when she heard a loud knock on another door. Sounded like Tracy's. She rushed to her own door and put her ear against it in time to hear a larger metal panel sliding open.

"I'll come for you when everyone else is getting dinner," a male voice said. No doubt the blond again. "He's taking you on a date. Here are the dress and shoes you have to wear."

With that, the panel slid shut, and footsteps stopped at her door. She heard a click, and then the footsteps headed toward the end of the hall.

Alex tried her upper panel. It opened this time, and seconds later she heard another panel sliding open.

"Tracy, I heard," Alex said.

"I'm supposed to go on a date with this guy tonight," she replied. "I don't want to do it, but I don't think I can get out of it this time."

The sound of metal against metal reverberated up and down the hall.

"It'll be okay," a voice said. Amy. "He'll be nice to you, like he was with Merrie. Just go with it. We all did, and we're okay."

"Why didn't any of you try to overpower him?" Alex said.

"Because it was made very clear that the other guy would kill all of us if we tried anything like that," a voice said. Marla. "Look, Amy's right. The date was okay, but it was because . . . well, because we got by easier than we thought, you know? I'm sure every single one of us wondered if we'd be raped . . . or killed. After that kind of threat hanging over our heads, the rest of what happened was a relief. It doesn't mean we enjoyed it. We were just grateful to be left alone . . . and alive."

"That's what I want you all to concentrate on," Alex said. "Marla nailed it. You didn't fight back because you were under threat . . . and because he made you feel grateful. But you shouldn't be grateful. All of this, the good food, the soft beds, the clean sheets and clothes, the books . . . it's all designed to lull you into a false sense of security. You're thankful because it's not worse than this. But I have a question for you."

"What's that?" Tracy asked.

"Where are the other women? We counted fourteen— now fifteen with me—as possible victims of these guys. Five of us are here. Where are the rest? Do you really think they let them go?"

"I asked him how many women were here," Marla said. "He wouldn't tell me, but he did say quite a few women had already been released. They were warned that if they said anything, the rest of us and their families would be in danger. He said when they let them go, they drug them and take them somewhere far away so they can't lead the authorities here. That's probably what happened to Sarah and Rhonda."

"But there's no evidence that they ever showed up," Alex said. "The FBI would know if they made it home. None of them has."

She heard only silence as the women digested what Alex said. She wasn't trying to scare them, but she wanted . . . no, she needed them to start fighting back.

"What should I do?" Tracy asked.

"Didn't one of you say he asked questions? Did he mention an amusement park?"

"Yeah," Merrie said. "One in a town called . . . Ashville. I think he's looking for someone he met there a long time ago."

The others recalled his talking about the park with them as well.

"I know about that park. When he asks you, Tracy, tell him that I mentioned Magic Land Park. That I *might* have said I went there when I was young. You don't need to be precise. And just go along with him. Let him know you're not the one he's looking for, but don't fight him. I need you to get him ready for me."

"You're going to pretend you're the one he's been searching for?" Merrie asked. "The reason we're all here? Are you sure that's a good idea?"

"He's going to keep hunting and abducting women until he finds her. This is the way to stop him . . . and I'm the only one who can do it."

# 40

Logan took small sips of the water the way the nurse had instructed him. Then he moved on to the coffee, carefully finding the cup with his hand. When he took the first sip, he couldn't remember ever appreciating coffee this much. Although hospital coffee certainly wasn't the best in the world, being deprived of it made this cup truly special.

The nurse had told him Dr. Schmeidler was on her way to see him. Logan tried to stay calm as he waited, but he couldn't help wondering if the surgery had cost him his sight. If so, his career with the FBI was over. He'd never met a blind agent.

His thoughts shifted to Alex. Why hadn't he heard anything from Jeff or Monty? The pressure of the surgery and her disappearance suddenly felt too heavy to endure. He started to breathe faster, but he couldn't seem to get any air. One of the machines hooked up to him began to beep. A few seconds later, the door to his room opened, and he heard several footsteps and voices around him.

"You're having a panic attack," someone said. It was the nurse who'd brought him the water and coffee. "I'm giving you oxygen."

Logan felt something placed over his mouth. A mask. Air. Thank God.

"You have to slow down your breathing," the nurse said. "Breathe with me. In . . . out. In . . . out. In . . . out."

Logan finally felt air getting into his lungs again. Another panic attack? He was an FBI agent. He had to get ahold of himself.

The nurse removed the mask. "How are you doing now?" she asked.

"I'm fine. Thank you. Sorry."

"It happens a lot, Agent Hart. Nothing to feel guilty about. Just try to keep your breathing regular. If it gets too fast, it messes up your timing. That's why you can't get any air when it hits."

"Okay. Thanks. I really appreciate it."

Logan felt a touch on his shoulder. "No problem."

He heard her step away.

"I hear you're having trouble seeing," another voice said. Dr. Schmeidler.

"Yes. But why?" Logan asked. "Please tell me this isn't permanent."

"To be honest, I can't be sure. But we're giving you a blood-thinning medicine in case blood clots are causing the problem. If that doesn't clear it up, we'll need to take a look to see what's happening."

"You're going to open me up again?"

"No, not necessarily. First we'll try an MRI." He could tell she was now leaning over the bed. "I'm shining a light into your eyes. Tell me if you see anything."

"Yes," he said, trying to choke back his emotions. "I can see some light."

"Good. This could be a temporary side effect from the anesthesia. In my opinion, that's what's happening. It's rare, but I've seen it before. With the blood thinner and some rest, let's see what happens over the next few hours."

Although it wasn't a complete victory, the word *temporary* gave him hope. "So now tell me about the surgery," he said.

He heard her pull a chair close to the bed. "Sorry. I need to sit. Got called in last night for an emergency surgery, and then I had yours this morning. The hospital frowns on surgeons who sit while they work."

Even though he wasn't in the mood for humor, he couldn't help but smile. He knew people well enough to realize she was purposely trying to lighten the mood. And that's when he knew what her next words would be. He felt as if he were falling and couldn't find anything to stop his descent.

"We got most of it, Logan," she said. "It's called a glioma. Yours is a grade two tumor."

"So it's cancer."

"Yes, and it can become very dangerous if left untreated."

"Now what?"

"Chemotherapy, radiation. But like I said, I was able to get most of it."

"What are my chances?"

"I can't say at this point, although I feel fairly confident that we caught it early. For now, we need you to go home and heal, and then we'll start treatment."

He wanted to make her tell him if he would live or die, but it was obvious she wouldn't give him a death sentence. Not yet, anyway. Besides, God would have the last word.

"Anything else, Doc?" he asked.

"No. Except I want you to stick to a healthy diet. Plenty of lean protein, healthy fats, fruits, vegetables, and whole grains. Limit sugar, caffeine, salt, processed foods, and alcohol."

"I don't drink."

"Did you hear the rest of it?"

"Sure. *Limit* sugar, salt, and processed foods."

"And caffeine."

"I'm ignoring that part. It will be tough."

"Is it tougher than dying?"

Logan sighed. "Okay. I hear you."

More light in the eyes.

"Any improvement?"

He couldn't stop the tear that ran down the side of his face. "Yeah. I can't make out your features, but I can see the shape of your body."

"Good. I think your sight will get better as the day goes on."

"I pray you're right."

"You have some visitors. Okay if I let them in?"

"Yes. Please."

"And I'll have some food brought in."

"I suppose it will be healthy?"

"All hospital food is healthy."

Although he couldn't see her clearly, he could hear the smile in her voice.

"Thanks."

"I'll be here for a while. I have some other patients to see. But I'll stop by and check with you again before I leave."

"Okay."

He heard her walk to the door, open it, and leave. This was serious. But what about the man who told him everything would be all right? What had he said? *"You need to know everything will be all right. Just have faith. God is with you."* He wanted to yell, *How is this all right?* But his anger wasn't from God. It was the enemy's attempt to rob him of his faith—the biggest weapon given to God's people against the plans and attacks of the father of lies.

Logan took several deep breaths, and then he prayed, first for himself. *Help me, God. I'm sorry for reacting this way. I want faith and peace, not fear. I choose to trust you.* This time when the words from the man who'd spoken to him echoed in his mind, he grabbed hold of them with every ounce of faith he could gather. Then, after putting his situation in God's hands, he prayed for Alex. Where was she, and what was happening?

He heard the door of his room open and could make out two shapes.

"Who's there?" he asked.

"It's us."

"Monty!" Logan was so happy he was here.

"I'm here too," Jeff said. "Nathan's in the waiting room. They only let in two at a time."

"Thanks for coming," Logan said.

"The doctor talked to me," Monty said.

Logan was silent for a moment. He knew Monty and Jeff were concerned, and he didn't want to ignore that, but he had other things on his mind.

"Look, guys. I know we need to discuss this, and we will. But right now I'm more interested in what's going on with Alex. Have you found her yet?"

"No," Jeff said. "They've combed the site, and nothing there points to her location. All we can do is wait to hear from her. She's armed and she's smart. She'll get out of whatever situation she's in, and she'll help anyone else still alive come home too. I have . . . faith."

"Faith?" Logan said. "Careful, Jeff. You'll end up one of us crazy Christians if you're not careful."

"Well, maybe that's not such a bad thing. When you get out of here . . . let's talk."

This was a real miracle. Logan had been praying for Jeff for a long time. He was a pragmatic guy, and to him, faith in God had always been akin to believing in unicorns.

"We're praying for you, Logan," Monty said. "I just know you're going to beat this thing."

Logan could hear the concern in his friend's voice, and it touched him. "I believe that, too, but I really appreciate your prayers. I'm not looking forward to chemotherapy and radiation. I'd rather not go through all that."

"Whatever it takes," Jeff said. "The outcome's the important thing."

Logan understood what Jeff was saying, but he wanted to get back to work. Wanted to get back to where he was when he felt good. When he was strong. With Alex.

"Your doctor told us not to stay long," Jeff said. "She said you need a lot of rest."

"Please keep me updated on Alex, though. I'd rest a lot better if I knew she was okay."

"I will," Jeff said.

"Hey, when they're ready to let you out of here, call me," Monty said. "Nathan and I will come pick you up. And I'm taking off a few days so I can make sure you get the rest you need." He chuckled. "And don't worry. I won't make a nuisance of myself. Just want to make sure you have some help until you're able to get along without me."

"Hey, thanks," Logan said around the lump that had formed in his throat. "I really appreciate it."

"Wow, I thought you'd fight me. I'm surprised."

"Not this time, my friend. I know I need some assistance."

He blinked several times, trying to hold back tears. One of the shapes came closer to the bed and reached out his hand. Logan grabbed it.

"Hey, I thought you couldn't see," Monty said.

"It's getting better and better. I'm certain my sight will come back. 'Course, then I'll have to look at you again. That's a little discouraging."

"Very funny. You just have no taste."

"Yeah, that's it."

"We'd better go," Jeff said. He walked up next to Monty. "You get back to us as soon as you can, okay? Everyone misses you."

"Thanks, Jeff. I appreciate it. How are Bethany and Todd doing with the profile?"

"They've been refining it with the newest information. I'm sure they've finished it and it's been given to the investigators at the command post by now."

"I'd like to read it, if possible. Or at least hear it?"

"I'll give Monty a copy. He can read it to you."

"Thanks."

"Hey, I'll call you later," Monty said, "and I'll be back tomorrow. The doctor said you'll probably be here a few more days."

"Okay."

"I'll talk to you soon," Jeff said.

"Hey. Promise you'll tell me the truth about Alex, okay? Don't try to protect me because of . . . this."

Both men were quiet for a moment, but then Jeff said, "Okay, you have my word. But I really believe she'll make it through. If anyone in the FBI can do it, it's Alex."

"I know you're right."

After they left, Logan prayed again. *You just have to bring her back to me, Lord. I've got to tell her how much I love her. I won't let the opportunity get away from me this time.*

# 41

The afternoon passed slowly, but it gave Alex time to go over her plan. It wasn't complicated, but it wasn't perfect either. So much had to come together. She was still a little concerned about being overheard, but she'd profiled people like these guys before. Overly confident. Convinced no one could defeat them. They probably hadn't even considered listening in on the women. Believed they weren't any threat to them so why spend the money or take the trouble to install something?

On second thought, she doubted cost was a factor. Tracy mentioned that this house was huge and that their prison was once a wine cellar. And then there was the amusement park. You needed money to create something like that. Would anyone in the BAU consider why the UNSUB asked Alex to meet him at an amusement park? Wonder about why he picked the Ghost Shack for their meeting and called himself the Ghost Rider? She prayed they were putting the pieces together. The rides here had to be purchased and delivered. It was a link to their location.

She felt some hope. It was a chance. A good chance. Should she just wait on them? That was the one thought that kept coming back to her. The only reason she wasn't completely convinced her plan was the best decision. What should she do?

Moving to the door, she pushed open the top panel. "Tracy?" she called. She waited a few moments and then called out again. She heard more than one panel slide open.

"Yes?" Tracy.

"Please don't change your mind about making him think I'm the woman he's looking for. If you want out of here, you've got to do it."

Tracy hesitated before saying, "But what if he hates this woman and decides to kill you?"

"I don't think he will. And besides, I can handle him."

"You don't know that for sure. And if you try to hurt him, he may retaliate by coming after one of us. Or all of us."

"Look, just tell him what I said. I know what I'm doing. You have to trust me."

"And just how do I work it into the conversation?"

"Tell him some of the other women mentioned the carnival rides. And that I brought up the place where they took me, another amusement park. That I said I'd been to Magic Land Park when I was younger."

"You were abducted at some amusement park?"

"Yes. An abandoned one. Oh, and whatever you do, don't tell him you don't like amusement parks or anything like that."

"Why?"

"Because I think he identifies with them. In a note he sent to us, he called himself the Ghost Rider, no doubt after one of the rides at that park. If you say anything negative about them, he might see it as an insult. I don't trust his temper." There was silence as the women were obviously taking in this information. "By the way, have you ever heard him mention the name Ghost Rider?"

Each woman said no. Interesting. She'd expected him to be using it.

"Okay," Tracy said. "How do you know so much about him? Do you know who he is?"

"No, but I'm a behavioral analyst. I work for the BAU."

"I don't know what that is."

"Some people call us profilers."

Alex heard Tracy's quick intake of breath. "You mean like that TV show?"

"Not really. Behavioral analysts don't run around arresting people and chasing criminals. We just create profiles for law enforcement so they can narrow their searches. They target suspects who fit our profiles. It's not exactly like what you see on TV."

"Well, if that's true, what are you doing here?"

*Good question.* "The UNSUB—that's what we call our unknown subject—saw me on TV. Just like you, I fit the description of whoever he's looking for, and he sent the FBI a message saying he'd tell us where you all were if I showed up at that amusement park."

"But you're not wearing something that will lead them to us?" Tracy said, her voice lowered.

"I was. I had a tracker in my jacket, but he made me take it off before we came here."

Alex didn't mention the knife. That was one thing she wouldn't say out loud even though she was almost convinced the men weren't listening. This was the second time she'd put something she wanted to keep from an UNSUB in a boot. Frankly, the idea was probably running on borrowed time. Although she didn't plan to be kidnapped by another psychopath, if she were ever in this situation again, she'd use a different tool to defeat him. Although she hated to think of this guy running his hands over her body, he probably had. The two places people don't think to look? Hair and shoes. The last time she'd hidden her phone in her boot.

"Okay, I'll do what you want," Tracy said. "I sure hope you're right about this."

"Understanding people like this guy is what I do. You can trust me." Although she wanted to calm the women and give them hope, Alex wasn't as confident as she sounded.

"We're all counting on you," Merrie said. "We don't know who will be . . . released next."

"I know. We'll all get out of here."

"Do you pray, Alex?" Tracy asked.

"Yes, I do."

"Will you pray for us? Now, I mean?"

Alex wasn't used to praying out loud in a group, but she did as Tracy asked. She asked God to protect them and get them all home safe. She also asked for wisdom to know what to do and how to help the women trapped here. As she prayed, she heard sobbing. Then when she finished, she closed the small metal door, sank to the floor, and cried as well. The darkness from the warehouse still swirled around inside her, grabbing at her mind when she least expected it. It was like being on one of those rides, like the one she'd walked into almost twenty-four hours ago. The monsters jumped out at you when you least expected it, and even though you knew they were there, each time it happened you couldn't help but scream in fear.

And now she was about to walk into another nightmare. Try to triumph over another man full of evil intentions. Was she too damaged to do it? She felt crushed under the weight of the responsibility to save these women.

*God, I can't do this alone. I'm not strong enough. If you don't help me, this won't work, and these women will die. Please, God. You're our only hope.*

# 42

Logan tried to rest, but he couldn't stop thinking about Alex. Finally, he picked up the phone and called Monty, thankful it had a voice feature since he still couldn't see well enough to read his contacts list.

"Hey, how's it going?" Monty said when he answered.

"I'm fine, but I've been thinking about the UNSUB. Did you see the final profile?

"Yes, but why?"

"They've got to check out the UNSUB's connection to amusement parks. Especially the one in Ashville. It means something to him. It might help them figure out where he is now."

"Yeah, they know that. I understand someone's come forward. Someone who might have known the UNSUB. He was a carnie and used to work special events at Magic Land Park. I don't have all the details, but I believe they have a first name. Now they're researching people connected to that park, including the carnies. Problem is most of them were paid in cash. No way to trace them."

"Okay. Please keep me updated?"

"Seriously, Logan, you have to concentrate on your recovery. If you can't do it for yourself, think of Alex. If she thought you weren't improving because you're worrying about her . . ."

"Yeah, I know. But right now getting her back is all that matters to me. She can be as mad at me as she wants as long as she makes it out of this alive." He sighed. "Monty, I can't help but think about how much she's been through. How much more can she take?"

"You introduced her to the One who can keep her safe. She has hope because of you. Now you have to let God be God."

"Not the first time you've reminded me of that."

"Then how about listening to me this time? Pray for her, brother. Let God do His thing. You're in bed, recovering from surgery and . . ."

"And blindness?"

"I wasn't going to say that."

"I know, but like I said, my sight's getting better and better. I truly believe I'll get it all back."

"I'll believe that with you. And I also believe Alex is coming home—and she won't be alone."

When had Monty gotten so full of faith? But he was right. Alex needed him to pray, not worry. He was determined to do better.

"Hey, bro, thanks. You make me feel ashamed. I just . . . well . . ."

"Why don't you just say it?" Monty said. "You love her. That's not anything to be embarrassed about, you know."

"You're right. And I intend to. But stepping out on that limb when I don't know how she feels is a little scary. It could break, you know. It's a long way down if that happens."

"Just jump off the limb, Logan. As far as I'm concerned you should have done it a long time ago."

"I agree. Hey, Monty, thanks again for everything. And—"

"Yeah, I know. Keep you informed."

"Okay. Talk to you soon."

He was moved by Monty's faith. Logan had been praying, but it was time for him to start praying differently. Not pleading for God to save Alex. Praying in faith. Thanking God for taking care of her. What was that Scripture in Psalm 91? *He shall call upon Me, and I will answer him; I will be with him in trouble; I will deliver him and honor him. With long life I will satisfy him, and show him My salvation.* He realized that the Scripture not only applied to Alex; it fit his situation too.

*I'm taking you at your word, Lord. Alex will call on you, and you will answer her. You will be with her in trouble, and you will deliver her. With long life you will satisfy her and show her your salvation. And that applies to me too.* As soon as he finished praying, a deep peace settled over him.

Logan quietly wept with joy and relief. It felt good to get the worry off his back. To know that getting Alex home rested on someone stronger than him or anything he could do. It gave him hope. And that was even more powerful than the profile he and Alex had worked on. If God gave Logan something to do, that was one thing. But otherwise, he just had to trust God and believe He had the situation in His mighty hands.

He grabbed a tissue from the beside table and wiped his eyes. Crying was getting to be a habit. One he wasn't really comfortable with. He chuckled to himself as he dried his eyes. His dad used to tell him it was okay for men to cry, but Logan grew up watching movies with strong men who never wept. Turns out his dad was right. He intended to tell him that the next time he saw him. Once he could travel, he'd go home for a visit. He missed his family.

For some reason, he had a hard time getting his eyes dry, as if they were draining. He wiped them several times until finally the tears were gone. When he looked around, he started crying again.

He could see clearly.

Alex spent the afternoon praying and thinking. She'd come to several conclusions about the man who'd kidnapped her. He couldn't have known the woman he was looking for well. He remembered her hair and her general eye color. He also had an idea of her build, but he wasn't certain about her facial features. Also, the song the men kept singing or playing in this guy's personal amusement park had something to do with her. Alex had finally remembered the tune's lyrics, but this woman's name couldn't be Daisy or he probably would have found her by now.

Alex sighed. She wished she had more information, but one thing she was certain of—he was obsessed. Delusional. He was fixated on finding someone who may not even live in the area any longer. And he hadn't considered that she may have cut her hair—or dyed it another color. But some overwhelming urge wouldn't let him stop looking for her. It was clear something traumatic happened with this woman. But what?

Alex needed specific information. Something more if she was going to convince him she was the woman he wanted.

Could she wrangle details out of him without his knowing it? His body language would help her read him. She wished she'd had more data before she was taken. Now she'd have to wing it and pray she could convince him she was the woman he'd been searching for.

Her mind wandered to Logan. What had they found during the operation? Was the tumor benign? Or . . . She had to get back so she could be with him. Hopefully, he'd changed his mind and called his family. She didn't want him to be alone. But as she lay there thinking about him, she realized she couldn't afford to concentrate on anything except what was going to happen tonight—and the UNSUB's reaction to it.

She suddenly thought of something. He was still the *unknown subject*. She walked over to her door and slid open the top panel.

"Has the man on the dates—the one who kidnapped you—ever told you his name?" she said into the hallway.

Finally, she heard someone slide her panel open. "No." It was Amy. "But he did mention the other guy. I think it was an accident. His name is Andy."

"He's the blond guy?"

"Yeah, the one who takes care of us. I think the main guy, the one on the dates, is the boss. He tells Andy what to do. He also cooks our meals. He told me that while I was out with him."

"What did he say exactly about this . . . Andy?"

"I'm trying to remember," she said slowly. "I think it was something like he hoped I liked the dress Andy brought me. After he said it, he looked a little upset. That's why I don't think he meant to say Andy's name."

"What was your answer?"

"What could I say? I said the dress was beautiful. It wasn't. And that stupid song made me hate it even more. They kept playing it over and over."

Two more panels slid open.

"What's the deal with this dress?" Merrie asked.

"Please tell me before I have to wear it tonight," Tracy added.

"I'm sure the woman he's looking for wore a dress like that," Alex said. "And that's why that Daisy song comes into play." She smiled to herself. One more piece of the puzzle.

# 43

Jeff was sitting in his office, looking over requests for assistance from law enforcement across the country, when Alice buzzed to tell him Monty wanted to see him.

"Send him in."

When Monty opened the door, Jeff motioned for him to have a seat. "What's going on?"

"I went to the CP to see if Todd and Bethany needed help with questionnaires or surveys," he said, frowning. "They may have a lead on the UNSUB. ASAC Williams pulled me aside and brought me up-to-date."

"She didn't have to do that," Jeff said.

"I know, but I'm sure she knew I'd share the information with you. She knows how concerned we all are about Alex."

"So what did she say?"

"They found the last people who ran Magic Land Park. Although it's true a lot of parks paid cash to the people they hired, these guys kept records. Not for the IRS, just for themselves. Williams had to promise they wouldn't turn them in. Of course, even if they did, it's so long ago, I don't think the IRS could do anything."

"Did they learn anything that might help?"

"A last name for this Lum."

"And that name is . . ."

"Jones."

Jeff's mouth dropped open. "Seriously?"

"Yeah. You can imagine how many Joneses live in this country. And even though Lum is unusual, it could be a middle name. Or a nickname. They're searching now. The owners didn't know the father. Lum told them he'd died a few years before he showed up at Magic Land Park. Oh, one other thing. I guess one night after the park closed, some of the carnies were sitting around talking. The owner was there, and they were all sharing about their families. Lum said he had grandparents who lived in Virginia, but he didn't really know them."

"That's it?"

Monty nodded. "Unless someone at the CP has magical powers, I'm not sure this newest information will help them find Alex."

"The grandparents might not even have the same last name. They might be his mother's parents."

"Yeah. Feels like we take one step forward and end up two steps back."

"What did they come up with as far as the dead kids?" Jeff asked.

"Emily Marsden was just a regular teenager. Loved to have fun with her friends. Enjoyed amusement parks and carnivals. Always went to the Memorial Day celebration at Magic Land."

"Any enemies?"

"Not according to her parents. But after checking with some of her classmates, it seems she was kind of a mean girl."

"That sounds right."

"Yeah. Liked to make fun of kids at school who weren't as cool as she was. So the way Mike said she treated Lum fits."

"I know the ASAC wants to keep me in the loop, but I'm still surprised she told you all this."

"I think she plans to personally fill you in at some point. They're just really busy. Two birds, one stone, I guess."

"Anything else?"

"No. I mean, they're looking for a connection between Lum Jones and these grandparents, but so far nothing. Without more information, they may be at a dead end."

"Great." Jeff was frustrated. Everyone was doing the best they could, but this wasn't getting them anywhere.

"They know what caused the explosion at the park. It was a basic homemade bomb. Something anyone who looked on the internet could put together. Nothing special that might lead them in the right direction. Ingredients you can buy at any hardware store. Or even online. You already know there was nothing helpful at the park. They did find out that the tunnel had been there for years. The owners knew about it, but it seems it was added by the original owner. Not sure why, but it could have been a way to get some of their workers out of the park if the police came around. Or they might have been smuggling something in. No way to know now. The guy who built the park died a long time ago, and they haven't been able to find anyone still alive who was there when the tunnel was built. Of course, that was over seventy years ago."

"So our guy knew about the tunnel, especially since he worked the Ghost Shack. He had this all worked out. What was at the other end of the tunnel?"

"Just a gravel road. No visible tire tracks. Nothing left behind."

Jeff leaned back in this chair and frowned. "It will take a miracle for them to find her."

Monty shrugged. "I believe in miracles . . . and in Alex. You know what she's capable of."

"Yes, I do. But unless she can find a way to communicate with us, it really will take divine intervention for her to get those women to safety." He took a deep breath. "Maybe we should pray for her?"

Monty's eyebrows shot up. "I'm sorry. Did you just say *we* should pray?"

"Don't look at me like that. You all have made an impression on me. I see your faith and your love for one another. And . . . well, I guess I owe the man upstairs something after He saved me from drowning."

"I'm happy to pray with you," Monty said. "But before we do that, could I tell you how to get God directly involved in your life?"

"Is this that ask Jesus into your heart thing?"

Monty gazed directly into Jeff's eyes. "Yeah, that's exactly what it is."

Jeff leaned forward and stared down at his desk for a moment, then said, "Okay, let's do this."

Dr. Schmeidler moved the light away from Logan's eyes. Then she straightened up and frowned.

"So you're telling me your eyes filled with tears, and then when they dried you could see?"

He nodded. "I know that sounds weird, but that's exactly what happened."

The doctor walked several feet away and turned over one of the papers on her clipboard before writing something on it. Then she held it up. "What does this say?"

He smiled. "It says *I would never try to confuse Dr. Schmeidler. I'm telling her the truth.*"

She let the clipboard drop to her side. "I don't understand it, but I'm thrilled."

"You told me my eyesight might improve on its own," Logan said. "Why do you seem so surprised?"

"Blindness caused by anesthesia heals gradually. But because of tears? And this quickly? Never heard that before. Let's just be happy you got this result. A nurse will add some drops to your eyes. Rest them. I'll recommend an ophthalmologist familiar with brain tumors. After you're home and doing better, go see him, okay?"

"You got it, Doc."

"How are you feeling now?"

"Better. Still some pain."

She nodded. "Not surprising. When I send you home, I'll also prescribe some medication that will help you. But let's get you off the opioids and onto an over-the-counter pain reliever as soon as we can."

"Sounds good. Don't know what I would have done without them before the surgery, though. The pain was horrendous." He studied her for a moment. "I was surprised when

Dr. Morton prescribed them. Did he tell you he was ordering an MRI? And did you think he suspected a brain tumor?"

"I know he did. We talked about it. Your symptoms were classic. I expected you to get an MRI much sooner, though. One of his staff dropped the ball. I wanted that test run two weeks ago. I think that woman lost her job."

"People are people, Doc. They make mistakes. Trust me, in my work I've seen it happen. Even when lives are at stake."

"As far as I knew, yours was. I can't make mistakes, and neither can my staff."

"If you believe that, you're probably setting yourself up for failure. I'm afraid my colleagues made a mistake that could cost a . . . a dear friend her life. But I know they didn't do it on purpose."

"You're not angry with them?"

"No, because I know the kind of people they are. We're all doing the best we can. Forgiveness keeps us going."

Dr. Schmeidler looked down at the floor for a moment before saying, "You're a pretty smart man, Logan. For an FBI agent." She grinned.

"And you're pretty smart for a doctor," he said with a smile.

"You keep improving and I'm going to send you home sooner than later." Her professional persona was back. "But you'll need someone there with you."

"My friend Monty is already prepared to stay with me for a few days."

"Okay. I'll stop by tomorrow and see how you're doing. Then we'll talk."

"Thanks."

She nodded, then walked out the door.

Logan picked up the phone and called Monty. After

telling him about the possibility of going home soon, he also told him about getting his eyesight back. After Monty stopped whooping and hollering, he shared something about Jeff that made Logan's eyes fill with tears for the second time that day.

# 44

Although Alex was worried for Tracy, she felt fairly certain she would be safe tonight. The women who'd gone out with the UNSUB said he'd treated them well—except for threatening to hurt the rest of the women if she didn't go along with their so-called date.

Alex was still confused about something. The man who'd abducted the women appeared to be kind to them during their time together. And Andy seemed to be concerned about their captives. Therefore, the threats seemed rather incongruous. So which one was really pulling the strings? Who was the one to worry about? Alex had considered trying to influence Andy to help them, but what if he was the one in charge? Maybe his attitude was just an act to cover his real intentions.

The other thing she couldn't understand was why the women who'd been on the dates were still here. If he was certain they weren't the woman he was looking for, why were they alive? She had a hard time figuring this guy out. He didn't fit any mold she'd encountered before. But it wasn't always possible to understand everything a psychotic killer did.

She sighed and lay back on her bed, trying to think. Alex hoped their date would be soon—before he removed anyone else. And she wanted a chance to spend time with Andy. If he wasn't running the show, what was he getting out of this? He didn't come across as someone caught up in the thralls of hero worship. There were well-known duos who committed crimes together, the most famous being Leopold and Loeb, but they killed for the thrill of it.

Then there was John Muhammad and Lee Boyd Malvo. Muhammad was the puppet master and Malvo his puppet. They shot several people, at least one in Prince William County. Alex couldn't compare the men holding them to this pair either. Could the UNSUB only think he was in control? Could Andy be the man behind the curtain? Could he be killing women without the other guy knowing about it? Still . . . the guy going out on dates didn't fit the psychopathic personality.

Alex got up and paced the room for a while. When she had her date, should she confront the guy about Andy? Was it possible he might agree to let Alex take the women away from here? But if she was wrong, that could be a deadly mistake too.

Which one was the monster?

One other question kept bothering her. Was the woman he was looking for dead? Had he already killed her? That would mean he was so disconnected from reality that she and the other women were in more danger than they could imagine.

Alex had kept the panel at the top of her door open so she would know when Andy came for Tracy. Now she heard the squeaky cart making its nightly journey, delivering dinner.

She watched as her lunch tray was removed and the dinner tray pushed into the room. After all the other rooms had been approached, the cart made its way back, stopping at what had to be Tracy's room.

"Are you ready?" Andy asked.

"Yes." Tracy sounded scared, and Alex didn't blame her. But she needed her to do exactly what Alex had told her to do. Her plan depended on it.

"I'll be back in a minute," Andy said. "Wait by the door. Do you understand?"

"Y-yes."

Alex felt so sorry for her. The pressure was intense. She waited until she couldn't hear the cart anymore, then approached her door and called out.

"Tracy, can you hear me?"

"Yes."

"Look, I know you're afraid. Don't worry. You'll be fine."

"But if I make him think you're the woman he's looking for, doesn't that make me inconsequential? What if he decides to get rid of me, like they did with Sarah and Rhonda?"

Another panel opened. Amy.

"Tracy, those of us who've been here longer than you would go first, not you. Try not to worry. Really."

Alex appreciated Amy's strength and determination to get out of this place.

"When you get back, I'll need to know what happened," Alex said. "I've got to understand the man you'll be with tonight. I have to make sure I approach this the right way when he takes me on a date. Do you understand?"

"Yeah, I think so. I—"

The sound of the door at the end of the hall opening again

cut her off. Panels closed, but Alex kept hers open a crack. She wanted to hear everything.

Keys jangled. "Let's go," Andy said. The sound of a metal door opening. Tracy's. Then two sets of footsteps walking down the hall. Andy began to whistle that song—*Daisy, Daisy, give me your answer do.* Again, was he a subservient lapdog or something more? Andy was the wild card.

And therefore the one Alex had come to fear the most.

She wanted to know the truth about him before she confronted the other man, and hopefully, that would be sooner rather than later. Then maybe she could find a way to take him down and find a phone. Although she had no idea where they were, the FBI could track the signal and get help to them.

But most of all, Alex wanted to see the two men together. It was the only way to understand them both so she could determine how best to control them. But, of course, given what she'd already observed, getting them in the same place at the same time would be a challenge.

—————

Tracy was instructed to walk in front of Andy. She pulled open the door at the end of the hall and walked up the stairs. When she reached the top, she stepped into the kitchen. She'd been here before, but this time she could actually take a minute to look around. It was huge.

"Go through those doors," Andy barked from behind her. "And don't turn around."

She pushed open the French doors that led to the large brick patio. "Sit down there," he said, his voice low. "Don't move from here, okay? There's no place to run. This place is a fortress. Of course, you already know that, right?"

Tracy didn't respond, but it was the truth. There was no way out. How did Alex think she could set them free? She wanted to believe her. Needed to believe her.

Then Tracy thought about her children and decided she would do what Alex told her to do. She was an FBI agent. Surely she knew what she was talking about. She was probably the only chance they had.

"For Matty and Cassie," she whispered.

# 45

Alex stood by her door for several minutes after Tracy and Andy left. Was she doing the right thing? Or was she endangering Tracy and everyone else?

Finally, she picked up the tray at her feet and carried it to the table. She removed the top and found a beautifully baked chicken breast with some kind of seasoning, mashed potatoes, fresh green beans, two bottles of water, the cup of tea, and a bowl with what looked like chocolate pudding. She stared at it all a minute, then got up and opened the upper panel in her door. All three women responded when she called out into the hallway.

"I have more questions," Alex said. "When you went on your dates, did he cook for you?"

"Yeah," Merrie said.

"Was it like the meals we get in here?"

"No," Amy said. "It was just hot dogs and fries. And then there was cotton candy and popcorn. And soda."

"Why do you want to know?" Marla asked.

"I'm just trying to profile this guy. He's a really good cook. But on the dates he falls back on the kind of food you'd find at an amusement park or carnival. Those things don't go together very well, do they?"

"No, but he said he thought simple food was appropriate for the park," Amy said. She hesitated a moment. "You know, now that you bring it up, I don't think the food was his choice."

So maybe Andy made the decision?

"And he never gave you his name?"

The women all said no.

"I asked," Amy said, "but he told me it didn't matter, and I didn't want to push it."

"Was Andy ever around during your date?"

"No," Merrie said. "Andy took me to the patio and told me to wait. He never came back. The dark-haired guy came for me then. He called Andy once, though. At least I assume it was Andy. The small train that runs around the perimeter of the park was out of gas. He apologized to me, then told Andy to fix it."

"And none of you asked him to let you go?"

"I did," Marla said. "But he told me not to talk about that or everyone would be punished. He seemed to feel bad about it, though. It was almost like he was trying to protect me. I know that sounds nuts, but that was my impression at the time."

Alex digested that for a moment. "Okay. Can you remember anything else . . . unusual?"

"One thing," Amy said. "When we rode on the Ferris wheel, he wouldn't sit close to me. Kept some distance between us. In fact, it was that way the entire evening. I was afraid this whole date thing was a setup for rape, so I was watching him closely. But it was like he didn't want to touch me. I found that weird."

"Okay, thanks. Any of you who pray, please pray for me. I'll probably only get one chance at this. It has to go right."

"Hey, I'm not a praying person," Amy said, "but in this situation, I'd be happy to. I . . . I just want to get home to my family."

"We all do," Merrie said. "I'll pray for you. Haven't done that since I was eleven, but since I've been here, my prayer life has certainly expanded."

"Same for me," Marla added.

Alex smiled. At least something good was coming out of this. "Hey, thanks," she said. "I don't intend to drink my tea until Tracy gets back. I want to hear what happened."

"But what if Andy notices?" Amy said. "I don't want you to make him angry while Tracy's out there with the other one."

"Even though he seems solicitous toward us," Marla said, "it could be an act. It's not worth putting Tracy in danger."

Alex sighed. "I'll think about it. But in the meantime, don't worry. Our days here are limited. We'll be rescued."

"I hope you're right," Amy said. "I don't know how much longer we can take this."

---

Within a few minutes the French doors swung open, and the man who'd abducted Tracy in the park walked out. Anger flared inside her, and she wanted to hurt him, but she knew the women downstairs were counting on her. She took a quick breath and pushed down the rage burning in her chest.

"Hi," he said with a smile. He really was handsome. One

of the reasons she'd allowed him to get close to her in the first place.

"Hello," she said, forcing herself to smile back.

"I'm sorry about this. I know it's uncomfortable. All I can tell you is I can't do anything about it. And as much as I hate to say it, if you try to get away or attack me, the other women will be hurt. Do you understand?"

She nodded, not trusting herself to speak. How could he threaten her like that and still think they were going on some kind of nice *date*? He must be insane. Of course, that would explain everything. He was crazy. And that meant she couldn't control him or trust anything he said.

She had to remember she had one job—make him think Alex was the woman he was looking for.

He held out his hand. "Good. Now come with me. I promise you'll enjoy yourself. I won't hurt you, and I'm not going to molest you. You're completely safe with me. You'll be returned to your room tonight in exactly the same shape you were in when you arrived here. Do you understand?"

"Yes." She put her hand in his even though touching him made her want to throw up. Then she stood and let him lead her away from the patio.

She steeled herself for the next few hours. Her intention was to get this over with and get back to her cell. Hopefully, this night was the beginning of the end for this guy and his friend Andy.

And it couldn't happen quickly enough.

# 46

Tracy went with the man into the backyard. She could see it more clearly this time. The whole place was even larger than she'd thought. So expensive looking. He had to be rich? If so, he had the means to keep women here as long as he wanted. She suddenly felt overwhelmed and couldn't help the tears that fell down her cheeks. She tried to keep him from noticing, but he did.

"Please don't cry," he said with a smile. "I promise it will be okay. We're going to have fun. You'll enjoy yourself."

"No. No, I won't. I want to go home. I miss my family. I miss my children."

"You have children?" He looked surprised.

"Yes, a boy and a girl." How could he not know that? Surely he'd researched her before abducting her. And she was certain her disappearance had been on the news.

He was silent as they headed toward the amusement park on the other side of a fence. He opened the gate, and they stood at the entrance to a small but impressive array of rides and booths. How could all this be here? Wherever *here* was.

Again, trees surrounded the entire property, standing like silent guards. This place had to be tucked somewhere inside one of the forests in Virginia.

She noticed a large generator at the edge of the park. She'd seen another one when they came out of the house. Had he installed them so he didn't need electrical services from a company that might notice this odd property in the woods? Did anyone even know this house was here?

"Let's go on some rides," he said. "Then we'll get something to eat and we can talk."

She wanted to slap him. But Alex told her to play it cool. To answer the questions the other women said he would ask and then direct him to Alex. Tracy still felt as if she was about to put Alex in danger, and she didn't like it.

He led her to a beautiful carousel with colorful, carved horses and sparkling lights. It must be worth a fortune. She hopped up on a black horse, her legs dangling to one side since she had on a dress. He climbed up on a red one next to her. He really was being nice, but she made herself remember he'd kidnapped her. And that he may be a murderer.

He clicked some kind of device in his hand, and the carousel was activated. The music was the same tune he'd sung after he'd jabbed her in the neck with the syringe in the park, the same one they'd heard Andy whistling.

*Daisy, Daisy, give me your answer do. I'm half crazy, all for the love of you. . . .*

Would that song be burned in her brain forever? "Why do you keep playing that?" she asked him. "You sang it when you . . . when you took me."

He shook his head. "I don't like it. I sing it because I have to. Please don't ask me about that."

That was odd. Was Andy making him sing that song? None of the women saw him as a criminal mastermind.

The carousel finally slowed. What now?

"Let's ride the Ferris wheel," he said.

She didn't respond, just dutifully went with him. The Ferris wheel wasn't huge, but it was a decent size for a privately owned amusement park. Where did this guy get all his money?

"I heard I'm not supposed to ask your name," she said as they got onto the Ferris wheel. "But what should I call you?"

He was quiet for a moment, then said, "You don't need a name. I'm right here."

"But you told Amy Andy's name."

"That was an accident. He was really upset about that slip."

He pulled the bar that locked them into the car and pressed another button on the remote he carried with him. As one of the women said, he stayed on his side of the seat and left a space between them. Tracy was grateful, but she was also confused by him. It was almost like he was just following orders. But whose orders?

As they rode to the top, she looked out over the area. She could see the electric fence that surrounded the property, but part of it disappeared into the trees. And the house was even more spectacular than she'd thought. Brick, with turrets and scrollwork all along the roof.

"You must be very rich," she said. She hadn't meant to say it. The words just slipped out. "I mean, the house. And the grounds are beautiful."

He nodded. "I'm grateful to be able to enjoy this property. It's much nicer than any other place I've lived. My parents were very poor."

"Well, you've done well for yourself." She turned to look

at him. As much as she detested him, she was struck again by how handsome he was. Longish dark hair. Blue eyes. Strong chin. Nice mouth. "I . . . I just have a hard time seeing you as the kind of person who kidnaps women and imprisons them. I mean, look at you. And this place? You can't have problems attracting women."

"I . . . I can't talk about that," he said, shifting in his seat, obviously uncomfortable.

"Okay. Sorry. I don't want you to discipline the women because I did something wrong. Maybe it would be better if I just shut my mouth."

He sighed and turned toward her. "I enjoy talking. I get lonely. Just don't talk about . . . leaving here."

"I'll try. But it's hard not to mention it. I want to go home. I can't imagine what my children are thinking. Matty and Cassie probably think I'm dead."

On a TV talk show she'd seen once, they'd said making yourself a real person to a killer makes it harder for him to take your life. She wanted this guy to know about her children. Even their names. She was a human being with a family. Not just a woman with long black hair.

"You won't die. If you're not the one he's looking for, you'll leave here. You'll just be told not to say anything about all this or your family will be targeted and the women still here will be hurt."

Did he realize what he just said? The one *he's* looking for? The man behind this was Andy, not this guy.

"Do you really believe Andy is letting the women go?" she asked softly. "Surely you know that's not true."

He seemed taken aback. "If you don't stop, I'll have to return you to the house."

"No. Please. I won't bring it up again."

"Time to move on," he said, reaching for the remote.

"Oh, wait," she said. "One more time around? It's really beautiful up here." She was telling the truth. The lights from the park twinkled in the dark, and even though she was tired of hearing the same song over and over, it added to the ambiance.

She took a deep breath. It was time. "One of the women said you abducted her from an amusement park."

"Uh, yeah. I guess so, but I don't want to talk about that either."

*I guess so?* So he wasn't certain about it. Maybe Andy was the one who'd taken Alex? Yet this guy was the one who'd abducted *her*. Strange. She had to keep going. "I . . . I'm confused about something. You seemed surprised that I have children. Isn't my disappearance on the news?"

He sighed. "I don't know. It's one of the conditions for living here. No TV or radio. Not even newspapers. But I have lots of DVDs I watch when I'm not working."

No live TV? Someone didn't want this guy to know what was going on in the world. Probably because whoever was in charge didn't want him to find out too much. Unless he was the world's greatest actor, something was wrong here. Tracy could hardly wait to get back and tell Alex what she'd learned. Surely it would be helpful.

A thought popped into her head.

"But what about your phone? You can keep yourself up-to-date that way."

"It's only set up for calls." He frowned. "I'm not comfortable with all these questions."

She noticed that he patted his pocket. An involuntary response to her question? That told her he was carrying his phone. That was important for Alex to know too. "You're right. I'm sorry. I just think you're interesting. That this place is . . . well, I've never seen anything like it."

He didn't respond, just nodded. Tracy realized she may have pushed him further than she should have. She took another deep breath. She had to finish setting the trap.

"The woman who was taken from the amusement park said her name is Alex. She also mentioned that she used to visit that same park when she was a teenager. Before it closed down."

He immediately straightened up in his seat and looked at her, his eyes narrowed. "What did you say?" He used the remote, and the ride slowed until it stopped at the bottom.

Tracy tried to act surprised. "She said she used to go to that park when she was a teenager."

"Are you sure she was talking about that park?"

"Yeah," she said. "What did she call it? Magic Land . . . or something like that. Why? Is it important?"

"No." His response was sharp, and he shifted once again in his seat.

"I . . . I hope I haven't said anything wrong. I wouldn't want to cause Alex any problems."

"No. No, you're okay."

He seemed fidgety. Nervous. She had a feeling their date would be cut short.

"Let's get something to eat," he said.

"Sure."

She followed him past a row of booths, most of them with games. They stopped at a food stand. He stepped behind the counter, then took out two hot dogs on buns, some chips, and two large cups that he filled with soda. After grabbing some napkins, he came out from behind the counter.

"Let's go over there," he said, nodding toward a couple of picnic tables set up not far from the booth.

After putting the food on the table, he said, "Excuse me. I'll be right back."

He walked away and pulled the phone out of the pocket he'd touched earlier. As he made a call, Tracy tried to listen, but his voice was so low she couldn't understand him. After he hung up, he came back to the table.

"So I take it you never visited the park she was talking about?" he asked.

Tracy shook her head. "No. We moved here from Kansas about six years ago. Maybe it was already closed by then? I'd never heard of it until Alex brought it up."

He looked worried, and his knee kept jumping up and down as if he were keeping beat to a tune no one else could hear. It certainly wasn't the Daisy song that kept playing over and over in the background.

Tracy was certain the bait was set and the trap was about to spring. For the first time since she'd been brought here, she felt some real hope.

# 47

lex sat at the table, picking at her dinner. She couldn't think about anything except Tracy's return. The silence in this place was disturbing. She usually enjoyed the quiet, especially when working a case. She didn't like distractions when she was creating a profile. But the silence here was . . . forced. The three women still behind the doors in the hallway were wondering if they'd ever see their families again. Contemplating what that meant. Trying to be brave. Attempting to believe there was a chance that life would go on after this place. But from experience, Alex knew they would never be the same even if they survived this.

She had to drink the tea eventually, unwilling to risk the consequences that could occur if she disobeyed. Maybe she could drink it and then go behind the curtain and force herself to throw up. But more than the tea could come up and clog the sink. The best idea was the one already in place.

Wait for her date. It was the only way. And after tonight, it was bound to come quickly.

She waited as long as she could, then drank the tea before turning the cup upside down to show the camera it was empty. Were these men skilled at drugging them? What if they gave one of them too much? It worried her, but she couldn't do anything about it now.

After covering the tray, she carried it to the door and placed it in front of the panel at the bottom. Then she went behind the curtain and changed into the nightgown they'd given her. She wanted them to think she was beginning to acquiesce to their scheme. Flannel. She hadn't worn a flannel nightgown since she was a child—before her mother killed herself. She brushed her teeth and then her hair. After that she got into bed and pulled up the sheet and blanket.

She began to think about their host, again wondering if this guy had already killed the woman he said he was looking for. Alex had actually worked a case once where a killer had spent his time searching for a woman he'd already murdered. He'd stabbed several other women who'd reminded him of her. The anger he'd felt toward his ex-wife didn't disappear after he took her life. He kept going, driven by the rage that still burned inside him. Was this the same kind of thing? It was a possibility, but it was also likely that the woman he was looking for was still alive. Which was it? She just couldn't be sure. And what would happen if he was confronted by someone saying she was the woman he'd murdered? Was the truth buried deep within his psyche? Would it come out when his reality was challenged? Would he react violently?

She needed to be ready for anything.

The personalities of the two men still bothered her. The

abductor, the man taking the women out on these so-called dates, was described as nice. Kind. Even gentle. And Andy seemed almost sorry for his role in their abductions. Both men seemed rather docile. Yet that didn't make sense.

So where was the Ghost Rider? The violent personality in charge? She hadn't seen him yet, and none of the women reported being confronted by him.

A thought struck her. What if Andy and the abductor were the *same man* with two personalities? No, that couldn't be it. One man wouldn't be able to do all this on his own. And that still left the Ghost Rider.

Then a new possibility drifted into her mind. What if there were three men? If that was true, this whole situation was even more complicated than she'd thought. Could she take down three of them? Were they all in more danger than she'd ever imagined?

When he came back from his phone call, he sat down but didn't seem very interested in his food. He ate about half of it and stared at the rest like he didn't know what it was.

"Is everything okay?" Tracy asked.

"I hope so."

"Can you talk about it?"

He shook his head and took another bite of his hot dog, then put it down and looked at her. "The women really are released," he said. "I know it may not sound true, but when they're taken away, they're drugged and dropped off far away from here. Since they don't know where they were, they can't lead the police to this location. And they stay quiet because they're afraid of being recaptured or their families being hurt."

"You can't really believe that. It doesn't make sense. Some-one would have spoken up. And there are only two of you—"

He glared at her. "That's enough. I mean it."

"Okay, okay." Tracy slowly ate her hot dog. It was really good, even if it didn't compare to the meals they were being served inside the house.

When she finished, she decided to try one more time to reach him.

"Look, I don't want to speak out of turn," she said, "but you don't seem like the kind of person who would normally do something like this."

His expression tightened. "I'm not. That's why I made him promise—" He shook his head. "Never mind." He pointed at her food. "Finish up. Then we'll get some cotton candy."

She forced a smile. "Sorry, but I'm not big on cotton candy. Too much sugar for me." The truth was she loved cotton candy, but she needed to get back to Alex so she could tell her what happened.

"Okay." He shrugged. "Would you rather go back, then?"

"Yeah, I would. And it's not because of you. To be honest, I'm not feeling great. Sometimes that stuff you put in the tea makes me nauseated most of the next day."

"Sorry. Not my idea either. I hope you enjoy the food when you feel better, though."

"It's very good. Do you do the cooking?" She tried to look like she didn't already know the answer.

He nodded. "I used to be a chef. That was a long time ago. Before things went wrong for me. I enjoy cooking again. I just wish it was under different circumstances."

Tracy frowned. "Why don't you do something about this?

Call the police? Help us?" She tried to blink away the tears
that filled her eyes, but failed.

"There's really nothing I can do. I'm sorry." He sighed. "I
really can't talk about this anymore. I guess we need to go."

"Wait . . ." She needed to tell Alex what she'd learned, but
now she realized she didn't want to return to that awful cell
until she had to. Surely a few more minutes wouldn't make
a difference. "Let's go on the rest of the rides. And I'll take
that cotton candy. I'm feeling a little better."

"Okay." He paused for a moment before softly saying, "I'm
sorry. I really am."

She wanted to put her hands around his neck and scream,
*If you were actually sorry, you'd get us out of here!* But she
knew if she overreacted it could hurt the women waiting
back at the house, all praying that Alex could get them out.
So she just nodded and wiped the tears from her cheeks.
"What other rides do you have?"

"The Tilt-a-Whirl and the train. And we have some booths
with games."

Tracy smiled. "Let's do it."

He seemed a little distracted, but she decided to ignore that
and try to enjoy her last moments of freedom. The breeze
was mild, and it was the kind of evening she'd enjoyed at her
parents' house, sitting on their deck in the backyard while
the kids caught lightning bugs.

They rode the train that surrounded the small park. It
allowed Tracy to see the entire perimeter. She'd hoped it
would provide something that might help, but all she could
see were trees until they were almost back to where they'd
started. A large shed was partially hidden behind the tree line.
What was inside? Something that could be used as a weapon?

She couldn't see a lock on the latch that kept it closed, but she had to be careful not to stare at it too closely. She didn't want to alert him to her interest. Someone had to be doing maintenance work on the park and on the grounds. It was possible there were shears inside. Something sharp. She'd tell Alex about it.

They rode the Tilt-a-Whirl—a little awkward since the air kicked up by the ride's rotation blew her daisy-dress skirt up a little. She put her hands on her lap to keep herself covered. She had no idea if he was looking since he was behind her, but he seemed totally disinterested in her as a woman.

It was also clear he wasn't going to help them. He must be too afraid of Andy. Or maybe he really was so happy living in luxury that he didn't want to risk losing his lifestyle. He'd said he'd once had it rough. There was really no way to know his motivation.

They played one game where Tracy threw balls into rings on a table. When she won, he gave her a stuffed cat. Once again, she was moved to tears.

"Sorry. It reminds me of my mother's cat back home. She looks just like this."

He looked uncomfortable again, but she wasn't going to push him anymore. It was obviously useless.

"Let's go back," she said, "and thanks for this. It was nice to get out of there for a while."

"You're welcome." He paused for a moment. "I really do wish I could do something."

"I understand," she said, even though she didn't. Right now all she wanted to do was to tell Alex what she'd learned. She prayed it would help them somehow.

As they walked toward the house, she decided to bring up

something else Alex had mentioned. "You guys have cameras in each room but no speakers. You watch us, but you're not listening. Can I ask why?"

He sighed. "He says it's not necessary because there's nothing you can plan that will get you out of here. But more than that, he worries that buying a system like that might get some attention from the authorities. He's very careful about not doing anything that might look suspicious."

More indication that Andy was running the show. She didn't know why, but her abductor seemed to be letting his guard down with her.

"But the cameras . . ."

"Were already in place when he inherited this place."

So Andy owned this property?

"That makes sense. At least it gives us a little privacy." She'd heard of people installing cameras in their wine cellars to prevent theft.

"So what happened to all the wine?" she asked.

"What do you mean?" He seemed flustered by her question. Was she not supposed to know they were being kept in a wine cellar? Had she just made a mistake? "I'm sorry. I thought maybe it was once a wine cellar, but I could be wrong. I wouldn't know. I've never had one."

He said nothing as he walked her inside the kitchen and then to the door that led downstairs. "Wait here. Andy will be here shortly."

"I will. And thanks. It surprises me, but I had a good time."

He smiled. "I'm glad. Good night."

He left through a door that had to lead to another room. She was tempted to open the drawers and find a knife, but she was afraid of ruining Alex's plan.

After a few minutes, the door her date had left through opened behind her. "Don't look at me," a voice said before she could turn around.

Andy. She kept her eyes facing the door to the cellar. "Okay."

"Now open the door and head downstairs."

She followed his instructions all the way to the door of her cell.

"After you get ready for bed," he said, "place the dress and shoes by the bottom panel of your door. Just like the trays. Your tea is in there waiting for you."

She pushed her door open and stepped inside, then winced as the key turned in the lock. She waited until she heard the door at the end of the hall close before sliding open the upper panel in her door. "Anyone awake?"

Silence.

She would have to wait until tomorrow to tell Alex what she'd learned.

# 48

"You're certain she said this Alex person had been to the park in Ashville?" Rider asked again.

"Yes, I've told you the same thing at least four times."

"You should have awakened me when you got in."

"You get mad when I do that."

Rider was irritated that he'd had to wait this long to discover they'd finally found the right woman, but he was also secretly overjoyed. She was finally going to pay for what she'd done.

"You'll take her out tonight," Rider said. "But once you're in the park, I'll deal with her."

"And then what?" Brent asked. "Then you'll let them all go?"

"I told you I would. Are you calling me a liar?"

"No, it's just . . . well, it's just something Tracy said."

"And what did she say?" Rider's voice rose with anger, but he didn't care. Brent was nothing to him. A means to an end.

"Never mind. I don't want you to hurt her. She's nice."

"Nice? None of them are nice. You didn't touch her, did you?"

"Of course not. You know I would never do that. They belong to you. You've made that clear."

Rider's resentment grew. Was Brent trying to hide something from him? "I want to know what she said to make you doubt me." He saw fear in the man's eyes. Good.

"She said that if you'd let the other women go, someone would have come looking for us. That not everyone would have kept quiet."

Was that all he was worried about? "That might be true, but no one knows where we are. And none of them have a clue how to find us."

Rider stared at Brent for a moment, looking for any signs of deception, but he didn't spot any. He wasn't really concerned. Brent was so dumb he couldn't pull the wool over anyone's eyes. Especially his.

He sat back in his chair. "So tonight we'll finally have her. The one we've been looking for all this time."

"What will you do?"

Rider glared at him. "Never ask that question again. Do you understand?"

Brent nodded. "Just don't forget about me when you finally have what you want."

"How could I do that? We're bound together. I could never get along without you."

"Or me without you."

Logan had been trying to sleep, but he couldn't get Alex off his mind. Why did he have to be stuck in a hospital where he couldn't do anything to help her?

The pain in his head had grown steadily worse, but he

hadn't pushed the button for more morphine because he wanted to be able to think clearly. He finally had to give in, though. He lay back on his pillow and let the drug bring him some respite.

But as it kicked in, he found himself praying for Alex with a sudden sense of urgency. As if she were in real trouble.

Tracy awoke to the sound of someone calling her name. At first, she thought it was her mother. She was so happy to hear her voice. But when she opened her eyes, she realized she was still in the same cell she'd lived in for days. She'd had to drink her tea later than usual last night, so she was still groggy. She hadn't wanted it, but this wasn't the time to make Andy and his pal angry.

She pushed herself off the bed, stumbled to the door, and then slid open the upper panel. "I'm here," she called, trying to push the sleep away. "Sorry."

"It's me," Alex said after a few seconds. "How did it go?"

"You were right. When I told him about you, he immediately made a phone call. I don't think this guy's in charge, by the way. He kept referring to another man who makes all the decisions. It must be Andy calling the shots. I know that's not what we thought at first, but our date doesn't act as though he likes what's going on. Unfortunately, he's too afraid to help us. And he's convinced himself that Andy lets the women go, although I tried to put some doubt in his mind."

"But Andy doesn't have the personality to be behind this," Alex said.

"Then the guy I was with last night is a fantastic actor."

Alex was quiet for a moment before saying, "Did you

happen to ask him why they don't seem worried about listening to us? I know I keep bringing it up, but if anyone overhears our plans, we're sunk."

"Yes, and it was exactly as you thought. They aren't really worried about what we say. He also said that the man who inherited this place is afraid to buy a bunch of equipment that might raise suspicions."

"I should have realized that," Alex said. "It makes sense. He won't do anything that might alert the authorities."

"But what about all that carnival equipment?" Amy asked. "Isn't that kind of odd?"

"I doubt anyone was suspicious about an amusement park connection until I was taken from the park in Ashville."

"Maybe the FBI is thinking about it now," Amy said. "Checking for unusual sales of carnival equipment."

"I hope you're right," Alex said. "Especially since he demanded I meet him inside the Ghost Shack at an amusement park and called himself the Ghost Rider in the note he sent."

"I suspect your date will be tonight," Tracy said. "But please be careful. I don't trust either one of them."

"I asked you all a question yesterday," Alex said. "About whether you'd ever seen Andy's face. And you said his hair always covers it."

"Right," Tracy said. "And last night before he brought me downstairs, he told me not to look at him."

"Has anyone ever seen the two men together?"

Each woman said no after a moment of silence. Tracy gulped at the thought that popped into her head. "Surely you're not saying there aren't two of them."

"I don't know," Alex said, "but I've wondered if we were being kept by one man. There's something called dissociative identity disorder. Something traumatic happens, and the identity splits into at least two personalities in an attempt to handle the trauma. One guy is the *good* part of the personality. The second personality handles his anger. His desire for revenge. But we've been dealing with two personalities—and neither one seems angry or vengeful. It's confusing. I'm trying to understand them before I'm faced with taking one . . . or possibly both of them down."

"But that's not possible," Amy said. "How could one guy take care of all of us?"

"It would be difficult."

"You're right, though," Amy said. "That long blond hair is always hiding Andy's face. And he never looks at us or lets us see him."

"Oh my God," Tracy said. "So if I'd taken him out last night, we could all be out of here now?" Guilt filled her, making her want to cry.

"No," Alex said sharply. "Even if there is only one person, his violent side could have come out. I'm sure his rage makes him strong. Very hard to handle. I can deal with that because I'm trained to. He probably would have killed you. You did the right thing."

"If there is only one guy, the split in his personality is really deep," Tracy said. "The guy last night? Nice, but weak. Like I said, he really believes Andy is letting the women go. He thinks the reason no one has turned them in is because of the threats against their families—and because they have no idea where they were."

"If they'd let them loose, someone would have contacted the authorities. The police and the FBI would have known about it," Alex said. "I'm sorry, but those women are dead."

"One other thing you need to know," Tracy said after a few moments of silence. "He had a cell phone in his pocket. He used it to call Andy. Or at least that's what it looked like. If you can get that phone away from him . . . It only works for calls, though. Seems Andy, or whoever is in charge, won't let him online or allow him to watch TV. Probably why he doesn't realize no one has really been let go from here. Oh, and this may not help you, but I noticed something else. A small shed not far from the park. You know, the kind you can keep lawn equipment in? Maybe there's something in there that could be used as a weapon. I mean, if you need it."

Just then the door at the end of the hall opened. Tracy left the small panel open just a little so she could get a look at Andy. Sure enough, when he walked past, all she could see was a man with long blond hair that concealed his face. He didn't look at her, and she didn't call out to him. It was best not to do anything to ruin Alex's plans.

She heard him approach Alex's door. Then came the knock. "I'll be here around dinnertime to pick you up. Put these clothes on." That was all he said before opening and closing Alex's large panel, then heading back up the hall to the main door. The voice was so different from the man last night. How could they be the same person? It just couldn't be true.

"Please be careful, Alex," Tracy said out into the hallway. "I'm not sure about this."

"Don't worry. We're almost out of here," Alex said. "Everyone just pray. Pray really hard."

# 49

The morning had passed slowly for Logan. But at least he was finally able to eat regular food at lunch—broiled chicken and green beans. He was surprised by how good it was.

He was trying to back off the pain medication, but it was taking longer than he wanted. When the pain was too bad, he'd push the button. Although he didn't like how it made him feel, the relief was almost immediate.

About one o'clock, he couldn't stand it anymore. He'd just pressed the button when a nurse walked into his room.

"How's the pain?" she asked.

"Not good. I don't want to keep pushing this button, but I can't help it."

She leaned over the bed and looked closely at him. "I think you need to see the doctor," she said. "I'll see if she's still in the hospital."

A few minutes later, Dr. Schmeidler came in. "Tell me what's going on."

"Sorry to bother you, but the pain in my head is getting worse instead of better."

She walked up to the bed and frowned. "I was leaving the hospital when I suddenly felt like I needed to check on you. I'm sending you down to radiology for a CT scan. I want to make sure you haven't developed a blood clot. Hold on."

She left, and a few minutes later two nurses came into the room. They disconnected him from a couple of the machines, but they kept his IV in. Then they scooted his bed and the metal stand holding his IV bag out of the room and down the hall, past some double doors, and into a room with a huge machine.

He prayed silently as they transferred him to the large round device and pushed him inside.

Alex spent the afternoon preparing for her date. This was it. Tonight it would be over. She washed her hair and bathed the best she could. Then she used the makeup provided in a small bag under the sink in the quasi-bathroom. It wasn't exactly what she was used to, but it would have to do. She dressed carefully and brushed out her hair. She assumed this was how he'd last seen the girl he was looking for.

It was difficult to put on the dress, but she had no choice. And at least it fit her perfectly, as did the shoes. The dress had something to do with his obsession. The woman who'd fueled his rage must have worn something similar. But the question now was, how many people did she have to worry about? Was there one guy? Two guys? Or could there actually be three?

She was determined to play whatever role she had to so they could get out of here. No matter what it took, Alex had made up her mind that this was the last day she would spend here.

Logan tried to watch TV, but he kept nodding off. At least if he were asleep, he might dream something pleasant instead of thinking about what nightmare Alex could be going through. He'd just decided to give in to sleep when Jeff walked in.

"Not planning to stay long," he said. "On my way home. But I need to bring you up-to-date."

"Thank you. It's all I can think about."

Jeff shared everything the ex-carnie had told Agent Williams. "And now we have a name," he said. "The guy we're looking for is Lum Jones."

"Jones? Seriously?"

"Yeah, unfortunately. No wonder he had a nickname."

"Which was?"

"The Ghost Rider. Or just Rider."

Logan sat up a little straighter. "Like from the note?"

"Exactly. That's how we know it's him."

"You know Lum is a nickname for Columbus, right?"

"Excuse me?" Jeff said, his eyes wide.

"Yeah. I only know that because of an old man who lived down the street from us when I was a kid. His name was Lum. He told me he was named after his father, whose name was Columbus. It stayed with me because I'd never known anyone named Lum before. Or Columbus, for that matter."

Jeff took his phone from his pocket and quickly made a call. "Hey, we could be looking for a Columbus Jones." He waited a few seconds before saying, "Yes, I know. But search under that name. It could be the grandfather's name. Maybe that's how we find Alex and the women. Thanks."

"Why do you think it could be the grandfather's name?" Logan asked. "You might be getting ahead of yourself."

"Not when the kid's father was called Junior. The ex-carnie thought it was because the dad liked Junior Mints, but I doubt that was the reason." He shook his head. "If I hadn't stopped by to see you . . ."

"But you did. And by the way, thanks for the flowers," he added, nodding toward the large bouquet delivered that morning.

"From everyone at the office. They just want you to know they're thinking of you."

"I appreciate it."

"Monty told me about your eyes clearing up. God really watches out for you, doesn't He?"

"He watches over all His children. I'm not special. I also believe He's going to bring Alex home."

"I hope so too."

Logan sighed. "The name Lum Jones is a long shot."

"I know, but at least it's something."

Logan's gaze locked onto Jeff's. "You've got to find Alex. I'm afraid . . ."

"After everything that's happened to you? How could you not have faith?"

Logan tried to blink away tears. Not just because he was worried about Alex, but because such words of encouragement had come from Jeff. "You're right. She just has to come back. She has to make it through this."

"I know, I know." Jeff stepped closer to the bed. "Everyone's looking for her, Logan. Some of the best investigators in the business. They'll find her. And I'll keep you updated the best I can, but the only reason I'm getting information at all is because Alex is involved."

"I know. Thank you."

"I do think those murders fifteen years ago are related to this. It's a good lead."

"I agree. What were the kids' names again?"

"Emily Marsden and Thomas Tedder, although Thomas isn't what they called him."

"So you're convinced that the guy taking these women killed those two?"

"Yes. But why kidnap women who look like Emily years later? What's he after? Surely he got his revenge when he killed her." He shook his head. "We won't know anything about his motives until we find the women and bring them home."

Jeff paused a moment before saying, "Before I leave, I'm going to ask you to do something I've never asked you to do before."

Logan frowned. What could he do from this bed?

"I want you to pray. I'm not sure how to do it, so I want you to pray while I listen. Is that okay?"

Overcome with emotion, Logan could only nod. He waited until he could find his voice, then prayed for Alex, asking God to bring her back safely. After that, he prayed for the other women. "Deliver them, Lord," he said. "Send your angels to surround them and protect them. And thank You that my friend Jeff is now my brother. In Jesus's name, amen."

When Logan opened his eyes, he caught Jeff wiping his cheeks with the back of his hand. "So Monty told you," he said. "Good. I want you to know that I'll be praying you'll recover completely and get back to work. It's not the same without you."

"Thanks. Trust me, I'd rather be at work than here."

"Monty says he's going home with you. He's determined to take care of you while you heal. I've given him the time off."

"Yeah, he told me. Thanks. I appreciate it." He sighed. "I need to call my family, but I want to wait until I can give them good news. My mother says my father is recovering well from his stroke, but sometimes she keeps things from me that she thinks might worry me. Just in case he's having a tougher time than she'll admit, I don't want to dump this on them right now."

"You know, if my kid did something like that, I'd come unglued."

"I hear you. I'll contact them soon."

Jeff shrugged. "It's your business, but I still think you're wrong."

"I've been wrong before, but I have to go with my instincts. Good or bad."

"Okay, I give up. So how are you feeling?"

"Better now. Seems I developed a blood clot, and I was in a lot of pain. Turns out my doctor was leaving the hospital when she suddenly felt she should check on me. Had my head scanned right away, and thankfully, they found it. Gave me some super-duper blood thinners."

"She just suddenly felt she should check up on you?"

Logan smiled. "Yep."

The door swung open, and a nurse looked in on them. "It's getting a little late, and Agent Hart needs to rest."

"I hear you," Jeff said. He reached over and patted Logan's shoulder. "You get some sleep. I'll let you know if I hear anything new."

"Thanks."

Jeff walked toward the nurse, who was holding the door open for him. "You take care of that man," Jeff said. "He's pretty special."

Something Jeff said suddenly popped into Logan's mind. "Hey, Jeff?" he called.

Jeff stuck his head back into the room. "Yeah?"

"Probably not important, but you said Thomas Tedder was called something else. What was it?"

"I guess his middle name was Andrew. They called him Andy."

# 50

Alex was ready. Dressed, looking as good as she could under the circumstances, the knife tucked inside her bra where it couldn't be seen but where she could get to it quickly. She'd decided to wait until Andy passed her off to the other guy. The nice one. That personality should be easier to subdue, although she still wasn't convinced Andy and her date were the same person. She was prepared for that possibility, but she was also keeping an eye open for whoever referred to himself as the Ghost Rider.

If only she could be sure if he was a third personality or a third man. There was no way to know, but she planned to have her date completely secured before any kind of violent personality could emerge. She'd dealt with dissociative identity disorder when she worked for the National Center for the Analysis of Violent Crime in Kansas City. They'd tracked down a spree killer who'd shot up a shopping mall. Cameras captured the event, so it didn't take long to find the guy. When they arrested him, he manifested four different personalities.

Turned out his childhood had been a nightmare of abuse and pain. His way of dealing with it was to create three other selves who knew nothing about the horror he'd endured. They were produced to help him tolerate his life. Unfortunately, one of the personalities was angry and violent. He was the one who'd shot several people before a security guard took him down, saving many lives.

Alex believed the man was truly ill, but even though a psychiatrist testified about his disorder, he was found competent to stand trial. Of course, he was found guilty. He'd been in prison a little less than a week when he was killed by an inmate who thought the man was trying to molest him. He wasn't. One of his personalities manifested as a child. Alex was certain he was just afraid and trying to find someone to comfort him.

She pushed the memory out of her head. She couldn't afford to feel sorry for the guy she was getting ready to face. She had to take him down.

With her panel open, it felt as if she'd waited forever when the door opened at the end of the hall. It was showtime.

―――

Logan felt as though someone was shaking him awake, and then he was overwhelmed with yet another strong desire to pray for Alex. He reached for the Bible next to his bed and searched for Scriptures to claim over her. Especially Psalm 91. He was determined to pray all night if he had to.

―――

After everyone else received their dinner trays, Andy opened the door to Alex's cell. He stepped behind the door so she couldn't see him. Fine. She'd play along for now. Besides, if he was also her date, she wanted his alter ego, not him.

"Walk to that door at the end of the hall. Don't look at me. If you do—"

"I know. Everyone will be punished."

"I'm glad you understand."

"Yeah, I do. I won't give you any trouble."

As Andy walked behind her, Alex had never been more determined in her life. She was going to get these women out . . . even if she had to die doing it.

"Open the door and go up the stairs," Andy said from behind her.

She did as he instructed and stepped inside a beautiful kitchen. It looked clean and organized, although she could tell someone had been cooking. The rest of the women would be eating now. How could one man do all this? Of course, he had nothing else to do. Obviously, he didn't have a job. This had to be his full-time gig. Still, she was bothered by the idea that they were dealing with just a single individual. What was she missing?

"Sit down at the table and wait. I'll get your date."

She lowered herself onto a chair, wondering when his other personality would show up. In the meantime, she scouted out her surroundings. Was there anything here that would help her? She thought about searching the drawers for other knives, but the one she had was more than sufficient. Made to be even harder than most metals. And if he caught her . . .

She decided to stay where she was.

She looked around for a phone or for keys, but she didn't see anything. A clock on the wall read almost six thirty. At least she knew what time it was, not that it made much of a difference.

*Everything will be all right.*

Alex looked around, but she knew no one was there. She smiled to herself and took a deep breath. "Thank you, God," she whispered.

Finally, the door opened, and a dark-haired, good-looking man appeared. Was this the personality who'd shown up at the amusement park? She doubted it. Based on what she'd been told, he was too weak. Too nice. This personality was probably closer to the way he was before whatever trauma he'd endured.

"Sorry about this," he said. "But I have to tell you that if you try to run or cause me any trouble, the other women will be hurt. And you'll be punished as well. Do you understand?"

She nodded. "I understand."

"Okay, let's go." He held out his hand, and she took it. She wanted to get him as far away from the house as possible.

He opened some French doors, and they stepped out onto a patio. Alex could see the amusement park not far from where they stood. Were investigators looking for this connection? With everything inside her, she prayed they were.

---

When Jeff's cell phone rang, he looked at his watch. Six-thirty. He was home, and Lisa had just called out for him to come to the dinner table.

"In a minute," he said.

She came into the living room. "Jefferson Cole, I want some time with you. If it's work . . ."

"You know I have to answer this. I'll be there as soon as I can. I promise."

Although his wife was used to the pressures of his job, he understood that she needed him to be available to her. Sighing, he answered the call.

"Hi, Boss," Monty said. "Todd just called. They've found a Columbus Jones Junior. Died almost eighteen years ago. Had a son.Columbus Jones the third. But they also found Columbus Jones Senior. Died about twelve years ago. Left everything he owned to his grandson. It's a huge mansion out in the boonies, about ten miles from here."

"That's where they are," Jeff said, excitement bubbling up inside him. "Are they sending teams out there?"

"Yes. SWAT and HRT. Hopefully, we'll have them soon. Oh, and the task force found something else. Someone bought a couple of the rides and some booths from Magic Land sometime after it closed down for good."

"And the buyer?"

"Columbus Jones the third."

"I'm surprised he used his real name."

"Probably had to since the purchase was expensive. Besides, he hadn't kidnapped anyone yet."

"So they're on their way now?"

"Yeah. I'll keep you posted as I hear from Todd. Williams was ready to send him and Bethany home, but they asked to stay. Then she told them to make sure you know she'll contact you directly as soon as the teams secure all the victims and Alex."

"She's aware Todd is calling you and you're calling me, then."

"Yeah. She's pretty sharp, and she knows how much this operation means to us."

"Okay. Thanks. I'm going to call Logan."

"Should you wait until they know something for sure?"

"No. I want him to be prepared for whatever happens. I owe him that."

"Okay. I'm almost to the hospital. You'll call him now?"

Jeff looked at Lisa staring at him from across the room. He sighed. "Yeah. Pray for me. My wife is giving me the evil eye. Dinner's ready."

"I can tell him what's going on."

"No. It needs to come from me. Talk to you soon." He disconnected the call and met Lisa's gaze. "They may have found them. We could have Alex back in the next hour or so, and I need to let Logan know."

She shook her head. "I'll put the roast back in the oven. It'll keep for a while." Then she smiled before heading back to the dining room.

Jeff was beginning to realize how blessed he really was. Just wait until he offered to pray over their meal. Maybe this interruption would be forgotten. Lisa had been praying for his salvation for years. The desire of her heart was to have a godly husband. Tonight she would finally see the result of those prayers.

# 51

Alex allowed him to lead her into the amusement park. "Let's eat first," he said. She could tell he was nervous. Tracy said they rode the rides first. This was different. Good. She didn't want to drag this out. She was certain it was because he suspected she was the person he'd been looking for.

She'd gone over and over a cover story. This personality might not be the one with the memories, but she had to be prepared for anything. And that was okay. She wasn't trying to convince him. She just wanted to stop him. And if he *had* killed the woman who'd caused him so much trauma, this wasn't the time for him to remember that. It might make him almost impossible to handle. She had to keep him stable.

She looked at the two large picnic tables he gestured toward. Metal legs. Large. Heavy. Good. That should work. She sat down at one of them.

He entered a nearby booth, then brought back hot dogs, potato chips, and soda. She didn't plan to be there long enough to eat. Then he sat down on the other side of the table. Shoot. She needed to be closer to him than that.

"Tracy said you told her you'd been to that amusement park before," he said. "Magic Land? The one where . . ."

"Where you kidnapped me?"

He looked uncomfortable. "I'm sorry that happened to you."

She wanted to tear into him, but this personality might not be aware that someone else was living inside of him. And she couldn't afford an introduction to the Ghost Rider yet.

"I'm trying to understand," she said. "But it's hard. To answer your question, yes. I went there when I was young. Particularly on holidays. It was fun."

"Did . . . did you have a dress with daisies on it?"

She nodded. "It looked a lot like this one. I couldn't believe it when I saw it."

He came around the table and sat next to her. "You've got to get out of here," he said in a low voice. "I mean it. He'll kill you."

She reached into her bra and took out her knife. Then she swiftly moved behind him and held the weapon to his throat.

"I'm not going anywhere," she said. "And neither are you."

Logan was praying when his phone rang, startling him. He picked it up and answered.

"Logan," Jeff said, "they think they've located the women. SWAT and HRT are heading out there, as well as police and ambulances."

"That's the best news I could hear," Logan said. "Do you know how long it will take them to get there?"

"This place is about ten miles out from Quantico. This is all secondhand information from Todd and Bethany. They're still at the CP."

"You've got quite an underground network there, don't you?"

"Yes."

"No guesses even?" He didn't want to push Jeff, but he couldn't help it.

"Well, it's not all that far, but they have to be careful. We could have a wait on our hands. They won't breach the grounds without being as certain as possible that they won't risk lives."

"You'll keep me updated, though. Right, Jeff?"

"I'll keep you both updated," a voice from the doorway said.

Logan looked up to see Monty walking into the room. "I'm the second link in the chain," he said with a smile.

"Tell him I heard that," Jeff said. "But Williams promised she'd call me directly when Alex is secured."

Logan repeated Jeff's words, and Monty grinned. "So it's a throwdown. Who gets to tell you the good news first? I accept the challenge."

Logan appreciated his friend's attempt to add a lighter tone to the conversation, but his stomach was still tied in knots. He was so glad Monty was here. He didn't want to be alone now.

"I'll let you go," Jeff said. "I want to keep the line open for her call."

"Okay. And thanks, Jeff."

"You bet."

He'd just hung up when a nurse opened the door and stepped inside. Logan was glad to see it was Donna.

"Before you say anything," Monty told her, "I know it's late, but we're waiting on some very important information. One of our team—a woman my friend is in love with—is close to being rescued from a dangerous situation. I'm staying with him until we know she's safe." He put his hands on his hips as if challenging her. Logan liked Donna and didn't want to offend her, but neither did he want Monty to leave.

Donna didn't say a word. She just came over and checked his vitals. "Your blood pressure is a little high," she said. "Try to calm down."

Logan waited for her to speak to Monty, but when she was finished, she just smiled at Logan. "I'll be back later. Glad I didn't notice anyone in your room."

As she walked toward the door, Monty said, "I know you can't hear me, but I think you're awesome. Just so you know."

She closed the door behind her, and Logan said, "Thanks. If I had to wait for news by myself, I think I'd go crazy."

"That's what I figured." Monty pulled a chair over and sat down. "Well, we can't just sit here and stare at each other. What do you want to do?"

"I don't know. If I turn on the TV, I won't be able to concentrate on whatever we're watching. I can't think about anything except Alex."

"Then I guess we'll sit here and worry together."

"First, let's pray. Then instead of worrying, we can *anticipate*."

"Is that a code word for worrying?"

Logan sighed. "I hope not. I know God loves her and that He's with her. Why do we worry even when we know that?"

"I'm afraid that's above my spiritual pay grade. But one thing I've learned? God knows how we really feel. And he understands the mountains we face. Faith isn't a show we put on to impress Him. Faith may not lower our blood pressure or chase away all worry. But hope in God is a powerful thing. It's the bridge to faith, and it puts those mountains on notice."

Logan shook his head. "When did you get so smart?"

"Must be the company I keep."

Logan smiled. "Okay. Let's pray and walk across that bridge together."

# 52

W hat are you doing?" he said. "I was trying to help you. I'm not the one you need to worry about."

Alex pushed him to the ground and removed her belt. Then she pulled his hands behind his back and wrapped the belt around them, making certain they were tightly bound. After that, she flipped him over and pushed him up next to the picnic table. The thing was massive. Extremely heavy. He'd have to turn into the Incredible Hulk to drag it around. Thankfully, the belt was leather. Strong. She looped the ends of the belt around one leg of the table and secured it. Then she pulled it as hard as she could. It would take a miracle for him to break it.

"You're making a mistake," he said. "You'll get us both killed. He knows you're the girl who made fun of him. He plans to kill you and then all the other women in the cellar. This isn't what I signed up for. I've been helping him for the last six years and . . . ignoring the truth about him because I didn't want to end up in prison. But this has gone too far."

"Look, I know you think you're telling the truth," Alex said, "but I believe you may be suffering from a mental disorder, and this is only one of your personalities."

His mouth dropped open. "You're wrong. You have to listen to me."

She ignored him and reached into his jacket pocket. She pulled out his phone and immediately called Jeff. She used the number given only to the FBI so he wouldn't ignore a number he didn't know. After a few rings she heard his voice.

"Jeff. Jeff, it's Alex."

"Alex! We know where you are. Teams are on the way. Are you all right? Are any of the women still alive?"

She sat down at the table, keeping some distance between herself and her captive.

"Yes to both questions. How did you find us?"

"We know the name of the guy who took you. We got it from an old carnie and a man who used to own Magic Land Park."

"What's his name?" she asked, staring at the man looking back at her. He still hadn't reverted to Andy . . . or the Ghost Rider. She was a little surprised. She figured by now he would be angry enough to really lose his cool and trigger an alternate personality.

"Columbus Jones," Jeff said. "I know it sounds ridiculous, but that's it. He was called Lum before he started calling himself the Ghost Rider."

"Because he ran the Ghost Shack?"

"Exactly. His favorite thing."

"Listen, Jeff. This place is surrounded by an electric fence, and he's running everything with generators. I'll turn them off so the teams can get in. Then I'll find the keys and let the

women out of their cells. Will you let whoever is in charge
know—"

"No!" the man said loudly. "You have to listen to me. He'll
stop you. He'll kill you. And then he'll probably kill me."

"What's he saying?" Jeff said.

"I think we're looking at a guy with dissociative identity
disorder. He's tied down pretty good, though, so he won't get
away." She looked at the man. "So your name is Columbus
Jones? No wonder you changed it to the Ghost Rider. Or
Andy."

But as she said it, the doubts she'd had earlier wiggled
around like little worms in her head. He wasn't acting the
way she thought he would. Could she be wrong? Was there
someone else here she needed to protect herself from?

"I have no idea what you're talking about," he said, his
tone bordering on hysteria. "My name is Brent. Brent Teague.
I was hired by the man you know as Andy to lure women
here. He felt he couldn't do it because . . . because of how
he looks."

"Alex, did . . . did he say Andy?" Jeff asked.

"Yeah. One of the three personalities I think we're dealing
with. Do you know what happened to trigger all this?"

"Yes. Years ago a girl with long black hair dressed in a
daisy-covered dress humiliated him in front of the carnies he
worked with, along with some friends the girl was with. She
lured him to the beer garden at Magic Land Park, pretended
she was going to let him kiss her, and then had her friend
pour soda on his head while everyone laughed at him."

"He killed her, didn't he?"

"Yes. Her and another young carnie who was with her.
Let's go back to Andy. That . . . that doesn't make any sense."

"Why?"

"The carnie he murdered? He was named Andy."

Alex had just turned to look at the man who was staring at her . . . no, past her . . . when she felt hands around her neck. Hands that choked her until she felt the world around her slip away.

---

After calling Williams, Jeff jumped into his car, praying as he raced to his office as fast as he could. Was Alex still alive? Was help coming too late? Agents from the FBI's Critical Incident Response Group planned to meet him in the parking lot and take his phone so they could track the call to Alex's location. He was certain the address would be the same one the teams were converging on, but he wanted to make sure they had it right. He'd told Williams about the electric fence and that it was powered by a high-tech generator.

She told him Hostage Rescue had already sent out one helicopter but would probably send out another. They could drop agents onto the grounds and disable the generator so the rest of the teams could enter the property.

He'd wondered if he should call Logan, but he decided to wait. The teams were so close. Why not wait until he could tell him the situation had been resolved? He just prayed the resolution would be good news. He still wasn't used to praying, but he prayed now. With all his heart.

---

When Alex opened her eyes, she was lying on the picnic table bench, face up, her neck raw and her throat sore. A few raindrops helped bring her all the way back to consciousness.

Grateful she was still alive, she lifted her head and coughed. The lights from the park's carousel flashed and music played. *Daisy, Daisy, give me your answer do. I'm half crazy, all for the love of you.* . . .

She looked around for Brent, but he was gone, and she didn't see anyone else. She'd been wrong about there being only one guy. What did Brent say? He was hired to lure women for Andy? Then she remembered Jeff told her the carnie named Andy was dead.

Brent wasn't the one with a split personality. Lum Jones was. He was certainly distanced from reality, but what reality?

She shook her head. She didn't have time to figure this out. She looked around for her knife, but it was gone. Then she remembered Tracy saying something about a shed just beyond the park that might have lawn equipment in it. She got up slowly, looking around again, but she still didn't see anyone.

As she made her way through the amusement park, she realized all the rides were running as if they had riders, but they were empty. It was spooky.

She'd just passed the train when she saw the shed. After scouting out her surroundings one more time, she sprinted toward it, praying it was unlocked. Where was the man called Andy? Why had he left her on that bench?

Why hadn't he killed her?

When she found the shed, she pulled the door open. Brent was lying inside, garden shears sticking out of his chest. She didn't have time to feel bad for him. She quickly looked around for something else but saw nothing that could help her. Even though she didn't want to do it, she grabbed the shears, pulled them out, and stepped outside.

She'd just turned when she saw the outline of someone walking toward her. "Stop or I'll kill you," she said as she held the shears out in front of her. "I mean it."

That's when she realized there were two figures. When they reached her, she saw that a man had Tracy, and he was holding Alex's knife to her throat.

# 53

"Drop the shears," the man said. "Now, or I'll slit her throat."

Alex let the shears fall to the ground. "Okay, okay. Please don't hurt her."

"I'm sorry, Alex," Tracy said.

"It's okay. It's not your fault."

"Back to the picnic tables," he ordered.

Alex couldn't make out his features in the low light, but she could see his long, shaggy, dark-blond hair. She was trying to understand him as quickly as she could. She'd need to know more about him if she had a chance of saving Tracy's life.

She led the way back to the picnic table and took a seat on the other side. It was wet from the rain, but she ignored it. He didn't seem to notice.

She kept her eyes on him, watching for a chance to do something. A way to rescue Tracy.

"Who are you?" Alex asked.

"Do you really want to know?" He leaned in closer, and for the first time Alex saw his face. He had a scar on his upper lip, the kind that came from cleft palate surgery.

"Quit staring at me. I know I'm hideous."

"Hideous? I don't understand," Alex said. "Are you talking about that small scar? It's barely noticeable."

His face turned dark red. "Liar!" he screamed.

The blood drained from Tracy's face. She was terrified.

It was at that moment Alex realized the truth. She'd read this man wrong, and it could cost Tracy's life as well as her own, and the women still locked in the cellar. He'd killed the kid he knew as Andy along with the girl who'd belittled him. Then, because he couldn't accept what he'd done, he'd become Andy and started looking for the girl who'd hurt him as if she were still alive, just older.

"Why did you kill Brent?" she asked, trying to keep him distracted while she tried to figure a way out of the situation. "Who was he?"

He shrugged. "I found him living on the street. He was good-looking and needed a place to live. I brought him here to help me find you. Because he was handsome, the women were never afraid of him. Of course, now I don't need him. I've found you." He sighed. "He had a good life here, but he betrayed me. After everything I did for him. I couldn't trust him anymore."

Then he laughed. "He even asked me not to kill you."

Alex wanted to feel some compassion for Brent, but she couldn't. Women were dead, and he could have stopped it. He'd allowed them to die so he could live in this big house and stay off the streets. His attempt to do the right thing had come too late.

"So you're the Ghost Rider?"

He laughed maniacally. "So you read my note."

"Yes. Now tell me what you want."

"I want you to watch Tracy die because you tried to ruin our plan. And then I want to kill you for what you did to my friend."

Alex decided to take a chance. She had to get his guard down for a moment. Make him forget Tracy. "Stop this," she said. "You killed your friend Andy, and the girl, Emily, who embarrassed you. You're really Lum Jones. It's time you faced the truth."

His face became a mask of rage. "You just cost this woman her life."

He raised the knife to Tracy's throat, but before he could cut her, Alex jumped up on the table and lunged at him. She heard the sound of a helicopter above her as they were all enveloped in a bright light from above. Backup was here.

It was then that he plunged the knife into her chest.

As the casket was lowered into the ground, Logan dabbed at his eyes, trying to stem the tears that had been his constant companion ever since it happened. Then he looked around at the assembled mourners, including Jeff, Alice, Monty, and several other members of the BAU. They'd all been there for him, and he was so grateful for their support.

His thoughts turned to how instrumental Alex had been in rescuing those four women. To no one's surprise, the bodies of the others were found in graves not far from the property.

Thankfully, Jones's reign of terror was over. After he stabbed Alex, HRT took him out for good. He'd died still believing he was someone else. After he'd murdered Andy Tedder and Emily Marsden, his personality had shattered in an attempt to protect the broken man he was inside. From what they could gather, he'd convinced himself that he would always be rejected because of a small scar he carried from a surgery he'd had when he was very young. He saw himself as disfigured and ugly. His rage and pain had built until it had to find release. And then when he inherited the mansion and money from his grandparents . . .

Logan's mother squeezed his arm. "Everything will be all right, son," she whispered.

Would it? He'd lost someone he loved with all his heart. It would take time to get to "all right."

The minister nodded toward where they sat, and with his mother beside him, Logan walked up to the grave and gently tossed a rose on top of the casket. Now he'd have to learn how to live with this hole in his heart.

He stepped aside so others could place their flowers as well. Say good-bye. His mother stayed where she was as he returned to his chair.

"We'll work through this together," Alex said as she leaned her head on his shoulder.

He turned and smiled at her, thankful that the knife had hit her rib, breaking it but not hitting any organs. Most people didn't realize that stabbing someone without hitting a rib was very difficult. You had to know what you were doing, and Jones hadn't. Thank God he was shot before he could try to hurt Alex again or carry out his threat against Tracy Mendenhall.

He was grateful for something else too. As soon as he heard his father's health had begun to decline, Alex had insisted they both fly to his family's home so he could spend time with him. Dad had loved Alex immediately and insisted Logan give her his grandmother's ring. She wore it now.

When Jeff let Logan know Alex had been taken to a medical center near where she'd been rescued, he'd left the hospital against doctor's orders. As soon as he walked into her room, he told her how much he loved her. She'd cried and then said, "Well, it's about time." He'd had to hold her gingerly so as not to hurt her, but it was the best hug of his life. And the kiss wasn't too bad either.

He was feeling better physically, and soon he'd start treatment for what was left of the brain tumor. He refused to call it "his" since he had no intention of claiming it. He was convinced that God was big enough to help him beat it.

After the burial they would be going to his parents' house, where friends and neighbors would gather to offer words of condolence. Then their friends from Quantico would fly back home. He and Alex wouldn't return to work for a while. They both needed to heal, and Logan was scheduled to begin radiation and chemotherapy treatments.

The minister said a few more words, and then it was time to go. Logan stood and took Alex's hand.

It was just starting to rain, and Monty came over and handed him an umbrella. "Jeff and I can share one," he said.

"Thank you. I should have grabbed one before we left, but I didn't think of it."

"It doesn't matter. We'll meet you back at your parents' house."

"You don't need to—"

"Don't even finish that sentence. We're brothers. I'll be there. Jeff is coming too. We can leave in the morning."

Logan could only nod, then watch as Monty walked away. It was as if his emotions were stuck in his throat and no words could get past them.

"Let's go," Alex said.

He held the umbrella over their heads as they walked together, her hand in his.

"You need to rest," she said.

"After everyone leaves." He squeezed her hand. "I want to be there for my mother."

"I understand, but I don't want you to overdo it. And when we get home, I'm going to make sure you do whatever the doctors say. I'll take good care of you."

"I know you will."

She looked up into his face, and when his eyes met hers, his love for her seemed almost too big for him to bear.

"I love you so much," he said.

She smiled. "But I love you more."

Logan wanted to kiss her, but it didn't seem appropriate at his father's funeral, even though Dad would have encouraged him to do it. But there would be plenty of time for that.

Challenges lay ahead, but whatever they had to do, the three of them would face it together. Logan, Alex, and the One who'd never left them. Who'd brought them through the fire and given them the desires of their hearts.

Logan smiled as Alex leaned into him, sliding her arm through his. The future was going to be amazing.

# Acknowledgments

Thank you again to retired Supervisory Special Agent Drucilla L. Wells, Federal Bureau of Investigation, Behavioral Analysis Unit. Your help is appreciated more than you will ever know.

Thanks to my editors, Raela Schoenherr and Jean Bloom. Raela, your guidance has been invaluable. I will miss working with you. I can't thank you enough for supporting me down through the years. And thanks once again to Jean Bloom for all your hard work and patience.

My love and gratitude to God for finding me a place to serve Him. I pray He will touch others through the gift He gave me. It has been and always will be for Him.

**Nancy Mehl** is the author of more than forty books and a Christy Award finalist, as well as a Carol Award winner, the winner of an ACFW Book of the Year Award, and the winner of the Daphne Du Maurier Award for Excellence in Mystery/ Suspense in the inspirational romance category. Her short story, "Chasing Shadows," was in the *USA Today* bestselling *Summer of Suspense* anthology. Nancy writes from her home in Missouri, where she lives with her husband, Norman, and their puggle, Watson. To learn more, visit www.nancymehl .com.

# Sign Up for Nancy's Newsletter

Keep up to date with Nancy's news on book releases and events by signing up for her email list at nancymehl.com.

---

# More from Nancy Mehl

When a renowned profiler is found dead in his hotel room and it becomes clear the killer is targeting agents in Alex Donovan's unit, she is called to work on the strangest case she's ever faced. Things get personal when the brilliant killer strikes close to home, and Alex will do anything to find the killer—even at the risk of her own life.

*Dead Fall* • THE QUANTICO FILES #2

---

# You May Also Like . . .

When authorities contact the FBI about bodies found on freight trains—all killed the same way—Alex Donovan is forced to confront her troubled past when she recognizes the graffiti messages the killer is leaving behind. In a race against time, Alex must decide how far she will go—and what she is willing to risk—to put a stop to the Train Man.

*Night Fall* by Nancy Mehl
THE QUANTICO FILES #1
nancymehl.com

When multiple corpses are found, their remains point to a serial killer with a familiar MO but who's been in prison for over twenty years—Special Agent Kaely Quinn's father. In order to prevent more deaths, she must come face-to-face with the man she's hated for years. In a race against time, will this case cost Kaely her identity and perhaps even her life?

*Dead End* by Nancy Mehl
KAELY QUINN PROFILER #3
nancymehl.com

FBI profiler Kaely Quinn visits Nebraska to care for her ailing mother. She can't help but notice suspicious connections among a series of local fires, so she calls on her partner, Noah Hunter, to help find the arsonist. Together they unwittingly embark on a twisted path to catch a madman who is determined his last heinous act will be Kaely's death.

*Fire Storm* by Nancy Mehl
KAELY QUINN PROFILER #2
nancymehl.com

◆ BETHANYHOUSE

# More from Bethany House

Coast Guard Flight Medic Brooke Kesler was caught in a mass shooting at a Coast Guard graduation—and little does she know that she overheard something that could expose the mastermind's identity. With targets on their backs, Brooke and her boyfriend CGIS Agent Noah Rowley must race to find the killer before he strikes again.

*The Deadly Shallows* by Dani Pettrey
COASTAL GUARDIANS #3
danipettrey.com

Allie Massey's dream to use her grandparents' estate for equine therapy is crushed when she discovers the property has been sold to a contractor. With weeks until demolition, Allie unearths some of Nana Dale's best-kept secrets—including her champion filly, a handsome man, and one fateful night during WWII—and perhaps a clue to keep her own dream alive.

*By Way of the Moonlight* by Elizabeth Musser
elizabethmusser.com

After moving to Jerusalem, Aya expects to be bored in her role as wife to a Torah student but finds herself fascinated by her husband's studies. And when her brother Sha'ul makes a life-altering decision, she is faced with a troubling question: How can she remain true to all she's been taught since infancy and still love her blasphemous brother?

*The Apostle's Sister* by Angela Hunt
JERUSALEM ROAD #4
angelahuntbooks.com

◊BETHANYHOUSE